VICTORIA PAULEY

ISBN: 978-1-0689207-0-7 (ebook)

ISBN: 978-1-0689207-1-4 (paperback)

Cover design by Opulent Designs

Headers and breakers by Aestheteam Designs

Formatted by Sullyn Shaw

Edited by Cruel Ink Editing & Design

Proofread by D.P. Editing

Map made on Inkarnate

Contents

Never stop fighting for what you believe in and
don't lose hope in a better tomorrow

Author's Note

I'm so excited to share the final book in the Silver City University series with you. I felt so many emotions with this one, and I hope you'll enjoy feeling all of them while you read Wings of Valor. While this is not a dark romance, the characters in this series all need to overcome their own issues. Some of these issues may hit close to home so please read the list below before diving in.

-Instances of prejudice between the different types of angels.

-Open door sex.

-Episodes of PTSD from past trauma with flashbacks of a witnessed death

-Death and torture

-Mention of the prior death of a parent.

-A difficult relationship with family.

-Demons intent on harm

Silver City University Map

1

THEO

The sight before me is painful to look at.

Hayliel sits on the front step, unable to move. She hasn't said a word since the Archangel Auriel blipped away. I don't blame her—the entire evening is more than unexpected. I can't imagine what she's feeling.

Meeting Raphael's family for the first time, then learning about the possible war brewing throughout the city, was bad enough. Add in the shit with Uriel and the discovery that one of the very rulers pushing for war is far more corrupt than we ever imagined, and it's a wonder any of us are coherent.

But to then learn that her family had been attacked and captured and are now being held as a bargaining chip? After everything my bright, shining firefly has been through—everything she's survived—this is the last thing she needs.

I take a step closer, wanting to get a good look at her face. She's pale, and the dark circles under her eyes are far more prominent than usual. Absentmindedly, she chews on her fingernails, something I've never seen her do before.

My heart aches at the sight.

As I watch her, my mind wanders to the four Archangels who rule the city. Are they all corrupt, or is it just Auriel?

Fuck. This is too much.

One thing's for sure, Auriel hides who he really is far too easily. In the few media appearances he's made, he seems kind. Like his only goal is making sure our lives are full and happy. But the man I just met? The one who threatened and harmed? He's nothing like that.

I glance once more at Hayliel. None of us know how to comfort her. Maybe there's nothing we can do—not unless we have a direct line to her parents.

It fucking pains me to be so useless.

Tilting my head, I beckon Raphael and Zeke to join me on the front lawn. "Raph, send something through the group chat. I'm going to message Castiel and loop him in." My best friend nods, quickly grabbing his slate and typing out a message while I do the same. What happened here changes everything. All of our carefully laid plans and thoughts on what was fucking going on have blown up in our faces.

"I think we should consider getting Azrael involved," Zeke

says, breaking the silence. Raph and I share a look that Zeke doesn't miss, but it prompts him to continue. "He already knows some of it, and even though the traps we've set to lure out the mole haven't revealed anything, he could still help us. Off the books, of course. But his experience would be valuable here. He could find something we missed."

While I don't exactly hate the plan, things are fragile. Our trust, for one. Without knowing who the mole is at the guild, it makes it hard for us to bring anyone from there into the fold. Or, in his case, further into the fold. Maybe the traps aren't working for a reason.

Raphael stays silent, which I appreciate. Things are still touch-and-go between those two, and the last thing we need right now is to be fighting amongst ourselves. "Let's not decide just yet. I don't want to rule it out, but I think we need to give it some thought and discuss it as a group. I'd rather he go through the cave tests before we blindly call him in, anyway."

Zeke grumbles, but he doesn't disagree. It's cute to see him being so reasonable.

The girls are the first to arrive. I'm honestly shocked Dina could get away from her dad, but from what I overheard the girls talking about the other day, he's more than happy to let her spend time with the *right* friends—like Mira. Purist asshole. Whatever. At least it worked out in our favor today.

"Oh, shit. Hayliel," Mira says, but Zeke beckons them to us instead. She looks like she wants to flip him the bird and ignore us completely, but Dina places a hand on her arm to stop her.

"I've got this. You should go see what they need."

I check my slate for the umpteenth time, not surprised when I don't have a single reply from Castiel. It shows he hasn't read it yet, which is par for the course with this guy. Sighing, I try not to let it bother me. He's not like the rest of our little group. The guy has real responsibilities and shit, but fuck. We need all hands on deck right now.

Dina and I each take a seat on either side of Hayliel, while Zeke, Mira, and Raphael go through the house one more time to look for anything we might have missed—clues about where they took her parents, or even confirmation that they're still alive. Anything to give my girl some hope.

I considered the possibility that Auriel would have taken her parents back to the barn, but that's too easy. He knows that place is compromised. Even if it were fortified by demon guards or who knows what else, I still don't think he'd take them there. Either way, I make a mental note to bring this up once we've gathered the group.

"They're crafty and eternally optimistic," Dina says to Hayliel, holding her close. "They'll get through this."

Hayliel never says a word. She just stares off into the distance.

She doesn't seem to notice the chill seeping in through the cement slab beneath our asses or the breeze that's picked up in the last ten minutes. She may be sitting beside me, but her mind is far away and out of my reach.

My heart shatters even more.

Ten minutes later, our search party returns empty-handed. Raphael shakes his head, telling me everything I need to know—we're no closer to helping her.

"We've been here too long. The last thing we need is the guild to show up and think we had something to do with what happened inside," Raphael says, causing Zeke to curse and pull at his hair.

"Are you sure we can't involve Azrael?"

I glance once more at my slate, hoping to find an unread message from Castiel, but my screen is empty of notifications. "Let's just get back to the cave, and then we can consider inviting him in."

"Fine. And Castiel? Has anyone heard from him?" Zeke asks.

I shake my head. "No response so far."

With a low voice, Raph asks, "Do we think he spilled the beans on what she is?"

We all exchange a look. I don't want to believe it or even consider it a possibility, but we may not have a choice. As if sensing our thoughts, my slate vibrates with a message from the man himself.

> **Castiel**: Shit. I'll be there shortly.
> **Theo**: We're actually heading back to campus.
> Meet at the cave in ten minutes.
> **Castiel**: See you then.

Tucking my slate away, I place a kiss on Hayliel's head and stand. "He's meeting us at the cave. We can discuss who we think blabbed once we get there. For now, we need to leave. It's not safe here."

It takes more than a little convincing to get Hayliel to leave her parents' home. Not that I blame her. If the roles were reversed, I probably wouldn't want to leave either. It's Zeke who finally gets her on board. Like a man on a mission, he strides back inside the house and comes out a few minutes later with an apron and a shirt—physical things from her parents that she can bring back to campus.

He might be an asshole, but he's a caring one when it comes to Hayliel.

Zeke gives the possessions to her, along with a gentle word about safety and plans. His words must break the mental dam she's built inside, because water suddenly pours from her eyes, and her listless body is wracked with sobs. Gently—far more than I've ever seen him be—he wipes away her tears and helps her stand. Her breaths come in sharp bursts that look painful, but she still holds her head up high. My strong firefly. Dina helps her get her wing jacket on, and as one, we take off.

How do we want to handle this? Raphael asks via the private mental connection with Zeke and me.

Carefully. She doesn't need the added stress, I say. For her sake, I hope it wasn't Castiel who betrayed us. That's a blow I'm not sure she'd ever recover from.

Zeke's reply pops into my mind just before we land, and it sends shivers down my spine.

One way or another, I'm going to get answers.

2

EZEKIEL

Restraint doesn't come easily to me.

The urge to act and find out who turned on us claws at me. If Castiel betrayed us—betrayed *her*—he won't like what's coming. Anyone who brings her pain will pay for it with their own. Mark my words.

I press my hands against my closed eyes, willing the memories of my own mother's torment to fade—but it's as if they're branded there. Images flash behind my eyelids: the day I found out Mom had been taken; the agonizing hours and days that followed as we tried to get her back; and finally, the moment I learned I'd never be in her presence again.

I don't want that for my hummingbird. She's too bright. Too

good. So if I have to threaten and maim to get answers, I won't hesitate. Not for her.

Back on campus, Theo stops me at the entrance while the others head into the cave. "Get out of my way," I growl, needing to be inside, to stand near her and protect her. If Castiel is in there with her, Theo's putting her in danger by keeping me out here.

"She needs us," he says. "All of us. So whatever anger and pain you're feeling right now, use it. But don't let it overtake you."

His words hit me like a slap to the face. "And what the fuck would you know of pain and loss, hmm? Move, Theo, before I make you."

"You aren't the only one who's lost a parent, asshole. I don't want her to experience that pain either, but she's fragile right now, and if you can't calm the hell down, then you can stay the fuck out here. Get your shit together before you come inside; she doesn't need *this*." He motions to my jittery state.

A little of my fury subsides as I watch him, catching sight of the pain he's buried. I sigh. "I'm doing it again, aren't I?"

Some of his frustration melts away, and he nods. "It's a good sign that you can see it this time. We've all got shit, man. It's the one thing we all have in common—aside from our love for that woman inside."

Fuck. How is it that Theo's always saving me from myself? "I'm sorry. Give me a minute, and I'll be in." Before Theo reaches the threshold, I call out, "And thank you."

Turning, he tosses me a soft, sad smile. "For what it's worth,

8

I wish we could have helped get your mom back."

He walks away, leaving me standing there wishing for the same thing. I give myself a few minutes to put my thoughts in order, trying not to let the memories of losing Mom take over. Just because she didn't make it doesn't mean Hayliel's parents will share the same fate. She's determined as hell, stronger than most—and unlike me, she has a loyal group of friends willing to do whatever it takes to bring her parents home alive.

When I finally walk into the cave, the silence is deafening.

Hayliel sits in a chair, staring at the wall. Castiel—who stands completely unharmed in the center of the cave, proving that the fancy rune Mira gave us must not work—looks confused, while the others do nothing to clear the air.

Shit. They've been waiting for me.

"Good. Now that you're here, can someone please tell me what's going on? Your message said someone took Hayliel's parents. Were you able to find them?" Castiel's gaze moves around the group. Is he that good of an actor, or does he truly not know?

"Not exactly, but we know who has them," Raphael says, not giving much away.

Castiel's brows furrow. "I'm not following."

I'm sick of constantly tiptoeing around shit. "Did you tell anyone about what Hayliel is?"

He reacts as if I slapped him. "Of course I didn't. What's going on?"

Hayliel's quiet, broken voice cracks the building tension.

"Archangel Auriel knows. He's behind everything going on in the city, and unless I join *Team Evil*, he's going to kill my parents."

The history professor can only stare at her, his eyes wide and mouth agape. I still can't tell if his reaction is genuine or all for show. "I'm so sorry, Miss Hayliel. The good thing is, they're still alive. But just to be sure these old ears heard correctly, you're saying one of the four Archangels has been working with demons?"

Hayliel goes back to staring at the wall. "Yes."

Castiel rubs his chin, more puzzled than ever. "For how long? And what is it he's after?"

Theo steps closer to Hayliel, placing a reassuring hand on her shoulder. "It's unclear. He didn't exactly go into the details of his grand plan, though he mentioned a cleanse of the undeserving."

It doesn't take a genius to figure out what that means. Fallen aren't safe anymore. Though, if I'm honest, we haven't been safe for quite a while now.

"Auriel didn't learn it from me, but I suspect I know where he heard it," Castiel says, and all eyes turn to him.

"Well? Don't stop there." Raphael crosses his arms over his chest.

A thought occurs to me—one I didn't consider before. Maybe it wasn't Castiel himself, but someone else connected to us. Someone we haven't even met. "Was it Phiel?"

It looks like Castiel wants to roll his eyes, but he doesn't.

"No. As I stated previously, he's trustworthy. Just before you messaged, Uriel approached me. He knew we'd been snooping through his things and wanted to rub it in my face that we couldn't get anything past him."

"Shit. That's not ideal, but it doesn't explain how Auriel knew of Hayliel being a Seraphim," Theo says, and it's like he plucked the thought from my head.

"Oh, but it does. It seems Uriel has a rare rune etched somewhere in his classroom that transcribes conversation. It's likely why he never took you to his class for detention"—he turns to Hayliel—"so there was never any proof of what he was doing."

That fucking asshole has been a thorn in our side since the beginning. It's time someone plucked him out.

Theo makes a noise in the back of his throat that has my brows darting up in surprise. "So, when we were snooping in his class and I mentioned she was a Seraphim, the rune would have transcribed it for him." His face is so pale the veins show through, making him look sick. "It's my fault. I did this."

The room grows silent as his stricken expression turns to Hayliel. In a voice so low I barely hear it, he says, "You're in this mess because of me."

"No," Hayliel replies, walking to his side with more gusto than she's had since discovering her parents are gone. "He'd have found out regardless. The asshole was already slinking around in the Fallen library, remember? This isn't your fault." Gone is the heartbroken girl from mere moments ago. In her place stands a woman who sees her friend hurting just as much as she is.

Something she can't bear to see without trying to soothe away the pain.

"But your parents."

"We'll save them. We have to. But it's not your fault, Theo." Hayliel's gaze hardens. "The only angels at fault here are Archangel Auriel and that piece of fucking shit Uriel."

Mira clears her throat, speaking for the first time since entering the cave. "So, what do we do now?"

3

HAYLIEL

Around me, the group argues about what our next step should be, but I don't bother joining the conversation. Instead, I just hold on to Theo's hand to reassure him that what happened isn't his fault.

The discussion grows louder, but I tune them out. It's late, and we're all worn out. Hell, it's our constant fucking state at this point. Yet despite the weariness, my damn brain just won't shut off.

Behind my eyes, the events of the night play on repeat. The sight of their blood on the walls will haunt me forever. And fuck, I can't even muster excitement about finally summoning enough sunfire to blast a demon to smithereens.

Maybe if I'd visited my parents earlier, I could have stopped this whole thing from happening in the first place. Now I need to decide.

My friends act like there's a choice. But with my parents in the grasp of that psychotic Archangel, there's only one thing to do. I have to give him what he wants.

Then there's Uriel. With every second that passes, my anger and rage edge closer to snapping. If he wants to pick on me and make my life on campus a living hell, that's fine. I'll make do. But to put my friends and family at risk like that? He deserves to pay.

"No!" all three of my guys snap at the same time.

"She's not giving herself over to that piece of shit," Zeke says, glaring at Mira.

The newest member of our group raises her hand in submission. "I get that I'm new here, but I care for Hayliel as much as anyone in this cave. It's not that I *want* her to do it, but we're discussing how to get her parents back alive, and it feels like we should at least put all the options on the table."

"It might be the only option we have—unless we can find out where my parents are and rescue them before the deadline. But seven days isn't a lot of time to sort that out." Six sets of eyes turn on me, all with varying degrees of emotion.

There's pain and worry from my guys, fear from Dina, a shrewd air of calculation from Castiel, and Mira almost looks proud.

"Listen to me, sunshine," Raphael says as he cups my face in his hands. "None of us want to see anything happen to you or your parents. We're going to do everything in our power to get them back, but sacrificing yourself is not an option."

"Besides, I don't exactly trust Auriel will stay true to his word and let them leave, even if you agree to his terms. We have no proof that he's trustworthy," Zeke says. The death glare he throws at Mira makes me think he wants to throttle her.

Little does he know, I've already come to the same conclusion on my own: trading myself is the best option for them—the safest one.

"I have to do something. And you can't tell me you wouldn't have given everything to trade places with your mom."

Zeke steps back like I slapped him.

Shit.

Every ounce of emotion drains from his face, and when he finally speaks, his voice is detached and cold. "I nearly did until Dad stopped me. Turns out they'd already killed her and just wanted more bloodshed."

I watch as Theo reaches out to squeeze his arm—something that would've seemed odd to me at any other moment but this one. Deep down, I know I should do the same. Offer him comfort and an apology for what I'd just said, but that would mean acknowledging the fact that maybe they're—

No. I can't think about that. I can't consider the possibility that they're dead already.

I.

Just.

Can't.

Ever the professor, Castiel says, "Look. It's been a rough day for everyone, and we're not going to get anywhere while emotions are high and we're all exhausted. Let's take the night to sleep, and we can regroup in the morning. Does that sound good?"

Sleep? After what I just witnessed? Not possible. But I don't want to argue anymore, so I go along with Castiel's idea.

On his way out of the cave, Castiel stops and offers me a reassuring smile. "We will consider every option to save your parents, Miss Hayliel."

I truly hope he means that. Mentally, I add his name to the list of potential allies I have to help convince the others that giving myself over is the way to go.

Mira is the next to leave, and just like Castiel, she stops by to speak with me. "Remember where you got your strength from. I've never met your parents, but if they're half as brave and bright as you are, they'll be fine."

Her words make my eyes sting with tears, but I hold them back. There will be time for that later—when I'm alone.

"Where would you like to sleep tonight, sunshine?" Raphael asks, his eyes roaming over my face.

Fuck. I forgot about our arrangement. All I want is to be alone with my thoughts, but I can't see them agreeing to that after what we've all just been through. So instead, I pick the next best thing.

"I'd like to stay with Dina tonight, if you're here until tomorrow?"

"Dad thinks I'm staying with my Pure friend, Mira, so I'm all yours until the morning," Dina says, then turns to the guys. "I'll keep her safe. I promise."

Raph, Zeke, and Theo look like they want to argue, so I do what any sane and reasonable girl would. I kiss them. One by one, I press my lips to theirs, keeping it light instead of deepening it like I would at any other moment. The spark that usually ignites at their touch is still there—but it's dull, hidden beneath my pain.

"I'll think of some excuse to give my parents for why we left," Raphael says, squeezing me a little tighter.

I groan. "Shit. I didn't even think of that."

He chuckles. "It'll be alright. And besides, who the hell cares what they think?"

Zeke clears his throat. "Don't think I've forgotten about our need to discuss looping Azrael in on the plan."

I turn to him, sure that I've missed something. If I'd realized this had been discussed earlier, I'd have agreed from the start. His lieutenant brain can surely help find my parents. "Let's get him to the cave tomorrow and have him pass through the rune. As long as he's not a threat, he can know everything."

Theo shares a look with Raphael. "Are you sure, firefly?"

"If you're hoping to avoid a trade to save my parents, then we're going to need all the help we can get."

I don't remember walking to Fallen house or entering Dina's room. It's like I blacked out, and now somehow I'm sitting on her bed. Mindlessly, I drink the water she gave me, staring at the wall and feeling more empty than I have in a really long time.

Dina sits beside me, nudging my leg with hers. "You said their telepathy skills were improving. Have you tried reaching out to them yet?"

Slowly, like the movement alone costs more energy than I have, I turn to look at my best friend. "I ... no. I didn't even think to use our mental connection."

Fuck. I'm an idiot for not doing this the moment we arrived at their house.

Mom? Dad?

Only silence greets me. Panic wells inside, but I push it down. I'd feel it if they were dead, wouldn't I? They could just be too far away. Maybe if I'd thought of doing this earlier, we could've found them already.

Stupid, stupid Hayliel.

Dina must sense that my attempt failed, because she says, "We'll try again in the morning. Here"—she hands me a little white pill—"to help you sleep. We'll face this with a fresh mind tomorrow, and to do that, you need to rest. Alright?"

I nod, playing along as I swallow it and move through the motions of getting ready for bed. My things are only across the hall, but I don't have it in me to go over there. I'll break down if I see photos of a happier time.

No.

I'll sleep. Rest.

Just like everyone wants.

And tomorrow, I'll make a plan.

I try to reach my parents every few minutes, but they don't answer, and I sink further into a dark pit in my mind.

Dina doesn't press me for conversation until we crawl into bed, and she curls up to snuggle against my back. "I love you, bestie. We'll bring them home."

All I can do is give a soft hum of agreement, but I know Dina gets it. She's known me long enough, knows that my parents are the glue that's kept me together all these years. Through the bullying, the shame, the years of being an outcast. I doubt Dina wants me to put myself in harm's way, but I know she understands why I'm so willing to trade myself to save them.

And I know that she'll accept my decision, even if it's one she doesn't approve of.

I hold tight to Mom's apron and Dad's shirt—finding comfort in the smell of home. Once more, I mentally call out to my parents, hoping I'll get a response. All I'm greeted with is silence—and the soft sound of Dina's sleeping form behind me as she lightly snores.

A lone tear rolls down my cheek as whatever medication she gave me kicks in, and I finally drift off to sleep.

4

RAPHAEL

Morning comes far too soon, and yet it feels like too much time has passed. I want to know how Hayliel is doing, but I don't dare risk waking her. After yesterday, I can't imagine she had an easy time falling asleep.

Sitting up in bed, I check my slate. There are a few unread notifications—one from the rune weaver, letting me know she received the deposit I sent her, which unfortunately used up most of my emergency funds. I don't dare ask my parents to refill it. I'll have to figure something else out to pay off the rest—along with a not-so-subtle reminder to send over the details ASAP.

Fuck. I'll have to put pressure on the others. Now, more than ever, we need those protective articles of clothing. Hayliel's parents are in jeopardy, and if I know anything about my sunshine, it's that she won't rest until they're safe. Even though it scares the shit out of me, her big heart is one of the many things I love about her.

The next text is from Raduriel—time-stamped from half an hour ago. Of course he's awake early on a Saturday.

> **Raduriel**: Mom was looking for you this morning. I covered for you and Hayliel. Just go with it if she calls.

Oh, goodie. Another mess to deal with.

> **Raphael**: How am I supposed to go with it when I don't know what excuse you gave her?

The moment I hit *send*, my slate vibrates with an incoming message from none other than my mother. Part of me doesn't want to open it. There's enough shit on my plate right now, so I'm not particularly interested in adding a tongue-lashing to it. But if Raduriel tried to cover my ass, the least I can do is play along—even if his motives are suspicious. I'll figure him out later.

Karena: Raduriel explained why you had to leave early. I wish you'd told me you started working with him and his colleagues. I'm glad you finally put aside your childish behavior and joined the adult world, Raphael.

Karena: That said, your little friend's outburst yesterday was awfully uncalled for. I hope you'll have a talk with her about manners. I expect a full apology for her rudeness if you plan to bring her back here.

Karena: Probably best to keep away from the riffraff and focus on your studies. Good grades don't come easily to everyone, so I expect you to put in the effort to make up for it.

I drop my slate before I snap it in half. Fucking bitch. If anyone needs a talking to about manners—it's her. As bad as her messages are, though, I imagine it would have been far worse if she'd woken up to find that I'd just disappeared without an acceptable excuse. I still can't figure out Raduriel's motives for helping us. Nothing about the last twenty-four hours has been easy to digest. I guess I'll just add this to the list.

Are you up? I ask Theo through our mental connection.

Yup. Heading to the cafeteria now to grab food for everyone at the cave. See you there?

I smile. *It's like you read my mind. Showering first, then I'll head straight there.*

Twenty minutes later, I walk through the cave entrance, barking out a laugh when I see the spread of food Theo brought. He wasn't kidding when he said he'd grab food for everyone. There's enough here to feed a small army.

Zeke's talking with Theo, the pair of them laughing as I approach. "What's so funny?"

"Theo just asked me what the plan is if Azrael ends up paralyzed by the rune, so now I can't stop picturing my big shot lieutenant wrapped in vines."

I smile, imagining the pissed-off expression on his face. "I'll admit I'd like to see it in action, but somehow I doubt he'd find it as interesting," I joke. "When is he due in?"

Zeke checks the time on his slate. "He left the Fallen district about five minutes ago, so he should be here any moment—if the wind is kind."

"We figured it might be best to get the testing part over with before Hayliel arrived, given what she's been through," Theo says.

I nod. She doesn't need to witness it if Azrael proves unworthy. Zeke's slate pings just as I grab a piece of bacon from the pile.

"He's at the front gates." The grumpy house leader looks nervous. I can understand why, given how strongly he's advocated for Azrael. For more reasons than just Hayliel and our plans, I hope he proves true. None of us need the added disappointment, and even though I don't always love the guy, I'd rather not witness Zeke losing one of his idols.

"You ready?" I ask Theo. He nods, and the two of us move to stand near the entrance, just in case something goes wrong.

When Zeke walks through the cave a few minutes later, I hold my breath. Azrael follows behind him, his face screwed up in discomfort as the dispel ward makes him want to run far away from here.

The banned rune glows blue, and I finally expel the air from my lungs.

Another ally for our girl. Let's hope he agrees.

"Theo, Raphael, this is Lieutenant Azrael."

"Nice to meet you both," Azrael says to us, then turns back to Zeke. "Want to explain why you've brought me to a heavily protected cave with a banned rune at the entrance?"

Zeke rubs the back of his neck. "That's why you're here. And since you're not tied up and paralyzed right now, it means we can fill you in on everything that's happened." Azrael looks like he wants to speak, but Zeke cuts him off. "I vouched for you. But with the way things are now, we couldn't leave anything to chance. I hope you understand."

"We need your help," Hayliel says, entering the cave with Mira and Castiel following hot on her heels.

"Happy to see you off the battlefield, Az." Castiel pats the lieutenant on the back.

"A little warning would have been nice," he grumbles, which only makes Castiel chuckle.

Theo motions to the trays full of food. "Grab something to eat, and we'll get started." He takes Hayliel's arm, leads her directly to the biggest pile, and helps her put a plate together. She looks exhausted—her eyes rimmed red like she spent all night crying instead of sleeping.

Mira brought a carton of freshly brewed coffee, so I get to pouring one for my girl. Today is going to suck, but the least I can do is help keep her caffeinated.

While we eat, we spill every detail of the past few months to Azrael—even repeating the small bits he already knows—and end with what we discovered last night. The poor guy looks green by the time we finish. I can't imagine this is easy for him. He works for the company that's supposed to protect angels—the very company made up entirely of the type of angels who are now being targeted.

Azrael's shocked gaze roams over Hayliel. "A Seraphim. But how? We thought God extinguished them all before he fell."

"It was a shock to us all. Hopefully you understand why we've been so secretive," Zeke says.

Hayliel sets her plate down. "Is there anything you can do to help me find my parents? I know there's so much more going on here, but I can't just leave them. And since these assholes don't want me giving myself over, I have to find another way."

I try not to take her words to heart. She must understand why we don't want her putting herself in danger like that. Not without exhausting every other option first, and even then ... I couldn't bear the thought of losing her to that wicked Archangel.

Azrael's entire demeanor shifts, allowing the powerful guild lieutenant rise to the surface. "You said there's a crime scene? Zeke, have you examined it?"

Zeke nods. "Last night, though I didn't do as thorough a job as I could have, given the situation. The attack we faced before Auriel's arrival may have also compromised the scene."

"Take me." Azrael turns to Hayliel. "I'm not saying I'll find anything, but I'll do my best. Is there anything I should know about the two victims?"

I catch Hayliel wince at his words, but it's Zeke who answers him first.

"They're two of the nicest angels I've ever met. Positive and accepting."

Hayliel gives a sad smile at his words. "Eternal optimists. Over the past little while, I've been working with them on building and strengthening their telepathy. I reached out all night without luck, so I'm not sure if the distance is too great or if something else is keeping the mental lines closed."

A visible shudder runs through her, and it has my heart squeezing.

An odd look flashes across the lieutenant's face before he says, "If I know anything about Auriel, it's that he keeps his word. If he gave you seven days and promised to keep them alive, he won't harm them. As for the distance, the guild might have something that could help. A totem that strengthens connections and allows for a greater range of communication."

Hayliel nods. "Oh, that sounds perfect. Thank you."

"We only have a limited supply at the guild, so it may not pan out, but if I can, I'll give it to Zeke. Now, we should head to the crime scene as soon as possible. Who's coming?"

5

HAYLIEL

I roll over in bed, stretching out the kinks of sleep.

The delicious scent of pastry drifts through the air, making my eyes pop open as I recall Mom promised to let me try one of her new recipes today. I dress quickly, hoping to catch my parents being cute in the kitchen—like when Mom hums while Dad watches her bake, just before it turns into a flour fight.

Their love is so pure, it's no wonder that's the kind I want for myself.

Once I make it to the top of the stairs, I breathe in and nearly drool. "Mom, that smells delicious!" I call out—but when I enter the kitchen, I realize something is very, very wrong.

Mom and Dad are bloody and tied up, each held by demons

with angel blades pressed to their throats.

"No."

From the back door, Archangel Auriel steps through with a smile on his face. "You're taking too long, my little seraph. Perhaps you require a bit of encouragement, hmm?" He turns to the demon holding Mom and nods. Before I can even react, the demon slits her throat, and I scream.

I jolt upright in bed and rush to the bathroom, barely making it to the toilet before emptying the contents of my stomach—dry heaving when there's nothing left.

Resting my forehead against my arm, I hover over the rim. A nightmare. That's all. It's not real.

Three sharp taps come from the front door, followed by the sound of someone turning the knob, trying to get in. My heart races, pounding like a drum behind my ribs. Auriel wouldn't come here, would he? Even if he did, I can't see him knocking. That asshole would just blip into my room without permission before doing something as civilized as knocking.

No. I can't go there. It's probably just Dina, checking on me after I convinced her to take the night off to wallow in solitude.

I rinse the acrid taste of vomit from my mouth and warily head to the door. On the other side, I find all three of my guys looking ready to fight. What the hell? My gaze travels past them to the mound of pillows and blankets on the floor. I freeze. "Did you guys—"

Zeke barrels past me, opens my closet, and checks the bathroom and the locked balcony door.

Raphael takes my hand in his. "We heard you scream. Is everything alright?"

I offer him a sad smile. "I'm fine. It was just a bad dream."

"Oh, thank fuck," Zeke says, pulling me in close. I take it all in—his worry, his joy that I'm unharmed. The way he's putting it all out there, no longer hiding behind a mask of indifference. What did I ever do to deserve these men?

"You had us worried, firefly." Theo places a soft kiss against my lips while I'm still trapped in Zeke's embrace. No one bats an eye at the shared affection.

"I'm sorry," I say when he pulls back.

"You have nothing to be sorry for." Theo taps the end of my nose affectionately. "Why don't you go shower, then we'll head to the cave for a quick meeting. Castiel got you a pass from Uriel's class today. None of us think you should be around him without one of us with you."

"He did? Wow. It's probably best if I just drop his class altogether. It's not like he'll let me pass the final exam." I unwillingly pull myself from Zeke's embrace. "You three should go get cleaned up. I'll meet you by the front doors in half an hour."

Raphael looks like he wants to protest, but I shake my head. "I'll be fine."

It takes another round of insisting before they finally leave. Part of me wishes they could stay, but I'm not good to anyone right now. My mind is toxic right now, and the last thing I want is to have my negative thoughts seep into them.

Wanting to be quick, I don't bother washing my hair. With

the way my thoughts are churning, what my hair looks like is the last thing on my mind. While I scrub myself raw, I try contacting my parents again with no success. It's like something is blocking us from communicating. I just have to hope it's only distance and that Azrael's tool will help.

By the time I'm dressed, I've tried twice more to reach my parents and am in an even worse mood than before.

A notification flashes across my slate, and I dive for it, hope rising. Maybe my parents found a way to get a message to me.

I sigh when I realize it's only Dina, letting me know she's got some family shit to deal with and won't be able to join us at the cave.

I wonder what her dad would think about the shit we've uncovered. Would he even care what the Fallen might end up facing? Or is he only concerned with his image? I doubt he'd mind that I'm now more than just the weird friend with strange wings.

Tucking my slate away, I grab my bag and begin the trek down to the main floor. The moment I step onto the last set of stairs, a shiver races down my spine.

Two familiar Fallen angels stand between me and the front door. Big Forehead and Thin Eyebrows. Just what I fucking need to deal with right now. With the two of them, it might seem like they've got the advantage—but with all the pent-up anger boiling inside me, it's *their* wellbeing I fear for.

Maybe they just want to talk. Doubtful, but still a possibility.

Big Forehead grins up at me, though it's anything but friend-

VICTORIA PAULEY

ly. "You're a hard beastie to track down."

"Maybe you're just not a very good hunter," I say, descending the last few steps.

"Watch your mouth, orphan," Thin Eyebrows says with a sneer, halting me in my tracks.

Blood roars in my ears like thunder. "What the fuck did you just call me?"

The pair of them step forward as one, but it's the bitch with overly plucked brows that answers.

"You heard me. Just like I heard your parents hated you so much they killed themselves instead of having to put up with you for another second."

Rage builds so heavily inside me, I black out.

When I come to, I'm outside. Two of my guys have Big Forehead restrained—his pained wails piercing through my fog—while the other pulls me off Thin Eyebrows. She doesn't make a sound. Her face is a bloody mess, and what little eyebrows she had before are now gone. Judging by the smell, I'm guessing I burned them off.

"My eyes! What the fuck did you do to my eyes?!" Big Forehead sobs, repeating himself over and over.

"Hey," Raph says, running a hand up and down my arms. I flinch. "It's just me. You hurt?"

I shake my head, anger gripping me too hard to speak. How fucking dare they? Of course that piece of shit Uriel would twist the story and tell his minions to use it against me as ammo. Why am I even fucking surprised? He's a rat bastard with zero morals.

"Take the bitch and get the fuck out of here," Theo warns Big Forehead, his usual soft voice completely gone.

Before he can scramble away, Zeke grabs him by the throat. "And if you so much as *think* about coming near Hayliel again, I swear to every being in this realm and the next that you won't like the consequences. Do I make myself clear?"

"Yes," Big Forehead squeaks out before grabbing his friend's unconscious body. Hoisting the bloodied mess over his shoulder, he stumbles down the path to the main hall. Whatever I did must've really messed up his eyesight, because the dude trips over everything—nearly dropping Thin Eyebrows more than once.

When they're far enough away, three sets of eyes turn to me. "What happened?" Raph asks.

I struggle to breathe. It feels like the weight of ten demons sits on my chest, though I know it's only anger. Looks like I didn't take all my aggression out on those two.

I try several times to answer but can't get the words out. Then the shakes kick in.

Fuck. I'm a mess.

"It's alright. Let's get you cleaned up first. Come with me." Raphael leads me to Somersault Falls, where I drop to my knees and rinse the blood from my hands. Cold water washes away the physical signs of a struggle, but the emotional wounds remain raw and festering. By the time I'm done, the knees of my uniform are wet and covered in sand, but I feel a little calmer.

Enough to explain, at least.

"They called me an orphan and said my parents killed themselves to get away from me." I fixate on the waterfall, unable to meet their gaze. Without looking at them, I sense their rising anger like a dark, warm cloud snuggling up to my own.

"Those motherfuckers. I'll show them what death fucking feels like," Zeke says. It's like he can feel the bloodlust rising in my veins because in this moment, that's exactly what I want. For them to know how much anguish I'm in. To feel how fucking hard I'm trying to keep myself from falling apart.

My mental connection with Theo flares, his anger matching mine, but in a far more refined way. "I want to harm them as much as the rest of you, but if any of us gets kicked out, our job of protecting Hayliel and saving this fucking city becomes all that much harder."

How the hell does he stay so clear-headed all the time? It's both endearing and, at this moment, slightly annoying. That's likely the rage talking, though, because he's not wrong. If any one of us gets expelled—or worse, imprisoned by the guild—we're screwed.

Scattered along the bottom of my bag, I find a hair elastic and pile my hair into a messy bun on top of my head. "Let's just go to the cave before I change my mind and spend the day in my room."

The thought gets more appealing with every passing moment, so depending on how things go, I may wind up there anyway.

Mira and Castiel are already in the cave when we arrive. I'm a little shocked not to find Azrael sitting with them, but it's probably harder for him to get away than the rest of us. Besides, I want him at the guild looking into the items they took from my parents' house.

He and Zeke took several blood samples from both angels and demons. They also took a few chunks of mud and wet sand they found inside the house, too. Azrael thinks he can track where they originated from. It doesn't guarantee we'll find my parents, but maybe it'll help me figure out where Auriel wanted the trade to happen, since the piece of shit didn't even leave me with a fucking destination.

How am I supposed to give myself over when I don't know where to go?

If Azrael finds out where my parents are being kept, I'll go there myself and bring them back, or I'll sell my soul for their freedom. Those are the only two options.

I just might have to keep the one I choose to myself.

"Miss Hayliel." Castiel approaches, looking just as tired as I feel. His hair, which is normally tied back, now frames his face. Maybe he cared just as little as I did for looks this morning. "I spoke with the principal about the possibility of dropping Wingology from your course load. He doesn't understand the want for it, considering how close we are to finals. For now, the best he could do is allow you to drop it as a major."

"It's still better than nothing. If any other professor taught the class, I'd love to continue, but I don't think there's any benefit to it while Uriel runs it. Besides, we both know he's going to fail me at the slightest infraction. Thank you for talking to him on my behalf." It's not as if I can convince the school to come watch me fly on the island, and as long as I'm in the arena with Uriel, I won't make any progress with the obstacle course.

Castiel nods. "I know it might feel like you're running away or we're giving up, but I promise that's not the case. This is a delicate matter, one I must handle a certain way if we want Uriel to get the punishment he deserves. I've been assembling a case to bring to Principal Cael, but I just need a bit more time before I can present it."

Words fail me as I comprehend just what he's saying. "I ... Thank you, Castiel. Seriously. You've been a friend from the start, and that means more than I can say."

Castiel blushes at my praise, and Zeke clears his throat. "I'm all for Uriel getting his due, so if you need anything from us, just say the word. Now, we only have a few days left before the deadline. Since we're all against Hayliel turning herself in and we clearly can't decide on a plan of action, could we consider an ambush? Perhaps we can capture whoever shows up at the meeting point—then the guild can do their thing and extract information for us."

I hate the idea, but I can tell the others don't feel the same.

Raphael nods. "They could even lead us straight to his hideout."

Theo at least looks pensive. "Maybe. But I think the risk would be too high. We'd still need to extricate her parents without sounding the alarm. Depending on whether they're brought to the swap point or being kept somewhere else—and who or what is protecting them—that may prove difficult."

"I won't risk my parents to save myself," I say defiantly. My life is not worth more than theirs. "Besides, we don't even have a location to meet at, let alone ambush."

Castiel strokes his stubble-lined chin. "What if I could get an audience with one of the other Archangels? Would anyone protest?"

"Uh," Raphael says. "I don't know about that. We could be jumping from one bad outcome to something worse."

While I agree with him, I'm also desperate. "Do you trust them?"

The nod Castiel gives is more telling than he realizes. "One in particular, absolutely. Let's just say he's saved my ass a time or two in the past. He'd never agree to follow Auriel. Not in this."

"He may not follow, but if he knew, would he stand by and do nothing?" Zeke asks, looking like he'd rather go with the ambush plan.

"The man I know would never agree to harming anyone, let alone innocents."

"Then I say get an audience. I'm willing to try anything and everything at this point. Maybe that's reckless, but it's that or give myself over."

"No!" Theo, Raph, and Zeke shout in unison.

"Then make the call, but do it fast. We're running out of time."

Castiel checks the time on his watch, then curses under his breath. "I'll contact him today. In the meantime, it may not hurt to have a backup plan—and maybe a backup to the backup plan." He apologizes and rushes out, leaving the rest of us to use the last ten minutes we have before class to discuss strategies.

But the more I overhear my friends hash out details of a possible ambush, the stronger my conviction grows. There's only one way to guarantee my parents' safety.

I need to turn myself in.

And it looks like I'm going to have to do it alone.

6

HAYLIEL

Two days have gone by without hearing from my parents.

Azrael says the long-distance totems aren't available, so I've taken to quick trips off campus, hoping some place in this goddamn city will bring me close enough to connect with them. So far, I'm out of luck.

According to Zeke, the samples they took were a dead end, too. Apparently the variety of sand and dirt is common in several regions of the city, so they're unable to pinpoint a specific location. The only good thing is that they confirmed the blood they collected belonged to my parents, and they didn't find any angel blade toxins in the sample. There's still hope.

To make matters worse, I woke up to a private message on my

slate. I stare at it once more, my hands trembling. Other than a cryptic list of numbers, there are no other details in the message. It has to be Auriel, but how did he get my information?

They're coordinates. And the exact time he expects me there.

I'd be foolish to go. Foolish to think this will solve all our problems. But how can I not when he dangles my parents' lives over my head?

I toss the device face down on my bed, unwilling to look at it any longer. Fuck. What would my friends do in this situation? I'd ask them myself if I thought they'd let me go.

Right away, I know Theo would look up the coordinates and survey the area, given the high probability this is a trap. Raphael would advise me to figure out what parts of the landscape I could use to my advantage, and Zeke would encourage me to do the opposite—figure out how my opponent would use the terrain against me. Mira would probably tell me to suit up with weapons, and I know Dina would already have a list of what to pack in a bag in case things don't go as planned.

Shit. This would be so much easier if I could just talk to them. I wish they understood. And I know, in a way, they do. They're only looking to protect me, but how can I think of myself at a time like this?

For the last twenty-four hours, I've been playing sick like a coward. Pretending I'm ill so I can hide away in my dorm room, skipping classes, and avoiding my friends while I figure out what the fuck I'm going to do. They've hated it, and I know they've done their best to have someone stationed nearby in case any of

Uriel's henchmen try something, but at least they're listening.

A knock on my balcony door spikes my heart rate. I've been jumpy as hell since the cloaked figure came for me, though I know now that was just Auriel. I wonder if he knew then what I was.

The knock sounds again, mere seconds before my slate vibrates on the bed beside me.

Slowly, like it's going to bite me, I turn it over, relaxing a little when I see Mira's name flash across the screen.

Mira: It's just me. Can I come in?

After tucking the paper containing all my secret notes under my pillow, I open the door.

She surveys the room, then asks, "How are you feeling? Any better?"

Right. I'm supposed to be in pain with cramps or something. Shit. What had I told them? I feel like an ass. Physically, I'm fine—and probably always will be since our immune systems don't allow for things like colds or sickness. But mentally, well, I'm a hot mess, and it hasn't been that hard to play it up for my friends. Still, I can't drop the ruse that I'm unwell.

"It's touch and go, though I think the solitude is helping," I say, trying my best to stick to as much truth as possible.

She leans against the wall, looking like a slightly more stylish, less grumpy, gender-swapped version of Zeke. It must be a *my father's a lieutenant* thing. "Well, I won't take up too much of your time. I just wanted to let you know I understand your decision, and if I can help, I will."

I stop breathing. She can't possibly know what I've decided. No one does.

Playing dumb, I say, "I'm not following."

One side of her mouth tilts upward in a half smile. "Please. I can smell your determination all the way from home. You're going to agree to work with Auriel in exchange for your parents' lives and freedom. It's what I would do in your situation."

My gaze narrows on her. This could be her way of trying to convince me to open up just so she can shut me down, but the more I think about it, the more I realize how very un-Mira like that is. She's open and sometimes downright blunt. Subterfuge isn't her thing.

"You would?" I ask tentatively.

"Without a doubt. Have they answered your telepathic calls yet?"

I don't get the sense that she's lying to me. She would absolutely trade herself in my shoes. But that still doesn't explain why she's here.

Shit. She asked me something, and here I am lost in thought. "No. It scares the fuck out of me, but I think I'd feel it if ... if they—"

"Trust me, you'd know." Our eyes meet, and I see a world of pain behind her green gaze. "My mom left when I was little. Just took off one day and didn't come home. She left me a note, promising to come back for me. Two weeks later, I was playing in the park when it hit me. The pain was almost unbearable. It felt like my chest was caving in. I knew, at that moment, that my mom wouldn't be coming back for me. Not in this life, anyway."

My chest tightens, making me feel even closer to this woman who sprang into my life out of nowhere. "I'm so sorry. Does what happened have anything to do with your situation at home now? I don't want to pry, but I'm here if you ever need a friend."

I want to ask why her mom left. What it was she'd been running from, or toward, but it doesn't feel like the right moment. Maybe it never will.

"It was a long time ago, and my circumstances now are a much longer story for when things aren't so messy. But it's why I sympathize with you. It's why I'm here offering whatever support I can." She glances at my slate, which has been vibrating nonstop with message notifications. "The others have good intentions. Hell, the guys are madly in love with you, and everyone else just wants you to be safe. I'm sure they won't be happy with me when they learn I knew and didn't try to stop you, but ..." She shrugs.

My gut urges me to take her words at face value. At this point, I'll take all the help I can get. "I appreciate that. And honestly, I could use a sounding board, if you don't mind? I just ... I need you to promise not to tell the others. The last thing I need is to worry about them stumbling in and ruining the plan. I don't want anyone getting hurt on my behalf."

She mimes locking her lips and throwing away the key. "It'll stay between us. But if you'd like, I can deliver a message to them after you've gone, when it's too late for them to stop you. Pass along your love, or even a plan to extract you, which, honestly, you should have as a backup just in case that shady fucker doesn't hold to his end of the deal."

I pat the bed and smile, reaching for my hidden notes with my free hand. "I'm really fucking glad you're here. Now this is where I'm at with a plan."

Turns out I'd been on the right track when I decided to research the coordinates. Mira confirmed it's exactly what she'd have done, and then we looked at the area together. Just past the point where the housing and farming district meet, there's a desert, and the coordinates Auriel sent are on the cusp of it. Pictures of the area are minimal, but it looks like he wants to meet somewhere far enough away from the city to not be seen or heard. There are a few places to be careful of. Little hidden spots I don't even think I'd have noticed on my own where Auriel could trap me or have his lackeys waiting to grab me—dense shrubs or large dunes of sand where the desert begins.

The heavy weight that's been sitting on my shoulders for days eases slightly with Mira's help. I'm grateful for her guidance and support. It's not as if she owes me anything, so the fact that she's here with me tells me everything I need to know about who she is.

It's enough encouragement for me to share my biggest fear with her. She's helped me with everything else so far. Maybe she'll have some good advice for this, too.

"What if ... what if he refuses to let my parents go? Given what he's capable of, I don't trust that he'll stick to his word. Knowing he saw Raphael, Zeke, and Theo with me—and isn't demanding anything from them—only makes me more concerned. Will he truly let them and my parents be, after what they know?"

She rests a hand on top of mine, offering me strength. "The bastard is an Archangel. Maybe he feels safe enough in the powerful good-guy image he has. With the way things are now, he probably doesn't think anyone would believe some youngsters or two Fallen adults."

"I fucking hate him and the way things have become," I say, dropping my head in my hands.

"Me fucking too, babe. We'll never know for sure what's going on in Auriel's mind. All we can do is plan for as many outcomes as possible—and hope none of them happens."

"Right. No pressure." It all feels like too much. Too many angels at risk with far too many shitty outcomes.

"Let's focus on small things," Mira says, tapping my notes. "We'll start with your parents. If you're worried he won't let them leave, why don't I wait nearby, far enough away that he won't sense me, and I'll help them get home safely?"

"I appreciate that, but I really don't want to put anyone else at risk, and that includes you. What if he attacks them and you get hurt in the process? I'd never forgive myself."

"Alright, then I'll check on them at home. Or you can tell

them where to go, and I'll meet them there. I understand you don't want anyone to get hurt, but you aren't alone. You can lean on me." Mira bumps me with her arm. "I promise I can take care of myself."

"Alright," I concede. "You can meet them at their house and bring the guys as extra protection." Maybe knocking the possibilities out one at a time isn't such a bad idea after all.

"Good." She smiles. "Now, obviously I hope he keeps his word and everything goes off without a hitch, but if it doesn't, there are a few general rules to live by. Be wary of food or drink that you haven't seen prepared. If I can figure out how to mix up a concoction, I'm sure Auriel has someone on his team who can, too."

A shudder runs through me at the thought—along with an idea. Fuck, I'm glad Mira's here. "That's a good point. And it brings up another option. The little blue vials you gave me to hide my powers ... if I take one before the meeting, it might help me get away in the off chance that things don't go according to plan."

Mira shrugs, clearly contemplating. "It probably wouldn't hurt, though it would give away that we have the means to disappear, so to speak. That may not be worth it—depending on how likely you think it is that something will go wrong."

Shit. She's right. Why is this so fucking hard?

"Here." Mira unsheathes the daggers at her hip, then does this little flip with them that looks effortless—and totally badass—before holding them out to me, hilt first. "In case things go sideways, I'd like you to take these."

I can only stare at her outstretched hands and the sharp blades she holds. "But these are yours. I couldn't possibly—"

"You can, and you should. Weapons are in short supply on campus, unless you want to take some of the training weapons from Malik's office?" She laughs at my scrunched-up face. "Precisely. And this is safer than Zeke trying to smuggle some out of the guild."

I hadn't even considered needing weapons. Ugh! Just how incompetent am I?

"Stop that," Mira says like she can read my thoughts. She places the daggers on the bed and takes my hands in hers. "You are so strong to even consider this sacrifice. Your bravery is inspiring. If this situation wasn't so close to home, you'd have no issues thinking of everything. It's understandable that your head is a little foggy. That's what I'm here for. To help. Please, take them."

My grip on her hands tightens. "Thank you."

"Don't mention it." Her smile turns serious. "Now, if the trade happens and you join his side but things take a turn later, remember your sunfire. With enough concentration, the heat of it should melt cuffs or bars—if it comes to that. Hopefully, it doesn't."

Yet another thing I hadn't considered. Would Auriel really turn me into his trained beast?

"Hopefully." I stare at my fingers, tracing the length of them, and consider confiding in her more than I already have. I've already gone this far. What's a little further? "There's something else. Something I haven't discussed with anyone, but I know the guys witnessed it."

Mira watches me with intrigue, though she keeps silent.

"I think I can teleport. At least, I did it at my parents' house and maybe one other time. Not sure I can do it on command, but maybe it would be useful?" Finally, I raise my gaze to hers. As always, Mira doesn't react the way I expect her to. She isn't upset with me that I've kept this to myself. She just looks excited.

"I swear, you're the coolest person I know." Her words make me laugh because *she's* probably the coolest person I know. Mira stands. "Do you feel up to practicing it a bit with me here?"

I can only stare. She really isn't going to tell me to do some research before attempting to travel through fucking air with my mind? I couldn't hold back the smile that spreads across my face if I tried. "Yes! Let's do it."

Mira picks up the blue university pen from the small coffee table and turns to me. The sight of that pen invokes memories of a time that was somehow less complicated and yet also more. Tutoring with Raph feels like a lifetime ago.

When I stand from the bed, Mira halts my step. "You stay there." She walks forward until she's closer, but still out of reach. "I'm going to drop this, and I want you to catch it before it hits the floor. Do your best to teleport forward instead of just lunging."

"Well, this should be easy," I say, deadpan.

She ignores my joke and counts down from three. I take a deep breath, and the moment she drops the pen, I will myself to move.

The pen hits the floor.

Shit.

"It's alright. This is unfamiliar territory for us, but we can figure it out together. Let's try again." Mira grabs the pen from the floor and begins another countdown.

We do this two more times before I manage to teleport anywhere. Unfortunately, my aim is off, so I smack right into Mira and don't save the pen from falling.

She laughs, and so do I. "Progress! Again."

We practice over and over again—until it finally feels like I'm getting the hang of it. Out of the thirty times Mira dropped the pen, not counting the first few where I sucked total ass, I caught it sixteen times.

My smile is bright as we continue training, moving on to harder challenges. Even if my abilities don't improve much beyond this, I feel ten times lighter than I did this morning.

Maybe I really can pull this off.

7

HAYLIEL

Mira's daggers lie sheathed and on top of the bag hidden beneath my bed. She insisted on loaning me her holster, promising that, like the daggers, she had plenty of others at home.

I suppose having a guild lieutenant as a father means access to things others wouldn't have. The story she shared with me yesterday holds steady in the back of my mind, and I vow that if I make it through this, I'll get to know her better. If there's anything I can do to help with her home situation, I'll do it. She deserves to be happy. And it's the least I can do to repay what she's done for me.

Heat flares beneath my flesh, rising from the core of power

living at my center. I think that means I need to release some of the churning sunfire that's only grown hotter since planning for this trade. You know, before I burn up and kill myself.

I really should imbue the daggers now. It would mean letting some power out, but I can't shake the nerves. My dorm room isn't exactly a fire-safe workspace. Scorching the floor isn't something I want to explain to anyone, either. Or pay to repair.

I can make it a few more hours without exploding, I think.

Wait. Is that how it works? Is it an explosion of sunfire or being consumed by it? Shit. This is depressing.

No. I'll be fine. And tomorrow, when I'm on my way to save my parents, I'll imbue the daggers. That way I can char whatever the fuck I want to without worry.

My slate vibrates at the same time I hear a commotion outside my door. I've been putting the guys off all week, cycling through a range of excuses for why I want to be alone. Even though I've denied them, they keep reaching out. And since I don't know what the future holds for me, I allow myself one more night with them.

Raphael, Theo, and Zeke wait for me in the hall of Fallen house. The original plan was that we'd all stay in Raph's dorm for the night, but because Zeke only has an hour before his shift, we're going to stay in his room. The fact he even offered blows my mind.

His leaving isn't ideal, but I couldn't exactly explain why I wanted him to bow out of work without raising suspicion.

I open the door and am immediately wrapped up in Raph's

arms. He kisses me like a starving man, stealing my breath and making my core ache with need. Theo grabs my chin and angles me toward his waiting mouth, where he swallows my low moan.

"Well? What are you waiting for, house leader? And don't even try to pretend like you haven't missed her these past few days," Raphael challenges Zeke. I want to laugh, but something about the charge in the air keeps me still.

Our eyes lock, and something snaps within him. Instantly, he's at Raph's other side, fisting my hair in his grip tight enough to shoot little sparks directly to my clit. I suck in a breath, and he pounces, using the opportunity to explore my mouth with his tongue.

If I thought I was hot before, it's nothing compared to this.

The kiss softens as he pulls back, which only makes me want them all more. Just not here. I have too many secrets hiding in here right now. "Take me upstairs. Now. And then I want all of you naked."

My words spark them into action, and I laugh when, not fifteen seconds later, we're standing in front of Zeke's top-floor room, where he struggles to unlock the door.

It probably doesn't help that I've got my arms wrapped around him from behind, stroking his dick through his pants. "Hurry up, Zeke," I whimper.

"Fuck!" he growls. "Don't think you won't"—he pauses to let out a low moan—"pay for this, hummingbird."

His words only make me smile and squeeze his length.

He finally gets the door unlocked, but I don't even have a

moment to think before he's facing me, gripping my cheeks in his big hands, and causing my lips to purse together. In contrast to the rough grip, he places the softest kiss on my mouth. "Go inside and strip for us. Put on a good show, and I'll make it worth your while." Then he drops all contact with me and backs up, letting me pass through the threshold untouched.

With a promise like that, I'll do whatever he wants.

I walk by Raphael and Theo, who watch me like they're not at all upset with Zeke's demand.

If it's a show they want, it's a show they'll get.

Waiting for them to get inside and shut the door is torture. *Could you walk any slower?* I huff through the bond.

So eager to strip for us, are you, little sun?

A shy smile spreads across my face. *I'm aching to have all your eyes on me.*

Theo stands in the open door, his gaze darting between Raph and Zeke, before he finally shuts it. *You're the only thing we see, firefly.*

His words cause my heart to flutter as I finally begin taking off my clothes. Theo stays by the closed door, Raph sits with his legs spread and his hand resting on his leg, and Zeke takes up his normal perch against the wall. Each of them watches me.

I close my eyes and hum a tune, slowly undoing the buttons on my shirt. My hips sway to the internal beat, and with every inch of skin I expose, I feel the eyes of my men searing me—tracking every movement with rapt attention.

When I've undone all the buttons, I hold the front closed and tease them with small glimpses. Not wearing a bra was probably the best decision I made today. The thought solidifies as I finally separate the two sides of my shirt, revealing my hardened nipples, and letting the fabric fall to the floor behind me. I keep my eyes shut, but the groans from the guys make me smile.

Continuing to hum, I kick off my shoes and pull down my leggings—let's be real, there's no sexy way to pull skintight pants off, alright?—until the only thing I'm left in is my underwear. I rarely wear thongs—wedgies are the devil's work—but I made an exception for this occasion.

I open my eyes to the sight of the guys fully dressed while I'm almost completely naked. Oh, now this is hot. The moment solidifies my want for tonight to be about them. The guys I'm obsessed with. I don't know if I'll survive without the three of them in my life, and with the outcome of tomorrow unknown, I need to show them how I feel tonight—so they never have to guess.

Extending my hand to Zeke, I silently beg him to approach first. The choice is easy. He only has a limited time with us tonight, but even if that wasn't the case, I need him to understand that I want him just as much as Raphael and Theo. His place within my heart is just as secure as theirs.

The reassurance is something I didn't realize he might need until only recently. Now that I do, everything makes a little more sense.

He strides forward with the confidence of a man who never loses. Now *this* is the Zeke who dropped in from the clouds and showed me around Fallen house. The same one who threatened to fuck me in the sky in front of everyone below.

Zeke wastes no time once he reaches me. He plasters me against him, his erection pressing against my stomach while he teases my lips with his tongue until I open for him. Then he ravishes me. He consumes me. Steals the very breaths from my lungs until it feels as if I might faint.

His attention moves down my neck, and I try to undo the button of his jeans and attempt to lower the zipper. Anything to free his cock so I can finally feel it against my palm. But his hand has slipped into my panties, his fingers sliding through my wet heat, making me fumble.

He groans. "You're soaked already. Is this all for us? Do you yearn to be filled with our cocks, hummingbird?"

A moan is the only response I can muster while he toys with my clit.

"Do you think you can handle the three of us at once?" Zeke inserts a finger inside my aching core, pumping it slowly. "One for Raphael." He adds a second finger, making my legs tremble. "One for Theo." I grip his shirt, a soft moan escaping me as he shoves in a third finger, stretching me. "And one for me."

He fucks me with his three fingers faster and harder, hitting a spot inside me that has my toes curling. Raphael and Theo watch on with utter fascination—each stroking their cocks. The sight of them mixed with Zeke's manhandling has me coming apart in his arms, drenching his hand with my orgasm.

"Oh, I think you'll manage all three of us just fine." My

core is still spasming when he pulls out of me and stares at his fingers coated in my pleasure. Without a second thought, he licks them clean, growling like a beast. "I missed your taste, hummingbird."

A shiver races down my spine. I need them. I need *more*. "Why the hell do you all still have your clothes on?"

Theo and Raphael take theirs off immediately, but Zeke only stretches his arms wide. "If you want me naked, undress me. But just know the moment my cock is free, I'm going to fuck you into oblivion."

His dirty words have more liquid pooling between my legs. I'm frantic, removing his clothes as quickly as fucking possible—or at least trying to. The bastard doesn't make it easy for me, using every opportunity to rub my clit through the fabric of my underwear.

When I only have his boxers left to remove, I shift my gaze to Raphael and Theo, who still haven't moved from their positions. Are they giving me time alone with Zeke? Is this a truce on their part to make him feel more comfortable?

Whatever it is, I appreciate it. Not because I want Zeke by himself. I'd gladly take them all at once, alone, or however I can get them, but this is new territory for us. For Zeke. And for them, too. We haven't exactly all gotten along, and the last thing I want to do is ruin this before we even have a chance to make it work.

I'll be sure to thank them for their efforts later.

Focusing back on Zeke, I drop to my knees before him and

pull down his boxers. His hard, veiny cock springs free. I can't resist sticking out my tongue and licking the bead of precum glistening at the tip.

"I'll have your mouth later. But right now, I need that sweet cunt of yours." Zeke lifts me into his arms with ease, and I wrap my legs around his waist.

His deft fingers shift my panties out of the way seconds before he plunges inside of me, filling me to the hilt.

Fucking hell. He feels just as good as he did during our first night together; it's like his cock was made to shatter my world. My fingers dig into his shoulders, mouth open as I'm stretched around him. He grips my ass, lifting me up and down, forcing me to ride him.

His biceps shift with the movement, the muscles rippling as my core spasms. But then he stops. He keeps me lifted so only the tip of his cock still penetrates me. I whimper, trying to shift myself down, to force more of him inside me.

He chuckles, placing a kiss on my cheek, and then glances at Raph and Theo. "Aren't we supposed to be sharing?"

My core clenches at his offer. Made of his own free will. For me. So I can have all of them to lick and touch and fuck.

Zeke must feel it, because he smiles and says, "Her greedy pussy agrees. It practically strangled my dick at the mention of sharing. She needs all our cocks, so get the fuck over here."

Raphael grins as he rushes forward, his eagerness causing more of my wetness to pool around Zeke's tip. Theo's steps are slower. More controlled. His excitement isn't as visible, but it's there all the same—in the darkening of his eyes. I feel it as he roams his gaze over every inch of my body, where I'm connected to Zeke, and where Raph now presses flush against my back, his cock dancing between my ass cheeks.

"Didn't I promise you'd take two of us at once?" he whispers in my ear.

A full body shudder flows through me when his fingers tease my pussy, slipping through the wetness and bringing it to my back hole. When he slips a finger inside, Zeke finally lets me sink down, and I take in every single inch of his cock.

"Oh, fuck." Through my hooded gaze, I find Theo stroking his pierced cock, his hungry gaze on us. I reach for him. His cock is too thick for my hand to fully wrap around, but I stroke him anyway, playing with the metal at the tip.

Zeke notices, and a laugh rumbles up from his chest, vibrating against my nipples and sending shock waves of pleasure through me.

"It's always the quiet ones who have a wild side."

Theo only smirks and pinches my nipple, making me gasp. "Take her to the bed. I want to fuck her mouth while you two fuck her ass and pussy."

Oh. My. Fucking. God.

I think I can get used to this bossy side of Theo.

Raphael removes his finger while Zeke takes me to bed. I straddle him and finally have control of my movements to rock my hips. Fuck, he feels good.

"Lube?" Raphael asks, his voice low, filled with desire.

Zeke points somewhere, but I can't focus, not when I'm this close to shattering.

As if sensing just how close I am, he grabs my hips and thrusts upward, hard and swift, sending me spiraling into my climax. His brow furrows, and I wonder how much longer he'll be able to hold himself back. Will my burly Fallen angel finally snap and take me as ruthlessly as I know he can?

Coldness drips on my back hole, causing my core to clench with anticipation. The sloppy sounds of Raph lubing up his dick have excitement running through me. I need this. To feel them all at once.

"Open up for me, firefly." Theo's thumb pulls on my bottom lip with a gentleness that has me melting. But I know he can be anything but gentle.

My tongue darts out to meet his thumb, and then I bite it, making him go wild. He grips my face and kisses me until the world disappears.

There's nothing else...only these three men.

My men.

Raph's cock pushes against my ass, and I whimper into Theo's mouth. He swallows the sound, his hand shifting to my clit while Zeke pinches my nipple. He pushes past the tight ring of muscles, and the burn is painful but perfect. I burn and burn, but it only heightens my pleasure, bringing me closer to my ruining.

He halts his advance, letting me get comfortable with the feeling of utter fullness. "Relax, little sun. Fuck. You're so tight.

You feel so good, baby."

Theo bends until his cheek rests on Zeke's abs, directly in front of my pussy, and licks.

He licks and nibbles and sucks until I'm coming apart again.

"Oh, fuck. Mmm, fuck. Your tight little ass is gripping me so fucking hard," Raphael says. He must've sunk all the way in, because a fullness unlike anything I've ever felt before settles over me.

"You okay?" Zeke asks, watching me.

Theo gives my clit one more lick before he stands, and I clench around the two cocks filling me up. The two men curse in unison.

I can only nod and reach for Theo, needing him to fill my last empty hole. Shit. I've never felt more alive than I do right now, and they haven't even moved yet. How am I going to survive once they do?

"Lean forward, hummingbird. Yes, that's it. Oh, fuck—that's it."

Blindly, I twist my head to face Theo's cock and lick him tentatively. His salty precum coats my tongue, making me moan.

"I swear to fuck, Theo. If you touch me with your dick, I'll kill you," Zeke growls.

"It's mine. You can't have it," I tell him, slurping the tip into my mouth and swirling my tongue around it.

"Fuck, baby." Theo slaps my ass, and that's all the others need to start moving.

Raphael fucks into me, which thrusts me against Zeke until

I can't breathe. I swear my soul has escaped my body, and she watches on with a gleeful glint in her eye. Pleasure blinds me, and it takes what little concentration I can muster to keep my throat open for Theo to fuck my mouth.

I moan around his cock. These small, unintelligible sounds that spur my three men on.

"Shit. Fuck. You're milking my cock so good, little sun. I can't ... I—" Raphael thickens in my ass, and then I'm flooded with warmth as the most intense orgasm I've ever experienced races through me. Euphoria bleeds through my veins, replacing every ounce of blood until all I am is feeling.

Carnal lust. Desire.

Zeke fucks up into me like a relentless animal. I shriek around Theo's dick, my core clenching and gushing as I'm thrown over another blinding cliff of ecstasy. Zeke's warm cum shoots inside me, and I turn lifeless.

But Theo isn't done. He pulls out of my mouth and caresses my cheek. Tenderly. Lovingly. Like I'm the center of his fucking world.

Without a word, Raphael drags his softening dick from my ass, the move agonizingly slow, while Zeke does the same until I'm nothing but an empty shell. A *happy* fucking empty shell. And even though I'm exhausted and sore, I won't be satisfied until all of my men are.

Gently, I'm placed on my back on the bed, my legs pulled until my ass reaches the side. "Fuck, baby. You're dripping." Theo spreads my thighs, watching as Zeke and Raphael's cum leaks from me. I feel it, still warm.

He drops to his knees and buries his face in my cunt. "Theo," I gasp in surprise as his tongue spears into me, forcing Zeke's cum back inside. It's possibly the single hottest thing he's ever done. When he comes up for air, he plunges two fingers inside me, then rubs the sticky mess over his shaft. I think I might come from the sight alone.

Raphael and Zeke, whose cocks are already half hard again, join me on the bed. They take turns sucking my nipples, playing with my clit, or kissing me until it feels like I might expire on the spot. And when Theo drives his giant cock inside me, I think I've died and gone to the great beyond.

He grunts and pulls out almost all the way before ramming himself back in. "I'm not gonna—*fuck*. I'm not gonna last long. Feels too good, firefly."

I barely have the chance to take a breath before everything shifts. Theo savagely fucks into me. His thrusts are punishing, brutal, and I fucking love it. I scream and scream, my throat raw and abused—just like my body. I jerk beneath their hands until I feel myself milking every last drop of cum from Theo's dick.

He shudders and moans my name, and it's the most beautiful sound I've ever heard. One I want to hear on repeat every single day for the rest of my life. From all of them.

I take turns kissing them lazily, and when Theo tries to pull out, I wrap my legs around his hips to stop him. "Just another minute," I whisper. "I need the three of you here like this for just a bit longer. Please."

Now that the bliss is wearing off, I know my time with them is coming to an end, and fucking hell if I don't wish I could stop it.

I'm not ready to give up what I've only just found. What I've finally, after so many months, managed to grab hold of.

Them.

Us.

Together as one.

They give me what I ask for, even as Zeke's slate blares an alarm, warning him he only has ten minutes before his shift starts.

I hold on to them for dear life and whisper, "I love you. All of you. I just ... wanted you all to know before anyone leaves." Before *I* leave.

My confession takes everyone but Theo by surprise. He professed his love to me not that long ago, but I couldn't say the words back. Not that I didn't share those same feelings, but I couldn't risk telling one of them and not the others. Now, more than ever, seems like the perfect time.

Raphael breaks through his shock first and *whoops* like he's just been told he won the lottery. "Say it again."

I smile. "I love you."

"This time with my name."

I grab onto his face and stare into his bottomless ice-blue eyes. "I love you, Raph."

"Fucking hell, sunshine. Do you know how long I've waited to hear you say that?" He kisses me, pulling me away from the others without caring that Theo's cock was still inside me moments ago, and crushes me in his embrace. "I think I've loved you since that first day in the cafeteria. It's only grown since. Becoming this tangible creature inside me that purrs in your presence."

Tears slip down my cheek at his confession, and he kisses me again until we both taste the salty wetness of my tears.

Zeke's slate goes off again. Five minutes. Not enough time for him to fly there, even at his fastest.

He still looks a little stupefied, like I can't possibly have this much affection for him. But I can. And I do. I knew my confession would hit him the hardest. So full of doubts, my house leader.

"Zeke," I whisper. Raphael lets me out of his hold so I can approach Zeke where he stands, now dressed in his guild uniform. I'm pretty sure Theo held it out for him, which I can't deny is adorable as fucking hell.

He shakes his head, clearing the cobwebs caused by my admission. He opens his mouth, then shuts it. Swallows and tries again. "Do you mean it, hummingbird?"

"Every word."

"But how? *Why?* I've treated you like shit ever since we ..." He rubs the back of his neck. "I haven't been good to you. How could you possibly love me?"

"I'm not going to lie and pretend like you haven't hurt me, Zeke. But even while you were glaring at me and being all grumpy, you still cared. You still tried to protect me when the demons attacked. You stuck around despite your misguided hatred of Raphael and Theo, and you found a way to put it all aside so we could work together. Hell, you were even willing to let me go and be with them, as foolish as that would have been."

"For the record, I would have hated it. But I just want you to be happy."

"I know. Even when you weren't trying, you were there for me. It's one of the many reasons I love you."

"I love you, too, hummingbird. Even if you scare the hell out of me half the time and get me hard *all* the time. I won't promise that I'll always be the perfect guy or that I won't revert back to Mr. Grumps"—he throws a look at Raph and Theo, somehow fully aware that's how they thought of him—"but I can promise to love you with every fiber of my being for the rest of our lives."

He kisses me again, dipping me on his knee and spinning my world on its axis. Only when Theo clears his throat does Zeke let go.

"The last thing in the world I want to do is leave, but …"

I nod, knowing if he stays, he'll only risk getting in trouble. We have enough of that already. "Be safe," I whisper, dropping another kiss against his lips.

He heads to the balcony but doesn't leave right away. Instead, he takes one more look at us, almost like he's taking a mental picture. "Make yourself at home. I'll be back in the morning." He looks at the guys. "And make her come a few more times, would you?"

His laughter trickles in through the closing door, leaving the three of us alone.

"You said it." Theo stands at my side, pushing the hair from my face as he stares at me like I personally placed every star in the sky.

"I'd have said it to you in the training room if I knew it wouldn't start a competition or hurt anyone's feelings."

"I know. But hearing the words from your lips is different than knowing you feel them."

"I love you, Theo. My quiet force."

"I love you too, firefly."

We curl back up in bed after changing the sheets since they'd gotten a little messy earlier. Contented between two of my men, I try to focus on the movie currently playing from the projector on the wall. It's about a guy who stays at a resort on the beach in an effort to get away from his ex-girlfriend, only for her to show up with her new boyfriend. If it wasn't the night before I go and do something reckless, I'd enjoy it.

But tomorrow things change.

I'm not even worried about school. Compared to everything else on my plate, it's taken a spot so far in the back of my mind I'd forget about it if I wasn't actively attending classes or staying on campus.

At least my final term projects are drafted and scheduled to send in the event I don't make it back tomorrow with my parents. It's not likely, given the psycho wants me on his side. I doubt he'll trust me to go back to regular scheduling.

Theo places a hand over mine, and I realize I've been chewing my nails. Shit.

"Are you okay?"

The real answer is that I'm far from alright, but that's not the response I give him. "Yup! Just a little tired, that's all. Three gorgeous angels wore me out earlier, if you'll recall."

They don't know how little sleep I've gotten over the past few nights. Mira's been helping me teleport, and we've gone over the plan a million times to make sure I don't miss any steps. I probably should have met with her tonight, but without knowing what tomorrow brings, I wanted one more night with my guys. One official night for the four of us to be what we always should have been.

"Why don't you get some sleep then, baby? Rest up before Zeke comes home and we ravish you again," Raph says, placing a gentle kiss to my neck that has my lids falling.

My friends, excluding Mira, think I'm waiting to meet Castiel's Archangel friend tomorrow. As if I'd ever put my faith in someone so blindly. Especially when that same being is an Archangel. They should have known.

I mentally shake my head. I've already thought through the pros and cons a million times. Tonight isn't about that.

"Sleep, little sun," Raph pushes. "Tomorrow will be hard. It's best you get some rest while you can."

His words make me pause. Does he know what I'm facing tomorrow, or is he just referring to what he thinks is happening?

"I find it strange that Auriel gave you a deadline but no location, time, or anything," Theo ponders out loud.

With my eyes still closed, I can't see the looks on their faces. Hell, I don't even know if they're watching me or just absently talking while staring at the movie. "He wants me on his team." I yawn and snuggle in close. "I'm sure he'll find a way to give me the details."

It's not technically a lie.

"We'll be ready," Raph says, his voice rough.

I drift off to sleep, knowing that none of us are ready for what tomorrow will bring.

8

EZEKIEL

I t's not often I work through the night like this. In fact, I used to enjoy doing so. But now, with so many threats against those I care about—and knowing the woman I love is tangled up in my sheets—I'm struggling to focus.

I still can't believe she loves me. After everything I've done, the way I've acted. She deserves better, and yet she chooses me. Sure, she chose Raphael and Theo, too, but the fact that I'm included feels like a victory. Even with those assholes.

As much as I don't want to admit it, sharing her with them wasn't the worst experience of my life. They'd been willing to take it slow and give me time alone with her as to not upset the grumpy fuck that I am, but I knew she'd want us all together in a big heaping pile.

It's what she deserves.

After checking the clock once more, my legs start to twitch. Azrael got a lead on a group of demons, and we've been chasing them all fucking night to no avail. We got back half an hour ago after we lost them again, and I'm getting tired of all this waiting.

It doesn't help that today is Hayliel's deadline with that asshole Auriel, and somehow, I'm supposed to make it through another hour here—waiting to chase demons, waiting to help Hayliel. Waiting. Waiting. Fucking waiting.

I've had enough.

With my slate and bag in tow, I stride down the hall to Azrael's office, knocking once before entering through the partially opened door. "Any news?"

He shakes his head. "Nothing yet, but we're working on it." Noticing what I'm carrying, he says, "Do you have somewhere else to be?"

If I didn't know Azrael, I might take his words as something they aren't. Rude. Condescending. But I know what he's doing. He's keeping his emotions out of things at work and truly asking if I have somewhere else I need to be. Now that he knows everything that's going on with me and my friends—with the city—I have no issues telling him the truth.

"Sorry. Hayliel's deadline is today, and all this waiting around is driving me insane."

"Go. We'll handle this from here. Make sure that slimy fuck doesn't get your girl." His eyes meet mine, and I read the sincerity in them. I'm one of the few angels he can trust at the guild, so for him to allow me to leave early is something I won't brush off lightly.

"Keep me in the loop if anything turns up, and I'll do the same," I say, and then stride toward the door I just came through. I barely make it past the threshold when I notice Lieutenant Atlas heading toward the balcony we usually use for quick escapes.

Hmm. Now where is he off to?

I follow behind, keeping my distance while checking the schedule on my slate. His name isn't on it until this evening, so why is he here?

No. Stop building conspiracies where there are none. Maybe he forgot something and just arrived to pick it up.

Opening my messages with Mira, I drop a casual question about her dad. She replies immediately.

> **Mira**: Dad left for work. Something about over-
> time. Why?

So maybe my message wasn't as casual as I thought, but her response makes me pause. I don't see anything about overtime on the schedule. I suppose it could be classified and far above my rank. I should really just let it go.

I should. But I don't.

Zeke: Oh. He's not on the schedule until this evening. The overtime must be above my pay grade. Thanks for the tip.

There. That shouldn't raise any suspicions, right? Mira's typing a reply, but I put my slate away and focus on Atlas. He's stopped at the balcony door, talking to someone who's just arrived.

"Yo. Lieutenant Atlas. I didn't think you were here today. Are you gearing up to join us or what?"

Atlas's voice is low when he responds, but I'm pretty sure he said he's off to a meeting and won't be back until his scheduled shift later tonight.

The guy he's talking to sounds disappointed, but moves on without spotting me, and Atlas slips through the door. I count to five before following, and for a moment, I'm afraid I lost him. Then the metal tips of his wings catch a shaft of pre-dawn light, and I find him again—flying away from the city.

Not wasting a second, I take off in the sky, following behind at a safe distance. I have less than an hour to figure out what he's up to, and then I have to make it back for Hayliel.

Easy.

But the farther we go, the more unease grows in my stomach. There isn't anything in this direction. No civilization. Nothing. Only the Godless Mountain.

But why would he go there?

The Godless Mountain was at the center of the battlegrounds

in the fight that put the Archangels in power and left Silver City without a God. Now, it's less of a mountain and more of a tall formation of rock reminding us of what happened here. The Archangels themselves banned the area ages ago, so what purpose could Atlas have to go there?

I hang back a little. This guy is a seasoned lieutenant of the guild and probably has senses far greater than mine. The last thing I need is for him to realize he's being followed.

It's not just for my safety, though, but curiosity as well. I want to know what's so special about the Godless Mountain. Maybe there's something here that can help us.

Atlas lowers his altitude until he lands near a pile of rubble. I watch on from the clouds as he spares a quick glance at his surroundings before continuing on foot.

Up ahead, the clouds disperse, so if I want to continue my tail, I'll need to do so from the ground.

Shit. As curious as I am about this area, I was kind of hoping to watch from afar.

I pick a spot farther back and dive quickly, flaring my wings at the last second to lessen the impact. No sounds greet me from the ground. Birds don't chirp in what's left of the charred and broken trees. Nothing scurries about in the destruction that litters the ground.

With nothing to mask my noise, I'll have to be even more careful.

What the hell is Atlas doing here?

Quietly, I walk by bones, worn-out fabric, rotten trees, and other debris. This place is eerie. No wonder they've made it off-limits. It's nothing but a graveyard.

A sound from up ahead has me stopping dead in my tracks.

No. It can't be.

A few more steps take me to the hollowed-out trunk of an old tree. I count my breaths, trying to steady my heartbeat into a normal rhythm. I manage—but it doesn't last.

Not when I peer around the tree and catch sight of who Atlas is meeting.

Except it's not so much a who as a *what*.

My mind races, slotting the connections into place as I watch Atlas and a fucking *demon* talk as if it's normal. Like they aren't warring species.

He's the mole.

Lieutenant Atlas is the fucking mole.

Does Mira know what her father's been up to? Did he plant her in our fucking ranks as a spy?

Oh, *fuck*. She used his keycard to help us steal amulets. She's the one who supplied the goddamn rune that proved we could trust her. Was that even real?

I have to get back. Now. Before we execute any kind of plan to get Hayliel's parents back.

Fuck. Fuck. Fuck!

Mira was involved in every conversation. The talks of an ambush. Castiel reaching out to one of the other Archangels. She knows all of it.

She wanted Hayliel to meet him. Sure, she said it was to look at all options, but what if it was more than that?

Turning, I get as far away as possible before taking flight, not wanting Atlas or his demon friend to see me.

We can turn this around. Use it to our advantage somehow.

Maybe offering Mira—or even Atlas himself—as a trade will help us get Hayliel's parents back.

Shit. Fuck! This is a mess.

The flight back passes in a blur. I'm constantly looking over my shoulder, worried I've been spotted, but I luckily land on my balcony with no one following.

There's still time to figure this out before we act on any of our compromised plans.

Placing my wing against the sensor, I unlock the door and step inside the dark room. Theo and Raphael are asleep in my bed. The space between them is empty. Likely where Hayliel once was, snuggled between them. At first I think she's in the bathroom, but when I look inside, it's empty.

I check the rest of my dorm room, including the closet, but there's no sign of Hayliel anywhere.

Where did you go, hummingbird?

Something churns in my gut—and I can't shake it.

"Raphael. Theo. Wake up."

Theo instantly sits up, but Raphael only mumbles something and rolls over.

"How was your shift?" Theo asks, his gaze darting around the room.

I ignore his question in favor of one of my own. "Where's

Hayliel?"

His brows furrow. "She fell asleep while we were watching a movie, and when Raph and I went to sleep, she was here. Maybe she's in the—"

"She's not. I checked." Not bothering to change, I grab the dorm's master key and stride toward the door. "Get him up. I'm going to see if she's in her room."

I don't bother waiting for his response. Something isn't right.

I race down the steps and slide the key into her door, but she's not here either. Where could she be? It's too early for her to have gone to class, and she knows well enough not to go anywhere on campus without an entourage.

Fuck!

I shut the door and pull out my slate, ignoring the unread message from Mira asking more questions about her father, and open the group chat.

Zeke: Has anyone seen Hayliel this morning?

Zeke: Where are you, hummingbird?

The only ones who read the message are Theo and Raphael. I tuck it back into my bag and head upstairs. There must be somewhere else we can look. It just doesn't make any fucking sense.

Where would she go without us? Did Uriel's minions get to her?

"Any luck?" Raphael asks once I make it back to my room.

"No. How did she seem last night after I left?"

Theo shrugs. "Tired. She fell asleep pretty quickly. We didn't think anything of it because of what went down. She was pretty worn out."

"Do you think something happened? We'd have noticed if Auriel took her from our arms." Raphael might say the words with confidence, but the look on his face tells a different story.

"We'd have noticed," Theo says, but his face pales. "My nightmare. It wasn't Serah, it was Hayliel. Dammit! What was it she'd said about Auriel yesterday, when we were talking about the lack of details?"

"Matching dreams again, just like the night she escaped the cloaked figure. That's not good." Raphael's brows dip low in thought. "She said something like, 'He wants me on his team. He'll find a way to provide details.'"

"You don't think—"

The vibration of all three of our slates halts Theo's words. Maybe it's her.

We scramble to grab them, but it's not Hayliel who's messaged in the chat.

Mira: Come to the cave.

"Do you think she knows something?" Raphael asks.

Seeing her name brings back everything I witnessed this morning with her dad. If she fucking did something to Hayliel, I won't hold back. I don't care that she's trained. I don't care if the others like her. No one hurts my hummingbird.

"Maybe," I say, unsure what to do. I consider telling them what I witnessed earlier, but that shit can wait until we hear what Mira has to say. We can focus on finding Hayliel and then deal with Atlas and the possibility that his daughter double-fucking crossed us.

"Let's go find out."

The campus is quiet as we leave Fallen house from my balcony and fly to the cave. It's still too early for most angels to be awake—yet Mira is, and she doesn't even go to school.

Honestly, I don't even know what she does when she's not with us. Does she even have a job? Or is her only job to spy on us and report back to her traitorous fucking father?

No. The focus is on Hayliel. I'll deal with Mira's betrayal later.

She's already waiting for us in the cave when we arrive. It takes every ounce of restraint I have not to grab her by the throat and demand she explain everything. Somehow, I manage to ask a simple question instead. "What do you know of Hayliel's whereabouts?"

She waves a hand toward the empty chairs. "You three might want to sit down."

We don't sit. How can we when the woman we love is missing? "Just spit it out, Mira. If she's in trouble, then we deserve to know," I say.

She sighs. "Fine. She agreed I could tell you after it was too late for you to do anything to stop her, so I'll get to the point.

Hayliel is meeting with Auriel. She's going to agree to work with him as long as he lets her parents go unharmed."

I don't blink; I'm completely dumbfounded as her words sink in. There's a split second of disbelief, but the more my brain processes, the more I realize how very true it might be.

"Why didn't you fucking stop her?" Raphael growls. I've never seen the cheerful blond so angry. He looks like he's half a second away from ripping into Mira with his bare hands.

Either she's oblivious, or she just doesn't care—because she rolls her eyes at Raphael. "Stop her? Do you even hear yourself? There was no *stopping her*. Hayliel was determined to do this and would have gone through with it entirely alone. Besides, she's only doing exactly what I would have done in her shoes."

Oh, gods. This was her doing. Mira's. She put this idea in her head and helped it come to life.

"This is fucking bullshit! You're supposed to be her friend. Instead, you've let her waltz right into harm without even trying to stop it," Theo says, fists clenched like he's trying really hard to keep his cool, but I can see the fear behind his eyes and the worry for our girl.

If only he knew how bad it really was … how deep this betrayal goes.

She scoffs. "You've got a lot of fucking nerve saying shit like that to me when I protected her a hell of a lot better than any of you. You think telling her *no* was protecting her? All you did was force her to keep secrets and try to do it alone. Fuck off. At least I gave her weapons and helped devise a plan instead of just trying to control her fucking life. The three of you need to pull your heads out of your asses and join reality. Hayliel was always going to do this. It's her fucking goddamn parents' lives on the line here."

"We weren't trying to control her," Raphael says, defeat in his voice.

I see her point, even if it pisses me off. Our intention was never to fucking collar her by removing her choices. We only wanted to keep her safe—something this traitorous bitch wouldn't understand.

Given everything I've learned today, I can't help but wonder if what Mira says is even true. Did she let Hayliel walk into what's surely a trap because her father asked her to? Does Mira truly care so little about the friendships she's made here?

"Call it whatever you want. Hayliel is going to do what she thinks is best. Now that everything is out in the open, she was hoping we'd all head to her parents' house and wait to make sure they arrive safely."

"Wait," Theo says. "How did she even know where to go?"

"Auriel got a message to her with coordinates and a time."

Way to fucking go, Theo. Asking the right questions. "And did she happen to share those coordinates with you?"

Mira's brows draw inward. "Maybe. But she knew you'd want it and asked me not to give it to you. She'd rather all of us wait for her parents at their house."

"And we'd rather she not walk directly into a trap with no backup. Tough *fucking* luck. Give us the coordinates, Mira."

I'm so fucking done with this chick today. Her next actions will give me all the information I need about where her loyalty lies. With Hayliel, or with her snake of a father.

Casually, like she can't sense how thin a line she's walking, she checks her slate.

"Fine." She taps around on the screen of her device, and I feel my own vibrate in response.

"You're just handing it over after that speech about how Hayliel didn't want us to know where she was going?" Theo asks, confused.

Mira shrugs. "For one, I can read the room. You guys won't let me leave without telling you. Second, I made my own promise to Hayliel, which I'll be keeping, even if I give up the location. Besides, the chances you'll make it there in time are slim, so I don't really count it as a betrayal of her trust. She'll understand once she remembers what possessive alpha shits you guys are."

I share the coordinates with Raph and Theo. *Let's go. We don't have much time,* I say through our mental connection. And as I pass by Mira on the way out, I whisper, "Don't think, for even a second, that this conversation is over. Once we get Hayliel back, there's a *lot* we have to discuss."

Mira and Atlas's schemes will have to wait.

It's time we bring our girlfriend back to safety.

9

HAYLIEL

Pre-dawn light hasn't broken above the horizon yet, leaving me bathed in darkness. In my rush to get out, I'd forgotten to grab the potion Mira mixed to hide my power signature. I suppose it might've been a waste anyway. I'm giving myself over to him. Hiding my power seems a little useless.

Still, I wish I'd brought them with me for *after*. A shudder runs through me, and I shake the thoughts away. I can't let myself think about what happens after my parents are safe and I'm stuck with Auriel. If I do, I'll go mad.

As I fly over the housing district and toward the desert-like wasteland where I'm supposed to meet Auriel, my mind races. I think of my parents, constantly trying to reach them with the hopes that once I'm close enough, the connection will solidify. I think of my men, wondering if they've noticed I'm missing yet and hating how I had to leave them. I hate how I had to keep them in the dark, but it was a necessary evil. They would have stopped me.

Dawn approaches, lighting up the sky just enough to illuminate something up ahead that has my stomach falling. A sandstorm. It's approaching quickly, blocking any view I might have had of what's coming.

Shit. Mira and I didn't even consider this a possibility. If I attempt to fly through that, I'll be blind, and given the high likelihood that Auriel has his little demon buddies with him, I don't need the additional disadvantage. I have to land, but where?

My gaze roams the area directly below me until I find a cluster of cacti and shrubs that will serve to hide me while I figure out my next move.

Dirt and sand shifts beneath my feet as I land, but this is no relaxing trip to the beach. This is my one chance to save my parents, to protect them the way they've always done for me. I hate what I have to give up, but for them I would do anything.

I eye the large shrub beside me that is miraculously thriving in the sunbaked land. The overthinker in me wonders if this is a sign. Will I become like this shrub, surviving despite the odds?

Pulling the blades Mira gave me from their sheath, I stare at them. They're light in my palms, and even though the blades themselves aren't very long, they're sharp as fuck.

With a deep breath, I connect to the well of heated power inside me and push it through the blades. I push and push, not stopping until they glow an incandescent gold with hues of yellow and orange. The shine is almost too bright in the dim morning light.

I can't stop the smile that spreads across my face.

If what little I imbued into the dagger with Zeke was enough to kill a demon, then the amount I just shoved into these should certainly do the trick.

Tucking them back into their sheath, I feel a little more confident and secure as I walk on toward the meeting place. I only check my slate twice, just to make sure I haven't gotten turned around in the vast emptiness—especially with my pre-planned markers hidden by the encroaching sandstorm—but I'm nearly there.

With each step, I tap into my mental connections, hoping to reach my parents.

They don't respond.

I tuck a strand of hair behind my ear—worried. With this swap, they should be closer than ever. Maybe it wasn't the distance after all. *No.* I can't let myself consider any other options. I just can't.

As the sun rises higher into the sky, the chill I barely noticed before melts away until my palms sweat and the little hairs that have escaped my braid stick to my skin. At least the heat inside of me has cooled off a bit since I imbued those blades.

I know I'm close when a sickly feeling washes over me. It

coats me like oil—dark and thick, reminding me of the way it felt in the library when the cloaked figure, now known to be Archangel Auriel, came to take me.

But that wasn't the first time we met. Only, he didn't feel like this then. His mere presence wasn't so weighted with wickedness.

How can his aura manifest in such different ways?

Whatever the reason, he's here, and hopefully that means my parents are, too.

That thought has me trying—one more time—to reach them, and for a second, I'm almost positive I hear *something*, though I can't make out any distinct words.

With one last big breath, I step around the dune I'd been hiding behind and find Auriel.

He has his staff, as expected. To his left stands three demons. A massively brutish looking one, a smaller yet still muscular one, and the scarred asshole that stabbed me. *Great.*

When I look to Auriel's other side, I have to stop myself from shouting *I knew it!* as my eyes land on none other than Useless fucking Uriel. He grins at me. There's this cocky tilt to his lips that makes me want to smack it off his face.

Motherfucking piece of shit.

My gaze continues past him, searching for the angels I came here for. My parents.

Auriel says nothing, watching me take everything in with a satisfied look on his stupid face.

When I don't find my parents anywhere, unease blossoms

beneath my ribs. "Where are my parents?"

"Nearby," Auriel replies smoothly.

"Well, bring them out. I'm here, as instructed. Now it's time to play your part." Surprisingly, my voice doesn't shake like I expect it to. I don't sound weak at all.

I sound strong.

Confident.

Even though I don't feel it. All I feel is his sickly presence and a fear that his promises were all lies to get me here. Maybe I'm just the foolish, naive girl who bought them.

Auriel grins wide, his perfect white teeth glinting in the desert sun. "There's been a change of plans, my little seraph."

And just like that, my stomach drops to my feet. "What do you mean? What changed?"

"I don't think I want to give them up. And I don't think you will either—once you know the new plan."

For a second, I can't find any words to give in response. Is he for real right now?

"I'm only here because you promised to free my parents. *That* is the plan. *That* was our deal."

"Yes, well, I've changed my mind." He holds out his hand to me. "Come with me as intended, and you can see your parents. They'll stay with you—with me—until after the cleansing. Until the world is free of the impure."

Questions bubble up in my mind ... questions that I have no answers to. Why would he need me and my parents to stay with him? What could have possibly changed to have him acting like this?

I came here fully prepared to sacrifice myself to save my parents, but I'm not willing to allow them to stay caged while our sacrifice means nothing. They are meant to be free.

"And after? What then?" I almost don't want to know the answer, but I need more time to figure out my next move. Mira and I never planned for this.

"Then we'll enter a new era. A better era. One where only the unsullied and powerful reign supreme."

He says the words with such confidence, like he truly believes all the bullshit.

His answer doesn't reassure me. It's not even an actual answer to my question. If the cleansing means what I think it means, I doubt he'd allow my parents and me any semblance of freedom. What was it he said? *Ridding the world of the impure.*

It's not very hard to read between the lines there. He wants to erase the Fallen from existence—and that includes my parents.

Once again, the weight of his evil presence presses heavily against me. I shake my head, trying to clear the fog begging to settle. "No," I say, not needing to think about it. "I want our original deal. Set my parents free, and you'll have me for whatever your twisted plan is."

Auriel only sighs. He glances at Uriel, who looks more than pleased at my refusal, then he looks over at the demons. If I weren't paying such close attention, I might have missed the almost imperceptible nod he gives them before he says, "I'm disappointed in you. I thought we could be a team. You and I against the world, as friends at first, and eventually maybe more. But I see now that you've spent far too long with the filth of Silver City. It's corrupted your mind. Tainted your soul. There can be no partnership for us."

After that, everything happens so fast.

Auriel steps back as Uriel advances toward me with an angel blade grasped in one fist and a needle in the other. *What the fuck is that?*

This asshole has had an issue with me since the very beginning, and it looks like he's finally getting the chance to act on his hatred of me.

But I won't let this bastard win. I'll do everything I can not to let him get the best of me.

My gaze darts to the black-and-red swirling orb in the handle of the blade he's holding. I hold my breath, legs trembling as I recall every ounce of pain and anguish I felt the last time that weapon was so close to me. Except, I think just as Uriel reaches me, as painful as that blade was, this asshole can't kill me. I just have to make sure he doesn't inject me with whatever the hell is in the syringe.

That thought is enough to bolster my confidence as I evade his first blow and land a solid hit to his kidney. I damn near stagger as I right myself, but I still landed the first blow.

Damn. That felt good.

A gasp escapes him. It's almost like he can't believe someone as weak and untrained as me would dare touch him. "You'll pay for that, foolish child." Then, he throws everything he has against me.

He uses his wings to make his blows more powerful, and although I do my best to block them, the force behind it is too much. On his next attack, I teleport barely out of reach—thank fuck for Mira's training—but it's not enough. His blade nicks my arm, and blood flows from the wound.

Fuck!

Every moment that passes gives Uriel a chance to study me. To learn my moves. And as much as I hate him, I can't deny that I'm impressed with how easily he can switch styles of attack. I just wish he'd stop fucking slicing me open.

"You worthless little bitch," he snarls as I evade him once more with teleportation.

I have no idea if he knows that's what I'm doing, but I hope he doesn't catch on.

"With you out of the way, your parents and the rest of the Fallen scum won't stand a fucking chance against us. And to think others thought you were so tough. Look how your blood coats my blade. Isn't it glorious?"

At this point, he isn't even trying to incapacitate me with the needle. The bastard is having too much fun with the blade. He manages another slice, this time to my leg, but I don't care. I can't. Not when he's threatening the ones I love.

Anger boils inside me with the heat of an erupting volcano. It builds and builds and builds until I can't focus on anything but Uriel. I move like a missile that's locked onto its target, dodging his blade and landing a solid kick to his gut that has him flying across the sand. He smacks into the nearby dune, and it's only the sound of his body thwacking against it that has me breaking free of whatever fucking trance just had me in its grasp.

What the fucking hell was that?

I don't get the chance to consider my own strength, because the three demons at Auriel's side snarl and approach.

As if by some instinct I shouldn't have, I reach for the twin daggers sheathed at my side and prepare for the fight of my life. I smirk when the asshole beasts look surprised to see my little blades glowing, but it's not enough to halt their advance.

To my surprise, though, they don't all rush me at once. They send in the thin one first, which almost seems like a gift. Damn. I don't know what this fucker did to piss them off, but the other two must hate him if they're sending him to fight me first.

We stalk each other in a slow circle, each of us waiting for the other to make the first move. They watched me fight with Uriel, and if they're half as smart as they think they are, they'd have paid enough attention to learn *something* about my fighting style while I know jack shit about theirs. All I know is that demons are vicious, brutal creatures who savor inflicting pain.

Up close like this, I can't help but study the way the creature looks. His leathery wings are tucked in at his back, and his horns are misshapen little stumps on the top of his head. I want to check out the other demons to see if their horns look the same or if this guy had someone hack them off, but I don't get the chance.

As if hearing my thoughts, the demon lunges for me with a

wicked snarl. I move out of his way easily, but he spreads his wings open, and I have to duck before the curved spikes at the end cut into my face.

Holy shit, that was close.

He manages to dig his claws into my shoulder. A scream of pain threatens to tear from my throat, but the rage inside of me takes over. I use his glee to my advantage, letting him haul me forward so his own force helps plunge my dagger directly into his heart.

And *poof*. Just like that, the creature is nothing but a pile of dust in the wind.

In a move that surprises even me, I grab the blade before it hits the ground. Mira would be proud as fuck.

Before the others can attack me, there's a shift inside my body as three tethers pull taut.

What the fuck are they doing here?

Without needing to look around, I know Raphael, Theo, and Zeke are close.

The brutish demon, and the scarred one, look pissed that I killed their friend—but they don't move to attack. They're waiting for something.

But what?

Fuck. Can they sense my backup?

A few heartbeats later, Raphael and Theo are standing on either side of me, but Zeke doesn't join them. Instead, I catch the slightest movement up ahead.

What the hell is he thinking?

My grumpy fucking boyfriend is trying to sneak up on an Archangel.

I don't know if the look on my face gives him away, or if they knew what he was doing all along, but suddenly, the demons move to attack.

Except it's not me they're after anymore.

No.

They turn to Zeke, who grunts as he's grabbed by an angel with metal-tipped wings.

The lieutenant moves too fast for me to get a good look at his face, but the tinkling of metal is unmistakable.

"No!" I shout as the guild lieutenant covers Zeke's mouth with his hand. Zeke tries to fight him off, but something is wrong. His movements are too slow. Too weak.

I blink, and suddenly the demons and the lieutenant—who's holding Zeke's ever-weakening form—are beside Auriel. I meet his eyes for the briefest moment, catch his smirk, and then they're just gone. Vanished, as if they were never there at all.

"Zeke!" I yell, racing forward to the spot where he just was, hoping for *something*. A rift in time and space. A portal. Fucking anything. But all I do is walk through sand and air.

I crumble to the ground, defeated.

This can't be fucking happening.

I look up at the sky and scream.

"Hayliel."

I hear my name and turn to find Theo and Raph.

"This is why I didn't want you here. This is why I told Mira not to share the location. Fuck!" I bury my head in my hands, a sob ripping from my throat.

How did things get so bad? And why can't anyone fucking listen to me? I throw my hands out on either side of me, and a stream of golden heat arcs across the sand, burning all of the vegetation in its wake.

"We'll get him back, sunshine," Raphael says, but I ignore him. We said the same thing about my parents, yet here I sit, covered in blood and sand and despair while they're held captive who knows where. Now Zeke is gone, too.

Theo clears his throat. "It's not safe here. We have to leave and tell the others what happened. About the mole and about Zeke."

I don't move. I *can't* move. My fingers sift through the sand, cupping a handful and letting it slip between my fingers. If only I could stop time. Turn it back. I could save them all. I could protect them all.

The flapping of wings has our heads turning and hope fluttering in my chest. Did Zeke escape somehow? Is he coming back to me?

But it's not Zeke.

The sight before me turns my stomach as I catch sight of four white wings spread wide.

Castiel lands beside the Archangel, face set in a grim line. It's not Auriel, yet I can't help the unease that settles over me.

An Archangel stole my parents and just took one of my boyfriends.

What the hell will this one do?

10

EZEKIEL

S omething slithers through my veins.

It mixes with my blood, much too fast for me to stop it, causing my limbs to fail me, making my mouth unable to form words and my eyelids so damn fucking heavy.

I need to tell them about Atlas. About him being not only the mole but Mira's dad, too. If I can't look into it, then someone else has to.

My mind is foggy, but I put all of my energy and focus into my connections.

Atlas is the mole. Do you hear me? Lieutenant Atlas is a traitor to the guild. And he's also Mira's father. Don't trust her. I don't know if she's working with him or not.

In front of me, no one's expression changes. Or at least, I don't think they do. Everything is a bit blurry. Whatever that asshole injected me with beckons me to close my eyes, to rest, to sleep and forget about the rest of the world.

But my world is standing with Raphael and Theo.

My world is trying to save the city on her own.

And my world is watching me fail her. Again.

That's all I seem to fucking do. So I push and push and push, willing myself to keep my eyes open, even just for a second. Willing myself to ignore the sweet whispers of slumber and lay my eyes on her one last time.

If they take me, that's fine. I only need to know that she's safe.

"Hayliel." Her name escapes my lips on a silent breath. I wanted her to hear me. She *needs* to hear me. To get out of here and be safe.

They can have me, but not her. Never her.

And then, just as the last vestiges of my strength leave me, the area seems to blink out of existence. Or maybe it's me that does.

I slump against Atlas and smile.

My girl is safe—at least for now.

And that's all that matters.

11

RAPHAEL

I should be paying attention to Castiel, or the Archangel he brought, but I can't tear my eyes away from Hayliel. She looks broken. Shattered. Something I never wanted to see her become.

She blames us right now. Mira, too. But I can't let that get to me. Out of any of us, Zeke is the most likely to survive. He's tough. Tougher than I ever gave him credit for. And I meant it when I said we'd get him back. For all his faults, he's still important to her. To me, too, even if I don't want to admit it.

Theo and I share a glance. Before Zeke was taken, he'd passed a message to us. Only to us. We know who the lieutenant is—the guild mole. And although knowing helps piece it all together, it doesn't solve our problems.

Lieutenant Atlas. The angel who saved our asses during the demon attack is working with the enemy. I replay every interaction in my mind as I struggle to pay attention to Castiel. The way Atlas told us to take the blade out when Hayliel had been stabbed—and how he promised to track down the demons who attacked us.

That motherfucker.

We have to tell the others. I press the thought to Theo, who looks to be paying attention to Castiel as much as I am.

He nods. *And find a way to contact Azrael. He needs to know who it is, and maybe he can help us get everyone back.*

Everything is a fucking mess.

Hayliel looks like she doesn't want to be in the Archangel's presence at all. She still sits on the sand, staring lifelessly at the tiny grains of it slipping between her fingers.

An empty shell.

Broken.

And even though I'm pissed that Zeke was taken, I'm still glad it wasn't her. I'm still happy it was one of us and not the angel we all love. The angel who has been through so much already. I just wish I could get rid of her pain. Wish she would trust us.

After what Mira said, though, I can understand why maybe she doesn't. We never wanted to control her. We only wanted to keep her safe.

"Are any of you listening?" Castiel asks, sounding annoyed

with us for what might be the first time.

"Sorry," Theo says sheepishly.

"We're all a little on edge, what with our friend being kid-napped by a psychopathic Archangel and not being any closer to getting Hayliel's parents back." There's more bite in my tone than I intended, but given the current situation, I'm sure he'll manage to forgive me. Or not. At this moment, I don't really care.

Castiel sighs but reads us well enough not to say anything. Instead, he crouches next to Hayliel. The Archangel he brought with him doesn't say a word. He doesn't step forward with Castiel. All he does is watch our professor talk to Hayliel in soft, reassuring tones, most of which I can't hear, but as the minutes pass, her shoulders relax a little, and she finally stands.

Good. This is good.

"Now, let me introduce you to Archangel Remiel," Castiel says, and my brows nearly reach my hairline. He's really just going for it, huh? "I know your trust of his kind isn't very high at the moment, but I've known him for a long time, and he would *never* go along with what's been happening."

My gaze darts to the Archangel we're being asked to trust. I wonder if he knows what we did in his offering tent.

"Hayliel." Remiel's voice is soothing. A comforting timbre that could lull me into a happy slumber, even under the worst circumstances.

Dangerous.

"I've often seen you in my visions," he continues. "So often that it feels as if I already know you."

Hayliel ignores his pleasantries and practically begs, "Can you see a way to help my parents? To save Zeke?"

"I see many things—most of which I cannot share, otherwise the future will shift. But there are possibilities, many of them, that may offer what you seek. I would like you to come with me to the Archangels' Sanctuary. There, we can speak more freely."

My first instinct is to laugh and tell him, absolutely fucking not. Isn't that where Auriel lives? Where he plotted to kill and maim angels? Where he conspired with demons right beneath their noses while they remained completely oblivious? Hell, for all we know, he could show up while we sleep and slaughter us all.

But what other options do we really have? Go back to school and take our exams like the world isn't fucking ending? Neither sounds particularly pleasant.

What do you think? As much as I'm wary of trusting Remiel, at least we could be close enough to make sure they're actually doing something, Theo says to us via our mental connection.

Hayliel's sigh rings loud in my head. *Uriel was here with them. The sicko was itching to stick an angel blade in my chest, so as shitty as it might be, I don't think campus is a safe place for me anymore.*

That fucking garbage ass angel, I hiss mentally. *Then I think we go, but we stay alert just in case. We can't let our guard down with another Archangel, even if Castiel swears he's trustworthy.*

Agreed, they say in unison, and then we turn back to Castiel and Remiel.

"We'll go with you," I tell them, not missing the look of relief on Castiel's face.

"But the rest of our trusted group should come as well," Hayliel adds, like she'd just thought of it. It's smart, though I can't say I'm not surprised that she'd want to see Mira again so soon after feeling betrayed.

Theo brings out his slate and begins typing, but stops to ask where they should meet us. None of us have been to the sanctuary before, and the only thing we know about it is that angels actually compete to win the chance to go there.

Remiel lists off numbers to the coordinates, and Theo dutifully types them into the chat and hits *send*. Before anyone can reply, Remiel spreads his four wings, signaling that it's time to leave.

We fly in silence.

Theo and I send small, reassuring comments to Hayliel through our mental connection, letting her know she's not alone, and by the time we arrive at the entrance to the Sanctuary, Mira is there. I don't see Dina anywhere, but I've come to realize that her father might just be more controlling than my family.

The angels guarding the entrance look annoyed, making me wonder just how hard Mira has been trying to get past them, but with a nod from Hayliel, Remiel confirms to the guards that she's with us.

Mira gives a sharp look to them that screams *told you so, asshole* but no fight breaks out. We're on the move, crossing through the threshold into the Archangels' Sanctuary. Something settles over me, causing the hair to rise on my arms and a shiver to race down my spine. If this is a protective rune, it's the strongest one I've ever felt.

I watch as Mira makes a beeline for Hayliel, her expression almost pleading. It's not a look I've seen on the confident angel's face before. But Hayliel only turns her back on Mira.

"Give her some time. She'll come around," Theo whispers to Mira, who looks like she wants to push but doesn't.

With the impending drama settled for now, I let my gaze focus on the elusive area that very few angels have the privilege of seeing. From outside the gate, the area appears to be nothing more than rocky mountain terrain, but inside, it's entirely different. There isn't much to see right away. A sprawling landscape surrounds a path that leads to tall castle-like walls and a massive arched gate. More guards are stationed at the next gate, which just seems like overkill considering how powerful the Archangels are, but what do I know?

I take one step, then another, fully intending to continue down the path to the high walls, but Remiel clears his throat. We all stop and turn to him.

"Now that we're within the shields that protect this area, I want to hear from all of you. Once we're behind those walls, things will escalate quickly, so I'd appreciate as much information as possible. Castiel told me some things about an uprising, strange demon behavior, and a supposed traitor among the guild and within our leadership. But I fear he only scratched the surface."

"Did he tell you I'm a Seraphim? Only recently discovered that bit, but now Auriel and his followers know, too. That's why he kidnapped my parents—so he could blackmail me into joining his cause." Hayliel's scowl deepens. "When I refused, he took Zeke, my ... well, he's very important to me. We have to get the three of them back right away. Alive."

Theo grabs her trembling hand, and I watch as she relaxes into his hold.

I give her shoulder a squeeze before sharing more of what we've learned. "We know Auriel is working with demons, and we suspect he's made some sort of agreement with the demon king. They're providing him with angel blades, though we're not sure what the demons are getting out of it."

"Very strange indeed." Remiel turns his midnight eyes to Hayliel. "And did Auriel give you any indication of what he's planning?"

She shudders. "A cleansing. Our best guess is that he wants to rid the world of the Fallen."

"Which is weird, because he's working *with* Fallen angels on his plan. How the hell does that make sense?" Theo's question has my brows furrowing—because he's right. That doesn't make sense.

"I have my theories on that, though none I can share at this juncture," Remiel says, and I have to stop myself from rolling my eyes. Of course, *he* can't share, but he expects us to spill everything to him.

"And the mole in the guild?" Remiel asks. "Have you discovered anything new?"

"No," Hayliel says at the same time Theo and I say, "Yes."

All eyes turn to us, but it's Hayliel who holds my gaze.

"How? When?"

"Zeke. He pushed the thought to us before ... before the connection was lost." I hate that my words make her flinch.

Theo must sense how close our girl is to falling apart, because he picks up where I stopped.

"The guild mole is Lieutenant Atlas."

His declaration is met with silence. Mira is the first to break the silence, her face ashen as she repeats, "Lieutenant Atlas is the mole. Are you certain?"

I nod. "Zeke's determination pulsed through our bond. And even if it didn't, we thought it over during the flight here."

"It makes sense, given what we've been through and what he was aware of. How he showed up at opportune times and seemed far too observant," Theo adds.

"Hmm." Remiel scratches at the scruff on his jaw. "I've heard the name before. What do we know of him?"

"Not much. Zeke would probably know more, but he never really talked about him. Only Azrael," Hayliel says, and it looks like the words cause her pain.

Remiel looks at Mira, who stays quiet. I'm about to ask her if she knows anything, but Theo interrupts my thoughts.

"We should probably update Azrael. At least we already know we can trust him, and he should know who he's working with."

Castiel folds his arms across his chest. "Absolutely."

"And Zeke's dad," Hayliel adds, pressing a hand to her heart like the act alone can reduce some of the pain. "He's a lieutenant, too. He deserves to know what's going on with his son."

"Wait." I turn to Mira as realization dawns on me. "Isn't your dad a lieutenant? If you think we can trust him, it might not hurt to at least warn him about Atlas so he doesn't get caught up in anything."

Before she can respond, Hayliel interrupts with a question directed solely at Remiel. "Were you aware that any of this was going on?"

He looks like he wants to avoid the question entirely, but he quickly realizes there's no getting out of it. "Not to this extent, no. Auriel has been in my visions over the years. All the Archangels have, for one reason or another, but I see so many that don't come to pass and saw nothing to make me think it would. Of course, we've always been aware of the history between angels and demons—and even knew their presence had increased over time—but that was not new. Recently we heard whispers of a Fallen uprising—talks of a truce made between the Fallen and demons. We were preparing for a fight with both, but we didn't realize, until recently, that the rebels were following one of our own. I fear this will come to a head far sooner than we expected."

"It already has," Hayliel says, her tone filled with annoyance. "We're well past that now."

Remiel nods, his expression stony. "It seems we are. We must make haste, then. Come. I'll take you inside, and then I must relay all of this to the others."

Castiel follows him, then Hayliel and Theo. Mira hasn't said a word, but her face remains haunted as she and I walk side by side toward the towering walls.

We're either heading into safety or stepping directly into the lair of our enemy.

12

HAYLIEL

The Archangel Sanctuary is like something out of a movie.

There's luscious green grass and bushes shaped like angel wings. Flowers and trimmed trees. Every inch is perfectly landscaped. And it all leads up to the high white stone walls and curved gate that's covered in flourishing green vines with multicolored flowers growing from them.

If it were any other day, the sight of it might make me feel something. Astonishment. Awe. Joy. Instead, I don't feel much of anything. Only pain. Loss. Fear.

I'm not sure what I expected to find as we finally pass through the large gate, but it wasn't this. The inside of their sanctuary is massive. Most of it appears to be stone or marble, with large columns lining the hallways that lead off in all directions. Even the railings are made of polished stone as they overlook the open room below. There is no ceiling above to protect it from the elements.

We take a turn and pass by a hallway with tall windows on all sides, with views of sprawling fields and a stunning garden tucked into the corner. In the distance, I see the burning embers of a tree. It stands out amidst the perfection that is the rest of the landscape, and it's not just me who notices.

"What's that?" Mira asks.

I want to be pissed that she's here and Dina isn't, but I know my best friend has a good reason for not joining us. Besides, it's not like Mira's question isn't a damn good one.

When Remiel answers, his voice betrays his dissatisfaction. "The demon blood tree."

My gaze darts to Theo as recognition clicks. Didn't Castiel say that's where those pouches came from, the one Zeke stole from the guild?

"Why is it burning?" Theo asks, hesitation lining every word.

"There is no proof, but I would guess Auriel is to blame. We believe he came by last night, grabbed what he could, and ran. I doubt he'll try to come back, but we're making alterations to our wards, so even if he does, he won't get far."

I want to ask why he'd burn the tree down completely if it's the last one of its kind, but the answer is obvious. If that tree can be used as a weapon against the demons, he'll take it from us, just like he tried to do with our remaining sunblades. Too bad he didn't account for someone to make new ones.

Me.

We continue on, passing rooms with plush pillows lining the many rows of seating and some with long tables where one might hold important meetings. It makes me think of what Raduriel said he does. Is this the type of room he was in when he learned of war?

What would my parents think of all this? Or Zeke? My chest squeezes at the thought until I have to clutch my middle just to make sure there isn't an open wound there.

Even though I know it's pointless, I try to reach them through the tether that connects us mentally.

And just like before, no one answers.

Remiel stops to open a door in a long hallway. We all pile into the room, and I'm surprised to find an empty sitting area. I expected him to take us to the others so we could discuss what's been going on, so what are we doing here?

He spreads his arms wide, and I notice a few more rooms built off this one. Their doors are shut, so I can't tell what's inside. "This is where I'll leave you to clean up and rest."

"What? No." I step forward. "We don't have time to rest while Zeke and my parents are in danger."

"I understand your concern, truly, but we must do these things in a certain manner. Wash up and grab a spare change of clothes from one of the bedrooms while I alert the other Archangels."

At my side, my hands are balled into fists as anger radiates off me. "We don't have time to waste, Remiel. They can't afford it. How can you not see that?"

I expect him to be mad at my outburst, but when our eyes lock, I see understanding instead. For some reason, that only pisses me off.

"It is not a waste of time to collect yourself and rest your body. In fact, it would be doing a disservice to them if you don't. Saving them requires we all be at our best. I'll call for you once the Archangels and our generals have assembled."

Remiel doesn't wait for me to respond—which is probably for the best. Rage is clouding my thoughts enough for me to make poor decisions.

Castiel offers me a sad smile, then follows him out the door while Mira disappears into one of the rooms on either side of the sitting room. Good. I'm too annoyed with her right now to have a productive conversation. I know it's not her fault Zeke was taken. And I know I agreed she could tell the guys what I was doing when it was too late for them to try to save me, but everything is too fresh to think realistically.

The heartache inside me doesn't allow for reason.

Raphael and Theo each take one of my hands and lead me into what might just be the most exquisite bathroom I've ever seen. A high, vaulted ceiling arches over a large sunken tub in the center of the room. Directly above it is a window that reveals dark clouds gathering in the sky.

Dreary—just like my mood.

"Come here," Raph says. He's standing near the tub where

hot, steamy water pours from the tap.

I'm still pissed at them for showing up, but I'm too damn exhausted and worn down to fight anymore. Without a word, I do as he says and allow him to pull off my dirty clothes. Even though they're covered in blood and sweat, Theo folds them into a neat little pile before setting them on the floor.

When I'm completely naked, both of them look me over with a serious gaze. I know they're looking for open wounds, but I can already tell there are none. All of my pain is internal, anyway.

They help me into the tub without ever breaking the silence. I'm grateful they can sense how much I need this. The quiet. I don't want to hear their apologies, their worries, or even their reassurances. I just need silence for a while.

I sink into the scalding water, letting out a long breath. Closing my eyes, I do my best to relax and just *exist* in this moment because even though I hate it, Remiel was right. We need to be at our strongest to get them back.

Raphael and Theo must have put something in the water, because it smells of honeysuckle and jasmine. After ten minutes of soaking, my aching muscles feel more soothed than they have in months.

At the sound of water splashing, I open my eyes to find both Theo and Raphael joining me in the tub. Theo pulls me forward so Raph can settle behind me. I relax into Raphael, letting him wrap his arms around my waist and press a kiss just below my ear. Theo sits across from us and pulls my left arm straight, rubbing a soft sponge along the length of it.

"We're sorry we made you feel you couldn't be honest with us," Raph says, his breath tickling my flesh and causing goosebumps to rise.

"We never wanted to control you. We just wanted you to be safe. But we realize now that how we handled it wasn't right," Theo adds, and my heart squeezes a little.

Then, as if they planned this speech in advance, they say in unison, "Can you forgive us?"

I want nothing more than to forgive them, and deep down I know I already do, but the loss I feel right now overshadows everything else.

"I think so," I tell them honestly. "But right now I'm angry. Angry at Auriel. At Uriel and the demons. At Mira for telling you where I was, and at the three of you for showing up. This is *my* mess. *My* responsibility. I went alone because I couldn't bear to see any of you harmed, and now the worst thing has happened."

A sob escapes me as flashes of Zeke's slumped form being taken race through my mind.

"But that's just it, sunshine. It's not only your responsibility. We're a team. Not just against the evil forces of this world, but here." Raphael places a hand over my heart. "The four of us are a unit. Against everything. Your enemy? Well, that's our enemy. Your problems? Also ours."

A single tear falls down my cheek, leaving a wet path in its wake.

Theo shifts the sponge from my collarbone to my right arm, his touch gentle and so full of love. "We shouldn't have tried to take away your choices, but we should also be allowed to decide for ourselves. About whether it's worth the risk of helping, of joining this fight. We all knew the risks of going to that meeting. And we were all prepared to endure the consequences, as long as you were safe. That alone is worth everything to us."

Tears flow freely as I realize they're right. I took away their choice just as they had done to me. And even though I *hate* that Zeke was taken, I'd be a hypocrite to be mad at anyone; I was making that same sacrifice. Allowing myself to be Auriel's pawn to save everyone else.

"I'm sorry," I whisper.

"And so are we, firefly," Theo says, placing my hand against his chest where I can feel his heart beating.

Behind me, I can feel Raphael's heart too, and I swear the three of ours are pounding in the same staccato rhythm, fully in sync.

I wish I could feel Zeke's, too. That thought sours the air around us, tainting it with pain.

"Hey," Theo says. "We're going to get him back. Your parents, too. But we do it as a team this time. With all cards on the table and all of us in the know. Deal?"

I nod, feeling the veracity of their words deep in my bones. "Deal."

"Good." Raphael places a kiss on my hair. "Now that that's settled, we just need you to do one more thing for us."

"Oh?"

I feel Raphael's smile against the column of my throat. "Lie back. Close your eyes. And let us take care of you."

I groan, not because I don't want to do as he says, but because my mind just isn't in it. Not knowing whether my parents are alright, paired with the fear of what might be happening to Zeke this very second—it's just too much. It's all too fucking much.

As if they can read my thoughts, Raphael says, "We want you to think of Zeke. Focus on your love for him and the connection you two have." He cups my bare pussy beneath the water. "Pretend it's his hand between your legs."

"And his mouth on your flesh." Theo leans forward to pepper kisses up my arm and across my chest, stopping just above my right nipple. "We think he'll be able to feel it. Your thoughts. Your love. So he knows we won't stop until he's back with us."

Water sloshes over my stomach as my breath turns choppy. "Do you truly think he'll sense it?"

Raphael teases my clit beneath the water, offering little nips of his teeth against the top of my shoulder. "We do, little sun. This thing we have, the bond we all share with you at the core, it's greater than anything we've ever imagined. Something powerful and undeniable."

Theo's lips wrap around my hardened nipple, his tongue flicking it before he sucks gently. Too gently. Still, a moan escapes my throat.

"No amount of distance can dull it," Theo says. "We'll only know for sure if we try."

As they continue to caress my body, I allow myself to think of Zeke. To push my love for him down the tether that links us and hope that, wherever he is, despite whatever he's enduring, he'll feel it.

Theo expertly strokes my clit beneath the water until I'm a writhing mess. Bliss takes over, and I whisper Zeke's name, begging our bond to carry it to him. Before the last shocks of pleasure leave me, the men I love move as one. Their fingers fight for dominance between my legs.

I watch as Raphael shoves two fingers inside me and pulses them against my sweet spot. His movements are slow. Controlled. What is he waiting for?

Then, I feel Theo's fingers at my entrance, and before I can comprehend what he's doing, he's pushing two of them inside to rest against Raph's.

I feel so fucking full.

Neither of them move their fingers. They allow my body time to stretch and adjust to this foreign feeling, all while lavishing other parts of my body with attention.

Zeke would love watching this. I could see him wanting to fuck my ass while both of them were buried in my pussy. A shiver races over me, and I gasp. Is that even possible?

Suddenly, they begin to move. At first it's little pulses from Raph and small thrusts from Theo. But with every passing second, it intensifies until I'm not even sure I'm still fully coherent.

I can't look away from the sight between my legs. Can't stop thinking of Zeke, wishing he were here to add his fingers to the mix. Then I'd be truly complete. Whole.

Theo pumps faster while Raphael's fingers tap repeatedly against this button of pleasure that makes my head spin. His thumb presses into my clit and little shots of electricity race through me.

It's so fucking hot. *I'm* so hot.

Pressure builds low in my belly, and it feels like I'm going to burst. I try to hold back, unsure of this new sensation.

"Let go, firefly."

"For Zeke. Let him know what's waiting for him when he comes home."

Their words trigger something inside me, and just like that, I snap.

A scream rips from my throat as my pussy flutters around their fingers. They don't relent. In fact, it seems to have pushed them into some sort of frenzy because they only fuck me harder with their fingers, throwing me headfirst into another mind-boggling orgasm.

When I come down, I barely manage to open my eyes. When did I even close them?

I'm no longer in the tub. Instead, Theo cradles me against his body while Raph dries me off with a fluffy towel. Exhaustion pulls at my eyelids, making them fall closed again, but I'm aware of being lifted and carried somewhere. They place me on a soft bed, each taking up a spot on either side of me.

I wish Zeke were here too, cuddled up with us.

Without effort, I find my mental pathway to him and cling to it as sleep finally claims me.

13

EZEKIEL

If sleep is peaceful, then why is my heart beating so fast?

I move my arm, trying to find a comfier position, but all it does is send a wave of discomfort through me as blood flow returns to my dead arm. I feel like a pincushion with how much it stings and tingles all at once.

As much as I want to groan, I keep quiet. If Hayliel and the others are sleeping nearby, I don't want to wake them.

I shift again, another round of imaginary needles pushing through my arm. Fuck me. I must've been lying on it for hours.

It's dark, or at least, I think it is. I can't really tell. Something feels off, but I can't place it. Right as that thought enters my mind, I catch a scent that turns my stomach. Copper and dust and something undeniably foul make me want to throw up. Then, as if someone flipped a switch, I'm bombarded with sound. Angels whisper somewhere nearby, though I can't make out their words. Behind their whispered voices, a steady hum grows louder. It's like whoever controls the volume doesn't care that it feels like my ears might start bleeding at any second.

I scramble to cover my ears and get away from that horrid scent, but I realize I'm not on a bed like I thought. My hands don't drift over soft linen; instead, I find hard, uneven stone beneath my fingers.

Where am I?

My head throbs again. I press harder against my ears, trying to stop the insufferable noise. There's a moment of peace, but it doesn't last. I feel the limp, wet strands of my hair beneath my hands and wonder what the fuck is happening. Why is my hair wet? Why am I on a stone floor? And why does my entire body feel grimy and slick with sweat?

I lick my dry lips and instantly regret it as the taste of salt, dirt, and something chemical coats my taste buds. Without thinking, I spit my saliva out on the ground, desperate to get the taste out of my mouth.

When I glance back up, a shaft of light illuminates my surroundings, making me freeze. Metal bars. Stone walls. And no sign of Hayliel, Raphael, or Theo anywhere.

Then it all comes back.

Hayliel's secret meeting with Auriel. His attack. Fucking Atlas.

I growl as everything hits me at once. The betrayal. The possibility of Mira working with her father against us. How close Hayliel came to getting hurt.

But she didn't. She's safe. And as long as she stays with the others and doesn't foolishly rush off to put herself in harm's way again, she'll stay that way.

As my heart rate settles, I blink a few times, still feeling groggy from whatever Atlas drugged me with. I might not be completely coherent yet, but that doesn't mean I'm useless. All I need is a plan to get the fuck out of here, but first I need to figure out where *here* is.

As more light filters in from somewhere up above, I can finally make out the color of the stone beneath me. It's beige—like sand. I guess Atlas didn't take me to the guild, then, considering I've never seen this type of rock there.

I try to check out the ceiling, but the motion makes my head spin, and before I know it, I'm vomiting on the floor.

"Are you alright?"

My body goes still. The voice is familiar. It almost sounds like my hummingbird, but that must just be my mind playing tricks on me. She can't be here. I don't *want* her here.

I spit more vomit-coated saliva on the ground and glance toward the voice. Two figures are in the cell next to mine. They're pressed up against the metal bars, watching me with concern.

Hayliel's parents.

"You're alive," is all I manage to say out loud. Inwardly, I'm desperately trying to let Hayliel know her parents are still breathing. When that doesn't work, I move on to the others, needing someone outside of this godforsaken cell to hear me, but the connections are too blurry. They shift in and out of focus, likely because of these damn drugs. Fuck!

"They haven't harmed us since the initial capture, so we're mostly healed. Though they like to keep us malnourished and quiet," Hayliel's dad says. Shit, what's his name again? Cal, maybe? Fuck these fucking drugs.

With worry etched across every line of her face, Hayliel's mother asks, "How the hell did they get you? Is Hayliel ..."

"Safe," I whisper. "She's safe, though I won't lie and say it wasn't close. Your daughter—"

A door opens, cutting off my words. Several sets of footsteps approach my cell, and now that my eyes have adjusted, I see who it is. Auriel stands with two demons at his back, the same ones who helped subdue me. Atlas isn't with them, and that just makes me angry.

"Ah. You're awake," Auriel says, leaning casually against his staff. "I see you've met our other guests. Splendid. Glad to see you'll all get along in your new home. Now, I just need to borrow this lovely angel, but I'll have him back before you can say *No, don't hurt him.*" He shifts the tone of his voice, mimicking a broken angel. "Not that begging will do you any good." He giggles maniacally.

Is it just the drugs still in my system, or does he sound crazed as hell?

That thought gives me an idea. I slump a little further, playing up the fact I'm still disoriented—which isn't really that hard considering I *am* lethargic and still fucked up from whatever they gave me.

Auriel unlocks my cell door, and the two demons yank me out. They don't even attempt to be gentle, not caring a bit that their grip feels like they might tear my arms clean off or whether they make my head spin with how they're throwing me around. Still, I bide my time. They're making the one mistake all kidnappers do—letting the prisoner out of their cage.

Auriel hangs back, allowing the demons to lead the way. With my head down, I search the long hallway for anything I can use to escape. I don't really expect to find a flashing neon exit sign, so when I see one glowing at the end of the hall, it takes a second for it to register.

Escape. I can escape.

Without a second thought, I tear my arms free of the demon's hold and race toward the exit. I nearly fall flat on my ass, tripping over nothing but my own two feet, but I don't stop. I'm so close I can almost taste it.

Freedom.

Her.

I shove the door open, bright light nearly blinding me. But it's not from the sun, and the door doesn't lead outside.

This is no exit.

I whirl around, but the two demons block my path with their large, leathery forms. They let Auriel pass between them, and I instinctively retreat farther into the room.

"It was a good attempt," Auriel says, like he loves watching the hope die in my eyes. The two demons shut the door, and it's only when I bump into something behind me that I realize just how screwed I am.

A lone chair with only a metal rod for a back sits empty in the center of the room. It's bolted to the floor, with several chains on either side. Behind it, along the far wall, is a table lined with instruments I know are going to cause me pain. Maybe if I can reach them first, I'd—

"I wouldn't," Auriel whispers in my ear. I whirl around, but he's not there. "See? You're no match for me."

I turn again to find him standing beside the table, his staff leaning against the wall while he holds what looks to be a pair of pruning shears. He opens and closes them, the *snip snip* sound making me want to throw up. How the hell did he get over there?

I plunge my hand into my pocket, searching for the protective amulet we've all carried since I stole them from the guild, except it's not there. When I look up, I find Auriel grinning. He must have taken it and my slate when I was unconscious.

Before I get the chance to do or say anything else, I'm grabbed from behind and forced into the chair. I try to fight the demons off. I kick and strain to free myself from their hold, but the drugs still flowing through my system keep me weak.

"Now, now. Calm down," Auriel says while the demons wrap a chain around my waist, tying me to the metal rod at my back. "We're only going to ask you a few questions about the

Seraphim girl. Answer them, and we'll bring you back to your cell with barely a scratch."

He wants information about my hummingbird? I'd rather die. "No."

Auriel only smiles. "Suit yourself." He nods to one of the demons, who hands him a vial of green shimmering liquid. I clamp my mouth shut, unwilling to let the bastard pour whatever the fuck that is down my throat.

With my arms and legs still free, I manage to dig an elbow into the stomach of the closest demon, but that only pisses him off. The demon holding the vial of green fluid grins, his sharp teeth glinting in the fluorescent lights as the other demon grabs my arms in a punishing grip. I cry out as he twists them the wrong way, giving the asshole demon the perfect opportunity to pour the contents down my throat.

I spit out half of it before they clamp my mouth shut, and I'm forced to swallow the vile liquid.

The concoction takes effect instantly. My back tingles, my shoulders ache, and then my wings spring free.

What the fuck?

The demons step back, giving Auriel room to walk around me. "Now, where to begin?" The piece of fucking shit trails a finger along my feathers until he's in front of me again. "An easy one first. What does the Seraphim intend to do about her parents?"

I glare at him, and he smiles. "Hmm, okay. What about ... ah. Got it. Where does she spend most of her time on campus?"

This fucking guy. If he actually thinks I'll give him any answers, he's delusional. I look away, but Auriel grips my chin, forcing my gaze to his.

"You will speak," he snarls.

"I will *never* betray her."

Auriel sighs. "Right. Of course. It's no matter. I was hoping you'd say that, anyway." He releases my chin, and before I can twist around to see where he went, I feel someone touch my wings. "For every answer you refuse to give, there will be a consequence. That's two so far, right, boys?" The demons only grunt in answer.

One second passes, then two, before a searing pain like nothing I've ever felt before shoots through my wings. It happens again, and I turn to find two black feathers floating to the floor. I grit my teeth to stop from shouting as my body tightens, preparing for another feather to be torn from my wings. But nothing happens.

"Answer my questions, and you might just have enough of these left to fly with."

14

HAYLIEL

I turn over in my sleep, snuggling into my guys.

They're warm. Too warm. But I stay sandwiched between the three of them, peaceful and happy.

My eyes flash open, showing only two bodies aside from my own.

Reality crashes into me.

My parents are gone. And Zeke is ... he should be here, at my side and in this bed. But this bed isn't mine, and Zeke isn't anywhere I can reach him.

Pain shoots through my chest, making it hard to breathe. It's too hot in here. I need to get out before I suffocate.

Grabbing my slate and the robe I find hanging on a hook

by the door, I put it on and tiptoe from the room. Thoughts and fears race through my mind as I step into the empty sitting room. Castiel and Mira must still be in bed or wandering on their own.

Good. I'm not quite ready to be around anyone just yet, especially not angels who can read me so easily.

The hall is blissfully quiet. I release a sigh and make my way toward the one place I think will help clear my head. The garden. I only get lost once, and when I step through the beautifully carved wooden doors, I know every ounce of effort I put into finding this place was worth it.

The space before me is an oasis. Somewhere nearby, a fountain gurgles. I follow the sound until I'm standing in front of the most exquisite creation I've ever seen. Silver and stone meld together to create a one-of-a-kind spout, with wings and angels coming off the top and reaching for the sky.

Around me, birds chirp and splash in the birdbath that sits in the corner as shafts of late morning light shine down. I can't stop the smile that spreads across my face, but it falls just as quickly. How did I sleep through the day and night? And how much suffering have my loved ones endured while I slept?

A slab of stone, stained green with moss, sits off to the side. Plush red cushions sit atop it, looking out of place but making the bench significantly more comfortable. I close my eyes as I sit and try to reach them, starting with Mom, then Dad, and finally, Zeke.

No one answers.

I can't even feel them anymore, as if the link that connects us mentally has been severed.

Torn apart.

A tear falls down my cheek, but I quickly wipe it away. Now is not the time to break down. I need answers, and to do that, I need to be strong.

When I finally feel stable enough to open my eyes, I spot Mira entering the garden. She hasn't noticed me yet, so I take the opportunity to watch her. She looks worn out, like she didn't sleep at all last night.

Could she be worried about Zeke? Or maybe she's upset with how I reacted yesterday.

I know the moment she realizes I'm here. Her body goes stiff, hand coming up to touch her throat. Even though I'm still pissed off about what transpired yesterday, I hate that this is what our friendship has come to.

"I'm sorry," she says, "I didn't realize this place was already taken."

"I think there's enough room for both of us to wallow," I tell her, tapping the empty cushion beside me. It's obvious she's beating herself up over what happened without me piling on.

She hesitates. "Are you sure? I know we aren't on the best of terms right now because of what I did."

I give her a soft smile. It's the most I can manage under the circumstances. "We're fine. My reaction yesterday had less to do with you and more to do with me. I'm sorry I made you feel unwelcome. After talking with Raphael and Theo last night, I think I understand them, and even you, a little better now. They shouldn't have tried to control me, but keeping my plan a secret from everyone was only doing the same to them. I get that now."

"I'm sorry you couldn't get your parents back."

My laugh is bitter. Poisoned. "It was silly of me to think he'd let them go. I should have known he'd go back on his word and change our deal."

Mira's brows furrow, and then she asks, "What did he want instead?"

"Everything." My chest turns hot as my inner fire grows, along with my frustration and self-hatred. "Instead of trading myself for their freedom, he wanted me at his side. He said my parents would stay with him too, so we'd all be together, but I knew, Mira. I just knew if I agreed, they wouldn't survive it. He'd force me to do something unforgivable, and they'd see everything. Even if he allowed them to live after, they'd never have looked at me the same again."

Mira puts her arm around me, pulling me into her. I go easily, needing the comfort and reassurance of her embrace.

I breathe in, counting to five before letting it out. "Looking back now, though, I probably should have agreed. At least then I'd see them. At least then I'd know they're safe. And maybe if I'd just fucking agreed, Auriel wouldn't have taken Zeke."

"It was a lose-lose situation, babe. Like, yeah, you could have gone along with his plan. Joined his army and seen your parents, but he'd more than likely only use them to control you. As for Zeke"—she shrugs—"he knew the risks. They all did, and you'd be crazy to think for even a second they wouldn't risk everything to get you back from Auriel. Besides, Zeke's a tough asshole. He'll handle whatever they throw at him—and maybe even be able to help your parents."

"Maybe." My slate vibrates inside one of the large pockets of this comfy-as-hell robe. When I pull it out, I find a novel-sized message from Dina. Heavy stones settle in my stomach as Mira and I read it together.

> **Dina**: I'm sorry I've been MIA. Dad is essentially holding me hostage at home until the school "does the right thing." Please don't reply to this. He's monitoring my slate, so I'll delete this message, but I had to warn you. Enough parents have complained to Principal Cael about you that he's called for an internal meeting. Today. Avoid campus, at least until you know what's going on. Love you, Hayles. I'll try to message you again soon.

It vibrates again with an email from the university. Looks like I failed Wingology class due to not completing the final exam. *Great.*

"Do I have 'garbage truck' written on my forehead, Mira? I must, because everyone keeps throwing their fucking trash my way."

"That goddamn piece of shit, Uriel," Mira mutters angrily.

"He was there, you know. With Auriel. The bastard was going to fucking inject me with something, and he looked more than happy to do it."

Mira goes still. "I've seriously had enough of that asshole. They should have removed him from the SCU faculty ages ago. He deserves to rot away in the dark cells at the guild."

A commotion outside the garden has us both turning to see what's going on. Raphael, Theo, and Castiel stand with Remiel. Everyone, including the Archangel, looks exhausted. Something tells me it wasn't just me that had a shitty night's sleep.

We might be in the sanctuary, but there is certainly no peace to find here.

"Ah, perfect. You're both here," Castiel says, offering me a half smile.

"What's going on?"

"It's time. The council is ready to see you now."

Remiel tucks his book beneath his arm and gestures. "Please, follow me."

"I, uh, need to change. I doubt anyone will take me seriously in a robe," I tell him, face flaming.

A frown pulls at Remiel's lips as he takes in my outfit. "I can only offer you five minutes."

Fuck. That's not nearly enough time.

"Try the thing," Mira says, pulling my attention.

"What thing?" I ask at the same time as Raphael and Theo.

"You know. The *thing*. What we practiced."

It hits me then. She wants me to teleport. The more I think about it, the more I like the idea. Far better than standing in front of a fucking council in nothing but a robe.

Besides, if it works, this will not only be the furthest I've ever teleported but also the most direct I've ever been.

Closing my eyes, I picture the room I left this morning. The comfortable bed and the stunning bathroom. A tingly sensation rolls over me, and when I open my eyes, a grin spreads across my face.

Holy shit. I did it!

I glance at yesterday's dirty clothes lying on the floor and contemplate whether or not I want to put them on. Are those stinky things really better than what I'm wearing? But Raphael and Theo weren't wearing the same clothes as yesterday. At least, I don't think they were.

I race to the closet and find a few outfits hanging up. None are quite in my size, but the cargo pants and long-sleeve shirt will do. Once I'm dressed, I let my lids fall shut and think about the garden and its bubbling fountain.

Mira's squeal of excitement is enough to tell me I didn't wind up in someone else's bathroom.

"You are one badass bitch," she says, patting my back, and then walks ahead with Castiel, who's looking over his shoulder at me with wonder in his eyes.

I guess I am pretty badass, huh?

"Feel like explaining what the fuck that was?" Raphael asks when it's just the three of us. If he's annoyed that I kept yet another thing from him, he doesn't show it. Neither does Theo.

"Oh, that? I guess I can teleport now, though that was definitely a first for me. The most I've done is moved within the same room and grabbed things before they hit the ground." The two of them look at me as if I'm a god.

"You astound me," Theo says before dropping a kiss to my temple.

Raphael takes my hand, leading me toward the others. "Do you have any more secret abilities up your sleeve?"

I shrug. "I don't think so. Well, actually ..." I whisper and feel them both look in my direction. "I can touch my nose with my tongue."

When I stick it out to show them, they both laugh and a little of the tension eases.

"How did you both sleep?" I ask.

"Meh." Theo shrugs. "We were worried when we woke up and you were gone."

He doesn't say it, but I can tell he's haunted by my sneaking out to meet Auriel. What kind of angel am I that I didn't even consider how they might react to waking up and finding me missing again?

"I'm so sorry," I say, slipping my free hand into his. "I just needed a moment alone, and you both looked too cute to wake up. But I've learned my lesson about keeping things from you guys. I won't run away like that again, promise."

"And we'll allow you to make your own choices, even if we don't agree with them. Though I do plan on being very vocal with my disagreements. Respectfully, of course." Raphael squeezes my hand, and I know that, despite the pain we've all caused one another, we're in a better place because of it.

We're going to be alright.

With our hands interlocked, we head deeper into the sanctuary until we reach what I can only assume is the council room. There are high-back chairs around a long oak table, and at the head are four seats that look like thrones.

My jaw threatens to unhinge and fall to the floor, but I keep it shut. The opulent room has high ceilings with beautifully drawn paintings covering its entirety. Plain robin's-egg-blue walls contrast with the luxurious items filling the space, likely the result of offerings during the Archangel Feast.

It seems wasteful to keep them hidden in here.

Remiel moves to join the two other Archangel's at the head of the table. Their wings are out, and if I thought looking upon one four-winged Archangel was a sight to behold, well, three at once makes me want to pass out.

The fourth throne-like chair is notably empty.

"Take a seat, everyone," one of the other Archangels says, his voice commanding yet gentle. Without needing to study his face for too long, I know who he is. Archangel Mikhael. The unofficial leader of the Archangels.

He looks exactly like his pictures. Sharp features, strong jaw, and kind eyes.

While the rest of the council gets settled, my friends and I don't move from our spot in front of the wall. I feel the stares of every angel in the room, but I don't back down. I meet each and every gaze, and even recognize a few angels—like Zeke's father, Kirach, and Lieutenant Azrael.

They look surprised to see us, and frankly, I would be too. But what hurts the most is watching the way Kirach's eyes drift from me to the others, searching for his son.

"The worst has happened," Mikhael says, drawing the council's attention. "Our once great and pious Auriel has slid into darkness, and because of his machinations, he and a group of Fallen angels are consorting with our greatest enemy."

The crowd erupts into conversation. Angels try to talk over other angels, all wanting their questions and thoughts heard by the Archangels. But it's Kirach who stands from his seat, the metal tips of his wings chiming softly. He says nothing, only waits in silence to be called upon.

"Yes, Lieutenant?" The room falls silent at Mikhael's voice.

"What do students from Silver City have to do with this situation?"

Every gaze in the room turns to us.

"Great question. It is from their courage and fortitude that we've uncovered this treachery." Gasps of disbelief fill the large chamber, but Mikhael ignores them. "Come, my friends," he says to us, motioning toward the row of chairs set up close to the Archangels.

We all take our seats—except for Castiel. He stands, surveying the room, and then begins to tell our story. He tells them everything—every attack, every loss. And when he explains how the traitorous behavior extended not only to the Archangels but also to the guild and the school, the war council begins to eye one another with suspicion.

I watch each angel closely, paying attention to the way they move and looking for anything that seems off. For all we know, one of them could be working for Auriel.

Castiel ends our story, leaving out yesterday's ordeal and my Seraphim status.

A woman with a sleek bun and pointed nose asks, "But why would they target her? She's only a student. A resident of Fallen house, as you just said. What could Auriel possibly want with her?"

When Castiel turns to me, I know what he's asking.

Public speaking has never been my strong suit. I've been the object of enough jokes and ridicule that I avoid situations like these. But this is one I can't walk away from. So I stand, nodding to Castiel, and take over.

"That's a fair question. What Auriel wanted was to control me. He figured out what I am, something I had only just discovered myself not too long ago, thanks to my friends. So he took my parents and offered me a trade. Agree to join his cause and he'll let my parents go free."

"And what are you, Hayliel Gracelin?" Mikhael asks.

Inside my head, I can hear the pounding of my heart and the blood racing through my veins. For the first time since I can even remember, I'm sure of who I am.

My voice doesn't waver when I answer. I don't tremble or fear being bullied.

This is me.

"I'm a Seraphim."

15

HAYLIEL

A t first, everyone is silent from shock. Then the disbelief kicks in, and angels talk over one another.

"It's not possible."

"A Seraphim? After all these years?"

"She lies to us!"

Archangel Shubael bangs on the arm of his chair, and the room falls into hushed silence. *Damn. That's a nice trick.*

"She speaks the truth," he says, gaze traveling around the room. "Remiel has seen it in his visions. Please, let her continue."

He turns to me, and I give him a cautious nod of thanks. Even though I'm desperate to learn more about these visions Remiel has had of me, I know now isn't the time. Besides, Shubael's interruption gave me an idea.

I take a deep breath and release my wings. Golden feathers shimmer in the light streaming through the window, erasing any lingering doubt of their authenticity. I count to thirty in my head, giving the council time to take it all in.

To my surprise, they all remain silent, but whether it's from shock or the fear of pissing off Shubael and the other Archangel's is something I'll never know.

Using it to my advantage, I pick up where Castiel stopped and explain the events of yesterday. Of how I tried to give myself over to Auriel in exchange for my parents. How I tried to do it all alone, thinking that he would keep to his word. And how I realized—very quickly—just how naïve I had been. When I tell them about my friends showing up and how Zeke was captured, I struggle to keep my composure.

My voice cracks when I say his name. This shouldn't have been how his father found out. I should have spoken to him earlier, warned him of what we'd be discussing. Fuck. How could I have done this to him?

Even though Raphael and Theo say Zeke knew the risks, I'm still to blame for his capture. Zeke's father will see it too, and then what? On instinct, my eyes find Kirach's, and all I want to do is go to him. Tell him how fucking sorry I am. Other than a new tightness around his eyes, his expression hasn't changed.

I wrap up my story quickly, needing to step back and out of the spotlight before I break down in front of everyone. No one speaks for a full minute before everyone erupts with thoughts at the same time.

"So, what is our plan to avoid this cleansing?"

"And how was this missed by Remiel? Did his visions not catch this?"

"Or did he know this whole time and say nothing?"

"How can we trust the guild now that Fallen angels have become tainted?"

Their questions are valid—most of them are the same ones I want answers to. Trust has been broken, and rebuilding it won't be easy. Not in a mess like this. Anyone could betray us.

Mikhael stands slowly but doesn't say a word. He doesn't have to. The moment everyone sees his tall frame lift from the throne-like chair and his four wings flex out wide behind him, the room quiets. As soon as it does, he tucks them at his back.

"As you know, over the last few decades we've been preparing for several things. Demons have been our main focus, but we've not lost sight of the Fallen involvement. What we did not anticipate, however, was Auriel's participation in such treachery. And let me assure you, the three of us feel his betrayal like a stab to the heart."

Mikhael sits and Remiel stands to take over. "We believe Hayliel's Seraphim status has sped up their timeline. They know once she learns to control her powers—once she truly recognizes what she can do—they won't stand a chance. It's why Auriel tried to sway her to join him. Why he took hostages who mean a great deal to her. He's afraid."

"So where do we go from here?" Theo asks. "And how can we help?"

I want nothing more than to hug him and show him just how much it means to me that he's taking our conversation to heart. How can *we* help. He isn't trying to keep me locked away in a tower while others put themselves at risk. Fat fucking chance I'd agree to that, and they're finally accepting it.

Each of us has to make our own choices. It's the only way it'll mean anything.

Shubael stands next, and I wonder if they have a schedule of who speaks or if they're that in tune with one another. "Now that we know who's involved, we'll take another look at our info in case we missed a key detail. We're looking for locations. Sources. Any clues that might reveal where Auriel is set up or where his next target is. We'll also consider making a city-wide broadcast, warning angels of Auriel's schemes. The last thing we want is to cause panic, so keep this to yourselves until you hear otherwise."

"And what of my son? And Hayliel's parents? Or the guild?" Kirach asks, his voice raw with pain despite his best efforts to hide it.

"We'll notify the guild immediately so they can revoke the lieutenant's access and keep an eye out for suspicious activity. As for the hostages, until we find a location, we're unable to do anything. But rest assured, we will work as swiftly as possible," Remiel promises.

His answer is unacceptable, and I open my mouth to protest

but Mikhael speaks first.

"Hayliel, Castiel, Raphael, Mira, and Theo, I think it best if you stay at the sanctuary. And Hayliel, we'll need you to master your powers and imbue as many blades as possible."

"But I can help find Zeke and my parents. I—"

"No."

I sit back in my chair as if he slapped me.

"You'll be more help doing the one thing no one else can do. And you'll be safer this way. We all have a part to play."

Even though I nod, I don't agree. And it looks like my friends don't either. The council's intentions remain to be seen. Are the Archangels on our side or Auriel's? Either way, we won't just sit by on the sidelines while my parent's and Zeke's lives are at risk.

Mikhael doesn't realize it, but his words have only added fuel to my raging need to help. He can underestimate me all he wants, but I know I can imbue swords *and* help bring them home.

And I'll do it whether the Archangels or their council approve or not.

16

HAYLIEL

We leave the war room with grim expressions on our faces and head toward the wing of the sanctuary dedicated to us. The one place we hope is private enough for us to talk about what the fuck just happened.

Mikhael told us to use the slate on the wall just inside our room to order room service. As if we're thinking of food at a time like this. Still. We need energy if we want to get anything done, so we order anyway.

Only after the food arrives do we risk discussing our options.

If the Archangels and their council think we'll just sit by on the sidelines, they're sorely mistaken. Maybe if I'd just let everyone help me in the beginning, Zeke wouldn't have been on his own and so easy to capture.

Fuck. I hate this!

I reach out to him again in my mind, trying my parents next when the connection doesn't go through. The others watch me. I feel it on my skin, their eyes tracing over me. Do they know I'm trying to reach him? Are they trying, too?

Theo shakes his head, and I wonder if maybe I said my thoughts out loud again. *I can't reach him either, firefly. I'll keep trying.*

I nod in understanding and push the tears away. Lately, it feels like all I ever do is cry. I'm always angry or sad. I'm tired of it.

"I can go to the guild," Mira offers. "If I can find a way to search Lieutenant Atlas's things, maybe I'll find out where he usually meets Auriel. It has to be somewhere they won't get caught."

"That's a good point. Zeke said your dad was a lieutenant. Maybe you can talk to him and see if he's heard anything?" Raphael asks.

An odd expression crosses Mira's face, but it's gone just as fast. "Maybe."

"Dina is basically under house arrest by her father, but if she's hanging out with you instead of me, he might not mind. It wouldn't hurt to loop her in on all this," I say, waving my hand around.

She nods. "I'll message her now and keep it chill so her father doesn't suspect anything."

Theo places a kiss on my cheek before stealing a fry off my

plate and popping it into his mouth. "If you're handling the guild, maybe Castiel and I can narrow down viable locations of their operations another way. It might even help us have a better picture of everything, depending on what we find."

"Splendid idea," Castiel agrees.

Raphael, being so observant, hands me a piece of bacon when he sees mine is all gone.

"Are you sure?" I ask, not wanting to take from him but really wanting another piece of the crispy deliciousness.

"I ordered extra." He drops a kiss on my cheek, and I snatch that bacon up like a lifeline.

Yum.

"Well," he goes on, "I'm still learning to trust him, but maybe I should contact Raduriel. The council isn't the only one with connections, and he seemed eager enough to help us the last time we spoke."

I take his hand. "Are you up for that? Because it's okay if you're not."

He gives my fingers a gentle squeeze. "I can put aside my past for this. Besides, trust needs to be earned—and what better way to earn some than by helping out in an end-of-the-world type situation?"

I giggle. "Right."

There's silence for a few minutes as Raphael uses a very old, very unused connection with his brother to let him know they need to talk. He's not even sure it'll work, but I know the second Raduriel responds by the look on Raph's face.

Good. Things are moving, and we're not stuck in a corner somewhere being told not to get involved. "We don't have many answers, but when has that stopped us?" I ask, trying to adopt some of my parents' optimism. I hope wherever they are, they haven't lost their hopeful spark.

"We'll get them back," Mira promises, and the others pile on in agreement.

I want to believe them. No, I *have* to. It's all I think about as I do my best to finish the food on my plate, despite no longer finding myself hungry. I bet my parents and Zeke are hungry right now.

When everyone has finished eating, Castiel's slate buzzes for the third time. As he reads it, his face falls. "It's Principal Cael. It would appear my presence is required on campus. Raphael, can you take over for me with Theo until I'm back? Hopefully, I won't be long."

"Of course. No problem."

I watch Castiel go, wondering if Cael is calling about what Dina mentioned. Some emergency meeting.

Fucking hell. The hits just keep coming.

Mira leaves, probably off to the guild, and my legs start to twitch. I can't just sit here. Raphael and Theo can look over maps, but I need to get some of this fucking energy out of me before I explode. Besides, when Zeke and I imbued at his house, all I needed was big emotions. And boy, do I have a lot of those right now.

In my search for the garden this morning, I stumbled across

a room filled with swords and daggers, arrow tips and curved blades, and even a few wicked-looking maces. That's where I head now, my strides steady and determined. I'll imbue as many as I can now and show the Archangels I won't be tucked aside.

The room is blissfully empty when I arrive. I grab a few swords off the rack, set them in a neat line on the table in the center of the room, and try to act like I know what I'm doing. One by one, I imbue them, keeping my focus sharp and fierce on the task at hand.

Before I know it, I've imbued six swords. They shine brighter than the small dagger I imbued with Zeke, and even brighter than the twin daggers I imbued for myself before meeting Auriel.

Not bad, Hayles. Not bad at all.

The well of power at the center of my being feels less full, less like it might devour me whole. Still, I think I can drain it more. We need enough for an army, which means I might have to be a little more deliberate with how much sunfire I'm pushing into each of these.

I'm pulling out another blade when the door opens and Kirach steps inside. All the air rushes out of me, and I freeze, unsure of how this will play out. Does he hate me? Blame me for Zeke's kidnapping? Gods. Last time he saw me, I was half naked in his workshop with his son. If he knew the trouble I'd get his only child in, would he have been so nice that day?

He doesn't say anything at first, only looks at the six weapons glowing on the table. There's no smile on his face, not even a glimmer of lightness. Not that I blame him. He already lost his wife, and now he's facing the same thing with his son.

"I'm sorry," I blurt, unable to stay silent a moment longer.

"What are you apologizing for, exactly?"

I swallow, taken aback by his question. "The only reason they're holding Zeke hostage right now is me. And after everything your family has already been through, I'm—"

"I don't accept," Kirach says, sounding detached and making my hopes plummet.

"Oh. Um ... alright. I understand." Without another word, I turn and put the fresh blade back on the rack, holding back tears until I can get the fuck out of here, but Kirach's words stop me.

"I don't accept, because you have nothing to apologize for."

I turn on him, unable to keep the bewilderment from my voice. "But he was only there because of me!"

"That might be true, but it doesn't negate the fact that you aren't responsible for the actions of others. Zeke made a choice, one I know he probably doesn't regret. Not if it means you're safe. I suspect he made that choice for someone he loves, and that's not something anyone agonizes over."

I can only stare, unsure of what to say.

How can he already know Zeke loves me, when even I didn't fully understand until recently?

He offers me a tight smile. "My wife made a similar choice once. It isn't easy, being the one sacrifices are made for."

My world tilts on its axis. Is that what really happened to Zeke's mom? Does he know? I want to ask him these questions, but Kirach keeps talking.

His jaw is set, determination blazing in his eyes. "But know this. We *will* get my son back, and whoever took him will pay the price. I haven't been the best father, not since my wife died, but I'm so proud of the man he's become."

"I think Zeke would really like to hear that," I tell him, my eyes stinging.

"Then we best make sure we get him back, hey?"

I offer him a smile and nod. Something tells me he'd be down to assist with our secret mission.

"Would you mind if I stayed to watch you imbue?"

His questions take me by surprise. Not just that he's asking, but he sounds genuinely intrigued. It seems like anytime someone wanted to watch me in the past, it was always with the hope they'd see me fail. His request doesn't feel like that. It's a nice change.

"Not at all," I reply, then pick up the blade I'd just put away, close my eyes, and coax my internal pool of sunfire to life.

Kirach has lost enough. *I've* lost enough.

We'll get Zeke and my parents back, even if I have to defy the entire city to do so.

17

THEO

Another day goes by without making any headway. Castiel and I just got back from following up on a possible Auriel sighting that didn't pan out, putting us right back to square zero.

I hate this.

"The rune weaver is done, and we have a very tiny window to pick it up," Raphael says, handing me his phone so I can read the message.

I pass over the location to read the time frame. We have an hour to waste before the deadline, then only a mere twenty minutes to show up for our gear before that window closes. "They don't give much notice, do they?"

"Looks that way." Raphael eyes me as I try to hand him his phone back but doesn't take it. "I thought maybe you could go."

"Okay," I say, raising my hand so he'll see that I'm holding his phone out for him, but he still doesn't take it.

"Okay? Just like that?"

"Why would it be difficult?"

"You didn't look at the location, did you?"

My brows furrow as I pull his phone back and reread the message, paying attention to the location they shared. *Fuck.* Only two blocks from my grandparents' house.

Noticing my reaction, Raph says, "I know you like to go home about as little as I do, but it would be a good opportunity to grab that book on the demon blood tree. Having more information would probably be worth it, given how little ash we have left."

Ugh. I hate that he's right. The last thing I want to do is go home, but we need all the help we can get, so it sounds like I don't have a choice.

"I can go with you, if you want?" Hayliel says, coming over to join us.

"That's a great idea!" Raphael adds excitedly, but I'm not so sure.

"Oh. You don't have to. It'll be super quick and probably not worth it at all."

"Do you not want me to go?" Hayliel asks, and I see through the mask she wears. She can't hide her disappointment from me.

Before I can respond, Raphael chimes in. "Theo would love for you to be there. He's just a little shy about his family, that's all. But you met Zeke's dad and my parents, and since we're giving this whole joint relationship thing a try, it makes sense for you to meet his, too."

Hayliel takes my hands in hers, squeezing them as our eyes meet. "I don't want to make you uncomfortable."

I hate that I'm making her doubt herself, but the last thing I want is for her to find out about my parents. Will she look at me differently if she knows what happened to my dad? Or how my mother hated me so much that she chose to leave instead of staying and taking care of me?

Raphael's voice fills my mind, his tone gentle and reassuring. *Hey. What happened to your father wasn't your fault, and your mother left because she's a coward. Don't let what's been happening lately drag you back into old thinking patterns.*

I try to let his words wash over me. I really do, but the worry continues to fester in the back of my mind. What if Hayliel blames me? What if my grandparents say or do something to set me off?

"It's alright," Hayliel says with one final squeeze of my fingers. "I should probably stay here and imbue weapons, anyway."

Fuck. The last thing I wanted to do was make her think I didn't want her there. Without knowing why, she probably thinks it's something she did. I swallow down my fears and take a deep breath. "No, no. I want you to come. It's just ... going home always makes me a little crazy, and I didn't want you to see me like that."

Her eyes search mine, and then she pulls me into a hug. When we separate, she cups my cheeks, forcing me to look into her eyes. "I am madly in love with you, Theo. Every facet of your being calls to mine, even the parts you don't want me to see. Even the parts you aren't fond of. Nothing will change that for me."

I have no words to give her in response. Nothing I say could even begin to compare to what she's just given me. All I can muster is a shaky "okay" before pressing my forehead to hers and closing my eyes.

"I love you too, firefly. More than anything else in this world."

When we pull apart, I find Raphael leaning against the wall with a shit-eating grin plastered on his face. Not that I can really blame him. Even when I doubt myself, he's never faltered or given up on me.

"You should get going. It's probably best if you stop at the house first. Don't need your grandparents questioning why you've brought so many clothes over for a quick trip."

"He makes a good point," Hayliel says. "I'll grab my bag, and then we can head out." She kisses me, then Raphael, and leaves the room.

"Thanks, Raph."

He shrugs. "You've done the same for me. Besides, with

everything so chaotic, I think it's best if we air out all our personal shit. We don't know what the future holds for any of us."

We arrive at my grandparents' house twenty minutes later, and I'm immediately hit by the same feelings I experience whenever I come here. Pain. Regret. Loss.

The house holds too many memories.

It wasn't where I always lived, though. I had another house before. Before I lost my dad. Before my mother gave up trying and left me on this very doorstep. Before my grandparents felt such dishonor to the family name.

A lot has changed since that first day. The angels who once put immense pressure on me to restore their name have backed off. But the pain in their eyes when they look at me has only diminished, not fully gone away.

I'm the reason their son is dead. I'm the reason they had to play parents when they were more than ready to enjoy not having to raise anyone.

"Theo."

Hayliel's voice sounds as if she's far away, but as I open my eyes and the fog of memories clear, I realize she's standing right in front of me.

"Are you sure you want to do this? We don't have to go in there. We can turn around right now and find some place to hang out until it's time to meet the rune weaver."

I brush a stray curl from her face and offer a weak smile.

"Sorry. I'll be fine in a minute." Pulling her into me for a hug, I release a long sigh when I feel her warm body mold to mine. I don't know how much time passes, but finally, when my heartbeat returns to a normal rhythm and it doesn't feel like I want to run away screaming, I give her a squeeze and step back.

Pushing the key into the hole, I unlock the door and step into the familiar space. No one rushes to greet us at the door, and for that, I'm grateful. It gives me more time to compose myself.

With everything going on between demon attacks, impending war, and possible death, I feel like a ticking time bomb. When will I go off? Who will I hurt when I do?

Being here only compounds on that feeling.

"Theo, is that you?" my grandmother calls out from deeper in the house.

Knowing we won't be able to get away without saying hi, I direct us toward the living room, where I know she and my grandfather must be.

"It's me," I call back. "I'm only here for a quick visit and to grab a few books for school."

When I enter the room, I find her. She's sitting alone on the couch, the convertible coffee table opened into a desk with papers covering the entire surface.

"What on God's Silver City is all of this?" I ask her with astonishment. I might have a complicated relationship with my grandparents, but I got my love of information from them.

"Oh, you know how we love to research, and with all the rumors flying around about special angels and their powers, we couldn't resist. It's great to see you. I wish you would have told us you were coming. Oh, and who's this?" My grandmother turns to Hayliel, her eyes taking her in from head to toe.

"This is my girlfriend, Hayliel. Hayliel, I'd like you to meet my grandmother, Lorna."

"It's an honor to meet you," Hayliel says.

"Likewise, dear. Javan will be sad to miss this, our Theo bringing a girl home."

"Where is he, anyway?" I ask, surprised to find he left her alone with all of this exciting research.

"Off on a secret rendezvous." She looks between the two of us, clasping her hands in her lap, and whispers, "He swears he's found information on the Seraphim everyone's been talking about lately."

Her words make me freeze, but I shake it off before she notices. Hayliel looks like she wants to say something, but I push a message to her through our connection. *No. It's better if we don't tell them. Not yet.*

She gives me a look that demands an answer but says nothing aside from, "A Seraphim? Aren't they extinct?"

My grandmother blathers on, and even though I try to listen, I can't stop my mind from wandering. How the hell do they know there's a Seraphim in Silver City? Is it Auriel trying to cause confusion among the angels? What's his end game?

"Oh, my gosh. Is this a young Theo?" Hayliel asks, breaking me out of my spiral.

"He was a rascal, I tell you."

"You don't happen to have more photos like this, do you?" Hayliel asks, staring at the photo of me wearing heels and a bow in my hair.

"An entire book. Why don't I get us some coffee, and we can look through it?"

"Would you mind?" Hayliel directs her question at me, but I'm at a loss for words. I know the book my grandmother is going to get, and I don't want to be around when she brings it out. I can't. But how can I explain to Hayliel that looking through all of those memories only causes me pain?

Shit. I should have told her the fucked-up details of my past before we came here. Deep in my soul, I know she wouldn't be so eager to bring that book out if she knew what it would do to me, but because she has no idea, I can tell just how excited she is.

Dammit. I can't say no to her.

Praying my voice holds steady, I say, "How about you two look through the book, and I'll grab what we need for school? Sound good?"

Her eyes meet mine, and I urge her to agree, to let me have this out, because I *can't* sit there and look at that fucking book.

When she nods, I relax a little.

"Come. Help me with the coffee while Theo does his business," my grandmother says, whisking Hayliel away.

I take a single moment to breathe before heading to the library. As I stand outside the door, I wonder if maybe I should have stayed with my grandmother and asked Hayliel to come find this book. But that would make me a coward.

Bracing myself, I push through the door and get hit with memories.

Anytime my parents and I would visit, this is where we all hung out. This is where we played trivia games and told stories. It's in this very room I found my love of knowledge. And although that joy remains, so does the pain.

For a moment, it feels as if I can still smell my father's cologne and my mother's shampoo. But that's impossible. Dad's dead and Mom abandoned me.

I find what I'm looking for on a shelf filled with books on demons. After stuffing the one I came for into my bag without reading it, I search the rest of the titles for anything that could be useful. *How to Take Down Demonic Forces* catches my eye, but after flipping through it quickly, I realize it's all the same shit we already know. Sunblades and sunfire are the best weapons to defeat them. Anything else will only incapacitate them for a short while.

When I'm done, I head back to check on Hayliel, grateful when I find they've put the book away. From the look on Hayliel's face, though, I can tell she knows the full story.

Even though we still have time to kill, we don't stay much longer. I just need to get out of here. Doesn't matter where, as long as it's not in this house full of ghosts.

Hayliel doesn't argue when we leave and head in the direction of the rune weaver. She doesn't push me to speak, which I'm grateful for, even though I know I'll have to say something eventually.

It's too early when we arrive in the yard of the house we're supposed to pick up our clothes from. I don't really want to loiter here, but the thought of going back to my grandparents' house is far worse than sitting outside a stranger's home.

Might as well get this over with.

"I take it you know?" I ask. "About my mom and dad."

Hayliel nods. "We don't have to talk about it. I'm sorry. I wouldn't have been so eager to see your baby photos if I knew."

I hate that she's apologizing as if she's the one who fucked up. "No. It's not your fault. I should have told you before. I was just, I don't know. In my head about it. It's not something I talk about with anyone."

"It's fine, Theo. Seriously. Talk about it or don't. I'm not going anywhere. You're stuck with me."

"So I don't repulse you?" I ask, the words barely a whisper. "I'd understand if I did. My own mother abandoned me because of what happened—what was my fault."

Another angel walks by us on the street, and I immediately stiffen. Hayliel pulls me farther into the yard, disappearing behind a row of hedges.

"Absolutely fucking not," Hayliel says with utter vehemence. "Just like with Serah, what happened to your dad isn't your fault. He was protecting you when that demon attacked, Theo. That's what parents do. What happened was awful, but it wasn't your fault. And the fact that your mom took off isn't a reflection of you. It's a reflection of her."

A moment of silence falls between us, and I swear I can read everything in her eyes. The truth of what she's saying is right there, along with love. Acceptance. Support. Despite everything she's learned today, she isn't running away. She isn't blaming me or pulling the plug on this relationship we've only just started giving our all to. She's here. She's staying.

Hayliel looks around with a smirk and then pushes me back until I'm leaning against a tall fence. There are no words needed between us. Want shines in her eyes, matching the heat in my own. I let her set the pace of the kiss until I can't hold back anymore.

"Take my dick out, firefly," I command, my tone gruffer than it's ever been.

I don't offer her any assistance while she frees my cock from its cage. The moment I'm free, I don't waste a second before lifting her in my arms and spinning us around so it's her back against the fence. Tugging up her dress, I push her panties to the side and revel at the slickness coating her pussy already.

When I sink home inside her, I swear I hear bells chiming.

"We only have five minutes, so I'm going to fuck you fast and hard while you play with yourself, okay, baby?"

"Yes," she moans, using her legs to impale me deeper inside her.

"Oh, fuck," I groan.

My grip on her hips is punishing, but it only seems to spur her on further. I pound into her, watching her suck two of her fingers before reaching down to play with her clit.

The sight short-circuits my brain. I don't care that we're in public, in some random backyard of the housing district. Neither of us tries to keep quiet. We only care about getting each other off.

Her mouth pops open, eyebrows creased, so I know she's getting close. My balls tighten, a shiver racing down my spine, but I won't come until she does.

"I'm close," she pants, moving her fingers faster.

I slam into her harder and harder, giving her everything I have and growl, "Come for me."

Sparks dance up my spine as I release into her. The walls of her pussy grip onto me, squeezing with her orgasm until it's almost too much sensation. By the Archangels, I love this woman.

"You're it for me, firefly," I tell her, still breathless as I rest my forehead against hers.

"I love you, Theo. No matter what."

We have one last moment of peace before we separate. I put my jeans back in place while Hayliel fixes her underwear.

"Can I ask you something?"

I glance at Hayliel, my curiosity peaking. "Always."

"Firefly. Do you call me that because of the blast of sunfire that happened the first time I fried those demons?"

Smiling, I touch her neck and stroke my thumb along her jaw. "No. It has nothing to do with what you are or your special powers. I call you that because of the light inside you. The one that brightens the lives of everyone in your presence."

A tear slips down her cheek, and I lean forward to kiss it away.

"What you are has never really mattered to me, not like that. But *who* you are in here," I place my palm over her heart. "That's what matters. Hell, you could be a human, a river troll, or even a demon. As long as you're you, there's no place I'd rather be than at your side."

Hayliel grins wide, but before she can say anything, the door to the house behind us opens, and a man steps out in an all-black suit. As we walk around the bushes, his gaze lands on us instantly—like he knew we were there.

Creepy.

He sounds almost bored when he says, "State your name."

"Theo. Hayliel. Picking up a package for Raphael."

The emotionless man looks us over twice before reaching inside the house to grab a black duffel bag. He places it on the ground and steps back. "The rune weaver appreciates your business." Then, without another word, he disappears inside and shuts the door.

"Did you see that?" Hayliel whispers when I return to her side with the bag in my grasp.

"See what?"

"I could have sworn I saw someone with blue hair inside the house."

"I didn't, but it might be best not to say that too loud." With her hand in mine, I tug her away from the house. "Who knows what they'll do if they know you saw something?"

Hayliel grimaces. "Good point. Let's get back to the sanctuary."

18

EZEKIEL

I come to in a rush of pain.

The ground beneath me shifts, and I almost crumble to the hard floor, but something catches me. Not something. *Demons.* It's the same two assholes who watched as Auriel pulled feather after feather from my wings. The ones who smiled through my pain.

If I were stronger, I'd kick their asses. But right now, all I am is a bundle of agony. My wings are raw from endless torture, and my muscles feel like I've just fought a thousand demons and lost.

I did, though. Lose.

My only solace is knowing that Hayliel is safe. Her parents aren't so lucky, but while a psychotic piece of shit may have them held hostage and confined, at least they aren't getting tortured and beaten for information.

Only me. And I accept that. Prefer it, even.

I do my best to stay conscious as the two demons drag my limp form somewhere. They're talking to one another, joking about how they can't wait for the next phase of the plan. Fuck, but what is it? I need to know.

We round a corner, and my wings catch on the wall, scraping over the oozing, featherless patches. Pain explodes in my back, and as I'm falling into darkness once more, I hear the demon chuckle and say, "Whoops. Didn't see the wall there."

I don't know how long I stay out for, but it can't have been for long because those fuckers are still holding me up when I wake. My strength is gone, so all I do is breathe. Through the pain. Through my fears and worried thoughts.

How much longer will this go on?

"I can't wait to see that thing go off! Shards of those angel blades will do most of the work for us. All we'll need to do is take care of the Fallen it missed," the demon on my right says with excitement.

The one on my left chuckles but says nothing.

Shards of angel blades? What does that even mean?

Blinding pain spears through me again as the demons shift their hold on me, and I swear I feel a pointed claw purposefully scratch against a tender spot on my wings.

I groan, and all they do is laugh. Squeezing my eyes shut, I try to breathe through the pain, but with each passing second I become more and more sure that I'm going to be sick.

"Not so tough now, are you?" the demon on my right says with venom lacing his tone.

"That's enough," the other one says. Just as I'm about to mentally thank him for the backup, he adds, "At least let him gain back his strength. I like it when they have some fight left."

So much for backup.

I'm abruptly dumped on the floor, and as the demons retreat and a metal door clangs, I realize I'm back in my cell. With no strength left, all I do is lie on the dirty floor, breathing hard.

"Oh, Zeke," I hear Maribella say. "They're still asking about Hayliel?"

A grunt is all I can offer in reply. Auriel has been trying to get me to break for days now. At least I *think* it's been days. It feels more like years. But it doesn't matter how long he tries or how hard he pushes. I won't break. Not on this.

She's all that matters.

Knowing I need to be strong, I force myself into a sitting position.

There's a shuffling sound that I immediately recognize as the pair moving closer to where our cages share a cell wall.

"Why are they doing all of this? And what does our little girl have to do with it?" Camael asks.

When I first arrived in this cell, I had a feeling Hayliel's parents didn't know their daughter was a Seraphim. I'm not sure why she didn't tell them, but so far I've respected her wishes and kept quiet on the subject.

"It must be about her wings, don't you think, Mari?" Cam continues. "Zeke, is that why they're after her?"

Shit. I don't have enough energy to handle this conversation.

"Yeah, I think so." There. That's not lying while also not giving away her secret.

Just like the last few times they've brought me back to my cell—bloodied and broken—Hayliel's parents tear off strips of their thin blanket and help wrap my wounds. I don't know if the potion they're giving me delays my healing, or if feathers are something that don't grow back once plucked, but the mending process is painfully long. Too long for me to ever fully heal by the time they collect me again. It doesn't help that we're underfed and barely hydrated.

"You'll run out of sheet if you keep using it on me," I tell them, not wanting to accept their care but too damn tired to fight them.

"Oh, hush," Maribella says, her hands shoved between the bars so she can tie a knot in the sheet. "You're much more important to us than the sheet."

Her words cause my eyes to burn, but I force the tears aside. Now isn't the time to break down and become a blubbering mess. I need to be strong. "You're important, too. Hayliel needs you both to get out of this."

"We will," Camael says, his tone allowing little argument. "Do you think she's safe?"

Do I? I fucking have to—I'll go mad otherwise. "I do. She's got her friends to lean on, and I know Raphael and Theo won't let anything happen to her."

"Who are they?" Mari's voice fades, as if she's underwater.

But she isn't, because I'm nowhere near water. I'm here, in pain, sitting on a grimy floor in a dungeon somewhere.

She ties another knot in the sheet over a tender section of skin, and I suck in a breath. Goddamn that hurts. "They're her boyfriends."

"What do you mean?" Camael asks, growing still. "Aren't you her boyfriend?"

Ah, shit. Note to self: don't fucking talk while in pain. Ever.

"Yes, yes. Boys who are friends. Sorry, I'm in a lot of pain," I say, hoping they'll buy the excuse. I guess that's one more thing to add to the box of secrets I have to keep on Hayliel's behalf. No way in hell am I telling Cam and Mari their daughter isn't just a Seraphim but also dating *three* angels. She can do that herself when we get out of here.

They seem to buy my story, and things grow silent as they continue checking over my wounds. While they work, I rack my brain for the details of what I overheard earlier. What was it the demon said? Shards of something, I think.

Fuck. Angel blades. What the hell does that even mean?

Not wanting to forget again, I tell Cam and Mari what I overheard, hoping they'll have some clue about what it means.

"No. They wouldn't," Cam says, his face paler than before.

"What? They wouldn't what?" Mari asks, studying her husband.

"I think they made a bomb filled with broken angel blades."

His words hit me like a sucker punch, knocking all the oxygen from my lungs as the rest of what I overheard clicks into place. "They intend to use it on the Fallen."

Shit! Now more than ever, I need access to my mental connections. I try to reach Hayliel, Raphael, Theo—anyone—but it doesn't work. It hasn't worked since I fucking got here.

Fucking fuck!

My gaze travels to the hole in the ceiling where light shines in, wishing yet again that I could figure out where the hell we are.

"Have either of you ever gotten a good look out there?" I ask, pointing to the window.

Pain barrels through me as I move, but I push through. I have to.

"Once when we first arrived," Mari answers. "There was nothing to see but a tower of rock and a sky full of stars."

Her wording makes me pause. "What do you mean by a tower of rock? Like a pole?"

Cam shakes his head. "No, not a pole. It's the strangest thing. Like the land that once grew around it had been chipped away."

Through my pain-addled mind, pieces slowly click together until I almost can't believe it. They've figured it out! "Is there anything else you remember about when you first arrived? Anything strange or different?" Excitement bubbles up my throat, nearly choking me.

They both reply in unison, sounding sad. "No."

"Well, nothing except the sand. I told Cam it's going to kill my desire to ever go to the beach again," Mari says, staring at her husband like she hates that she's lost that joy—but maybe, just maybe, she won't always hate it.

I don't bother trying to stop the victorious grin that spreads across my face. "I know where we are."

Silence greets me at my admission for only a moment before Cam and Mari press forward.

"How?"

"Where?"

Watching them clamber toward me only makes me smile harder. "The rock tower you saw is what's left of the Godless Mountain. And because of the sand, we have to be somewhere between the desert and that mountain. I bet we're in some old underground system from before God was overthrown."

"That makes sense," Cam says. "I don't think it took long to get here when they first grabbed us, but I honestly just assumed I passed out."

"How do we get this information to Hayliel?" Mari asks, effectively wiping the smile from my face.

"I've been trying to reach her and the others every day, but my connections don't work."

"We've been trying too. Sometimes it feels like we've connected to her, but we never get a reply."

I look between them, stunned. Holy shit. I completely forgot that Hayliel had been working with them on developing telepathy. "They haven't given you anything to block your mental paths?"

"No," Cam huffs a derisive laugh. "We're just lowly Fallen,

remember? We wouldn't know anything about our abilities."

Mari squeezes his hand affectionately. "I, for one, don't mind that they're underestimating us."

I nod. "Me neither. Let's try before—" The sound of approaching footsteps has me cutting off my words. Fuck! They can't be coming to drag me back already, can they?

A demon—different from the two who brought me in earlier—enters, carrying two trays of food. He goes to Cam and Mari's cell first, pushing the tray through the slot at the bottom of the cell. When he comes to mine, he's more forceful with his shove, causing the cup of water to spill on the stone floor, with the stale hunk of bread following it.

"Oops," the demon says with zero fucking remorse.

It should piss me off, but I'm too tired to care. I'm just glad he didn't give the same treatment to Hayliel's parents.

The fucker gets angry when I don't give him any sort of reaction. He slams his fist against the bars of my cell and then exits the room. Asshole.

After the demon leaves, Cam grabs their tray and offers me some of their food.

"No, no. I'll go get mine in a moment. Thank you, though."

Cam rolls his eyes. "It wasn't a question, Ezekiel. Eat it."

"He's right," Mari adds. "You need your strength."

I smile and take it, thinking of how they sound so much like Hayliel.

Gods, I miss her.

"I'll eat while you try reaching her again." I pick at the bread, doing my best to eat despite how tired I feel. The effort of simply chewing the stale bread is almost too much for me, but I do it anyway because Cam and Mari are right. I need to keep my strength up.

Disappointment fills their eyes when they finally meet my gaze.

Mari runs a hand through her disheveled hair. "I don't understand why we can't reach her. We were doing so well before."

"Distance," I croak, my mouth too dry from the stale bread.

"Well, there's nothing to be done about that," Cam says, and for the first time since I've known him, he sounds pessimistic. Not at all like the glass-half-full type of guy I've grown to know.

Something nags at the back of my mind—a memory of a time when distance was my downfall, too. What did Dad have me do back then?

"There's something we can try," I tell them, my voice garbled. I clear my throat, but it's only when Mari offers me a drink from her cup that I'm able to speak again. "Thank you."

She nods. "What can we try?"

"Boosting. Whoever's strongest with telepathy will try to reach Hayliel, and the rest of us will focus on boosting their ability."

Cam's brows crease together when he asks, "That's a thing?"

"It is, but it's not without risks. The schools don't teach it because it's easy to siphon power by accident. I've only boosted once before, so take a minute to think it over. There's zero pressure from me."

They say nothing for a moment, and I like that. I like that despite the shitty situation we're in, they're still looking at all sides of the issue and considering the risks. It says a lot about them that they can stay calm in such a terrible time and not just rush into something.

When Mari finally speaks, I trust her answer.

"We're willing to try."

"Then let's get started before anyone comes to check on us." For the first time since being taken, I feel hope.

"Mari's had the most success communicating in the past, so she'll try to reach Hayliel. How do we boost her, exactly?" Cam leans in, eager to learn. I wonder if he's this excited to try telepathy in general, or if this is a special case.

"Mari has the easy part. She'll find her connection with Hayliel and grab onto it in her mind. Cam, you and I need to find the well of power inside of us. What it looks like is different for everyone. For some it glows, for others it's just a sensation of raw energy."

Our cells grow quiet while we let Cam search for his power. I remember the first time I had to find mine. Mom taught me early, wanting to give me an edge in a world where Fallen weren't treated equally. It took me forever to locate it, so I'm a little surprised when Cam finds his within minutes.

"It was kind of like following the trail of breadcrumbs," Cam says with a shrug and a satisfied smile.

"Hey, whatever works! Alright, so once Mari is ready, we'll each grab her hand and try to slowly—and *very gently*—press our power through her. It'll feel a little weird on both sides, but weird is okay. If it starts to hurt, we need to stop. Is everyone ready?"

I locate my own source of energy, finding it far emptier than I hoped. Shit. I don't let the worry show on my face, not wanting to put undue pressure on anyone. Hopefully whatever Cam can offer will be enough.

"We're ready," they say together as a unit.

It takes a few tries, but eventually, Cam and I manage to successfully funnel our power through Mari. Her hair damn near stands on end from the force of it.

"Mari, you need to use the power now. Don't let it sit there too long, or our powers might get the wrong idea and attack one another," I tell her, watching as her face lights up with bliss.

She doesn't say anything, doesn't even react. Fuck. If we lose her to the power, we're screwed.

"Mari, honey," Cam says. "Even more than saving Zeke and ourselves, we need to warn Hayliel about the bomb. Only you can do that, my love. It's up to you to save our girl."

His words bring her back to herself and away from the power hungry core at the center of her being. "I'm sorry," she whispers.

"It's alright," I reassure her, not wanting her to feel bad for even a second. Power is addicting, especially when you're not used to it. "You're doing great. Now use all that power to reach out to Hayliel."

With her brow furrowed, she concentrates until excitement flashes over her features, but it's gone as quickly as it came. "I feel her, but it's like I'm still blocked. I don't think it's enough."

19

RAPHAEL

It's been days, and still the council refuses to act.

Hayliel is going out of her mind. We all are. Her parents are counting on us. Zeke, too. And don't get me wrong, I'm all for being smart with our plan this time. Honestly, it's something we've lacked in the past, so I can certainly see the benefit—but this is too much.

Other than our first brief chat, I haven't heard from Raduriel. Castiel has been extra cagey since returning from SCU and refuses to tell us what happened, but I get the sense that whatever it is, it isn't good news. He's thrown himself into research with Theo, but they haven't found anything concrete, despite following a few hopeful leads. They've narrowed it down to the cliffs or the desert, both of which are far too large an area.

Mira's lucked out at the guild, though she confirmed there's a strange vibe there, not that we can do anything with a vibe check. Dina is back at school but her father continues to track her movements. Most of her communication happens through Mira, who passed along a devastating piece of news. Uriel is back, teaching as if he isn't consorting with the enemy.

It pisses me off.

The only one of us who's truly succeeded in their goal is Hayliel. She's imbued an impressive number of blades—more than half of the entire supply at the sanctuary. I've watched her every chance I've had. The way she imbues so effortlessly boggles my mind. Every day, she grows more and more into her abilities. She's used this time to test out her endurance and find out just how much power she can use before it's depleted.

It's safe to say my sunshine has one hell of a deep well.

Would be nice if she could fucking use it on more than just weapons. Instead, we sit around while angels talk and stew. Half the time they don't even let us in the council room. Remiel, Mikhael, and Shubael have all apologized, spouting some political bullshit for why we aren't allowed to join.

We're all at our wits end.

At least we have an in with Azrael and Kirach, but they aren't always in the meetings, either.

The lack of progress is really starting to irritate us. I can see it now in the way Hayliel imbues. Theo and I watch as she shoves her power into weapon after weapon, never once breaking a sweat. Part of me wonders if the Archangels are doing this on purpose. Getting her riled up and frustrated so she can imbue more for them. At this point, it wouldn't surprise me.

What does surprise me, however, is the knock on the door that arrives as Hayliel is finishing up with her last blade. If it were one of the Archangels, they wouldn't knock. Neither would our friends, so who could it be?

"What now?" I grumble as I head toward the door.

"Optimism, Raph," Theo says with a wink. He's my best friend, but damn, he sure knows how to get under my skin. It's not his fault, though. He's only trying to keep our spirits up.

Trying and failing ... but still trying.

I open the door and stare into a pair of familiar eyes.

"Rad?" I whisper, surprised to find him here. Briathos stands behind him, offering me a nod.

"Good to see you, brother," Rad says, peering over my shoulder.

I break free of my stupor, grab the pair of them, and pull them inside. "What the hell are you doing here?"

"Holy shit. Even the guild doesn't have this many sunblades," Briathos says in awe.

Raduriel isn't distracted by the blades. He looks confused, and for some reason that only pisses me off more. "You needed me, so I came."

"I needed information—information you could've given me telepathically. But of course, you had to fucking show up. Hoping for center stage, I bet." Rage bubbles inside me. I do my best to contain it, but with everything else happening, I feel like I could blow any second.

"No. I just wanted to help."

How can someone so smart be so completely clueless?

"Well, let's hope no one saw you gallivanting around, or else we're screwed. They sidelined us, and if they find out we're working our own angle, they'll put an end to it."

"Raphael," Hayliel says gently, coming toward me while Theo makes his way toward my brother and his friend. I'm vibrating with energy and more anger than I can even understand. I feel foolish, but I can't stop it.

Hayliel's soft hands skim up my chest to cup my face. "Hey," she soothes, rubbing her thumbs across my cheeks and forcing me to meet her gaze. "Breathe with me, baby."

Part of me wants to slap her hands away and bolt, but that would be irrational.

I breathe in and out, doing my best to calm down. Fucking hell. My brother gets under my skin like no one else. I should probably go to therapy and deal with this cloud of overshadowing doubt whenever he's around, because I can't fucking live like this. Hayliel shouldn't have to deal with me in this state.

When I've come down enough to be rational, I place a kiss on Hayliel's forehead. "Thanks, sunshine."

"I got you," she whispers back.

"Did anyone see you come in?" I finally ask my brother.

"Just the guards." Before I get the chance to chew him out again, Rad adds, "And all I told them was that I'd found out my brother was here and wanted to make sure he was alright. We can play up that angle to the Archangels if they ask questions."

Briathos steps into my line of sight. "The information we have, it's dangerous, Raphael. Your brother and I only wanted to offer our help, so you and your friends don't have to face it alone."

"Or take over," I mutter, earning a sharp glance from Hayliel and Theo.

Shit, shit, shit. I'm mucking this all up.

"No," Rad says. "We'll stay behind if that's what you want. But we're here for you if you need us."

I hear his words, but I don't believe them. When has my brother ever sat on the sidelines? Never. How else would he get all the clout and praise from our parents? Ignoring his last statement, I say, "Well? Care to share with the class? Tell us what you know."

"Please," Hayliel and Theo tack on as one, making me feel like an even bigger asshole.

"It's not good," Briathos begins, but Rad cuts him off.

"Wait. Why are you guys hanging out in a room filed with sunblades?"

Seriously? That's what he's worried about? "Not important, Rad."

"Right, okay. As Briathos says, it's not good. It turns out that one of the Archangels, Auriel, is a traitor. There's been a lot of discussion recently about what the best course of action is to take him and the demons he's working with down."

Briathos nods. "It's being kept very tight-lipped. I don't think they know who to trust at the moment, so not even the guild is fully aware. I guess someone there was aware of Auriel's plan and even helped him a few times."

So far, they aren't giving us anything we don't already know. A tingle of satisfaction works its way through me. For once, I know more than the legend that is my brother—take that Mom and Dad.

Still, I ask, "If it's so tight-lipped, how do you know all this?"

"We called in a few favors." When I don't reply, Rad goes on. "They're finalizing a plan to trap Auriel and put an end to this mess once and for all. Apparently, the Archangels have the means to end him, should it come to that. Which is wild, because if you ask me, there's no other way out of this if he truly is responsible for what they're saying. Now this last piece is only a rumor, but apparently Remiel said the possibility of reform is there. Slim, but there. They're hoping to avoid the death route."

Hayliel rolls her eyes, fists clenched. "So their focus is on Auriel. What a fucking joke."

Shit. The information hadn't clicked in my mind. I was too focused on the fact that I'd one-upped my brother, and I wasn't really listening to what he and Briathos were saying. But this is bullshit! The lives of Zeke and Hayliel's parents aren't a game. They were supposed to be helping us get them back.

Theo takes Hayliel's fisted hand in his, gently prying until he can entwine his fingers with hers.

"Clearly we're missing something. Why are you all so pissed?

Hell, why are you even here at the sanctuary?" Raduriel asks, staring straight at me.

"You know, I'm asking myself the same question. Why are we even fucking here?" These walls suddenly feel like a cage, keeping us trapped until we can be useful. Is that what they're doing? Using Hayliel to make weapons. Using Hayliel to take down Auriel. All while not doing a damn thing for the angels we love.

Hayliel's soft voice floats into my head. *I think we should tell them what's really going on.*

I don't trust them, I push back. In truth, I just don't trust Raduriel not to fuck it up and make everything about him.

He's here, Raph, Theo says through our mental connection. *He and Briathos are here, offering support, and Rad even agreed he'd stay out of it if that's what you wanted.*

Your brother is making an effort, just like he did when we met with him at your parents' house. I think we should do the same. And we're running out of options, Hayliel says, giving me a pleading look that dissolves my reluctance.

Okay.

I glance between my brother and his friend, then say, "We're pissed because there are angels who mean a lot to us that have fallen behind enemy lines. The Archangels and their council were supposed to be planning how to get them back safely instead of focusing all of their attention on fucking Auriel."

"Zeke..." Briathos says. "At the guild, they've given four different stories about why he hasn't been around. He's been taken, hasn't he?"

"Yes," Hayliel whispers. "My parents, too."

"Well, since we can't rely on the Archangels or their council for help, it looks like we're going to have to do this ourselves," I say, fully prepared to go against the rulers of Silver City. Their priority might be Auriel, but ours lies with the family that was taken from us. Auriel can rot for all I care.

Rad runs a hand through his hair and turns to me, exasperated. "If you were in trouble, why didn't you come to me? I'm on your side here, Raph. I always have been."

The laugh that bubbles up from my throat is loud and unstoppable. "That's rich, coming from the brother whose shadow I've been sitting in for years. Your sole focus is on making Mom and Dad happy, and you stopped caring about me a long time ago."

"Raphael—"

"No. I used to look up to you. I wanted to grow up and be just like my big brother. But then nothing I ever did was good enough. Not compared to the perfect Raduriel. You reveled in our parents' love and support while never once sticking up for me or protecting me like you promised you would. Gods, it bothered me for so fucking long. It still does. But you know what I've learned recently, dear brother? I'm enough all on my own. And just because I'm not the perfect son our parents want me to be doesn't make me a disappointment. Maybe to them. Maybe even to you. But not to me. I'm proud of what I've accomplished and the angel I am. I don't need our parents' approval—or yours—anymore."

My heart pounds so hard in my chest, I swear it must be visible through my shirt.

Raduriel says nothing. He looks pale and somehow both shocked and appalled. Hayliel moves closer, tucking herself beneath my arm and giving me some much-needed support. *I'm so proud of you, Raph*, she says through our connection and I relax against her, feeling the heaviness of this confrontation ease.

"I ... Raph," Rad finally croaks. "That was never my intention. I wanted to save you from their expectations, not drag you down."

A snort escapes me, sounding loud in the quiet room. "Oh, really? Saving me from their expectations meant always doing what they tell you to, never messing up, and constantly bragging about it every chance you got?"

"Well, yes, actually. I thought if I did everything exactly as they asked, when they asked, they'd let you live your life without the weight of their expectations. Because it *is* a weight, Raphael."

"I fucking know!"

"I'm sorry." Rad reaches out a hand to me but thinks better of it and pulls back. "I'm sorry I failed you. I only ever had good intentions."

"Well, intention means shit if you don't back it up with action, and you never once stood up for me. Not when Mom compared my friends to yours. Not when she implied I was an idiot because my grades weren't as perfect as yours, or that I was a lazy piece of shit for not having a billion extracurriculars. Silence is a fucking choice, Rad. And it's the only one I've gotten from you in a really long time."

Briathos clears his throat, and fuck, I forgot he was even here.

"We both failed you. I should have spoken up, too. I'm sorry."

I watch in awe as a tear tracks down my brother's cheek. When was the last time I saw him cry?

"I'll do better, Raph. I promise. I'm sorry it ever got this bad. All I wanted was for you to have a normal life out from under their thumb, not become the problem myself. Can we start over? I want to help you get your friends back, even if it's from the shadows." His voice is pleading. "This will be on your terms."

I assess my brother, looking for any signs of bullshit, but I don't see any. Even though I just drug up all these old hurts, I think I might actually believe him.

Turning to Hayliel, I'm about to ask her what she thinks when I catch the look on her face. "Hayliel, what—"

"Raph," she whispers. "I know where they are."

20

HAYLIEL

"**B**reathe with me, baby."

He resists at first but then sucks in a breath. I watch Raphael calm down before me like magic.

He kisses my forehead, and I cherish the moment.

"Thanks, sunshine."

"I got you." And I do. Whatever he wants to do about his brother showing up here, I'll support him. As shitty as it is that Rad and Briathos have shown up, it's not exactly a bad thing. Not for our cause, and maybe, depending how the rest of this interaction goes, maybe not for Raphael either. Though I'm not sure he'll see it that way.

He needs to work out this shit with his brother before it

festers into something too toxic to escape from.

I watch the conversation unfold and Raphael's anger rise once more. Theo and I only step in a few times when the progress of information is at a standstill, but the moment they mention the Archangels' plan to trap Auriel, I lose all semblance of cool.

"So their focus is on Auriel. What a fucking joke." Blood boils in my veins as I think about the bullshit they've been feeding us. Theo takes my clenched fist and gently tugs until I let go. It doesn't fix everything, but his presence helps.

A little.

Raduriel asks why we're at the sanctuary, and I almost want to laugh. Good fucking question, buddy. Can we tell them why I'm here? That I'm practically a pawn being used to make weapons all while being lied to? What would they do?

I push my thoughts through the joined mental pathways with Raphael and Theo. *I think we should tell them what's really going on.*

Raphael responds immediately. *I don't trust them.*

He's here, Raph, Theo says. *He and Briathos are here, offering support, and Rad even agreed he'd stay out of it if that's what you wanted.*

Your brother is making an effort, just like he did when we met with him at your parents' house. I think we should do the same. And we're running out of options. I give him a look that I hope portrays I'm not saying we need to forget everything his brother has done, but we can meet him halfway in this. And we really

187

need more allies we can trust.

He responds with a single word. *Okay.*

Raphael explains why we're upset without really explaining, but somehow Briathos puts the pieces together.

"Zeke…" Briathos says. "At the guild, they've given four different stories about why he hasn't been around. He's been taken, hasn't he?"

"Yes," I whisper. "My parents, too."

"Well, since we can't rely on the Archangels or their council for help, it looks like we're going to have to do this ourselves," Raph says, and I nod.

Here I've been, imbuing weapons for them because I thought they were taking care of the situation, but all they're doing is giving the bad guy more time to do bad guy shit. What is it with all these Archangels letting me down?

My thoughts are interrupted by Raphael's raised voice as he blows up at his brother. It's maybe not the perfect time to put all their crap on the table, but it's long overdue. These two guys should have sat down and had a conversation a long ass time ago. I'm glad I can be here to offer him support now.

I press my body to his, wrapping an arm around his waist and letting him feel my presence. *I'm so proud of you, Raph.* It makes my heart burst knowing that he's finally believing in himself and stepping out of his brother's shadow. Knowing your worth isn't easy, I can attest to that. Hell, I'm still trying to figure mine out. It's a path lined with land mines of self-doubt, but from what I've learned about myself so far, and from what others have helped me realize, it's worth it.

Regardless of what blows up in our faces, we have to just keep getting up. Keep doing it afraid. It'll make victory so much sweeter.

I do my best to pay attention to the important conversation in front of me, but a mental tug pulls my thoughts.

Mom.

I go still as her words filter through my mind, her voice raw but strong. *Haylie-bear, can you hear me?*

Mom! Where are you? Is everyone safe? I almost can't believe this is real, but it's her voice. The one I grew up with reassuring me through everything.

We don't have long to talk. Zeke and your dad are ... me reach you. Your boyfriend found out where ... Underground between the desert and the Godless Mountain. There's a bomb with ... You ... to get everyone to safety.

Her words keep cutting off, but the ones I manage to hear make me smile. Dad and Zeke are alive. They're somewhere underground between the desert and the Godless Mountain. And there's a bomb about to go off somewhere. Is it where they are?

We'll come. I'm going to save you, Mom. It's so fucking good to hear your voice.

I love...

Her words cut off as the connection drops. No! I wanted to tell her how proud I am of her and how much I love them. But I guess I'll just have to do so in person.

Raphael turns to me with a question in his eyes. Whatever he was going to ask disappears when he sees the look on my face. "Hayliel, what—"

"Raph," I whisper. "I know where they are."

It's like my brain is on autopilot. I don't wait to fill the others in, I just head full speed toward the council room, where I'll demand backup from the rulers of Silver City if I have to. It's time they take action and do what they promised they would from the start.

Theo and Raduriel keep up with my frantic pace and walk beside me. Raphael is only a few steps behind with Briathos. They're talking, but in my panicky state, I only catch snippets.

"Things haven't been so great for your brother, either. He's been under your parents' thumb ..."

There's a pause, and I don't hear what Raphael says in response, but I can guess.

"I'm not trying to make this into a 'whose trauma is bigger' competition. I just want you to understand that it hasn't been easy on either side."

Maybe not the best time for Briathos to have this conversation, but I guess sometimes the best moment never comes and we have to take what we can get. Even if Rad had it rough, they're brothers. They're supposed to stick together. Maybe if they'd handled it as a team, things would be different.

The distance to the council chambers isn't long, but it feels like an eternity passes by the time we reach the large door. I grab the handle, but Rad tries to stop me from barging in and goes off about hierarchy and needing an invitation.

I'm about to bite his head off when Raphael interrupts.

"Rad, don't. Let her do this her way."

It's more than obvious how much Raduriel wants to disagree, but he stares a moment longer at his brother and finally nods, stepping back.

I push through the door and cause a bit of an uproar inside.

"What is the meaning of this?" a council member says, looking from the Archangels to the group and back again.

Remiel, with his visions and glimpses of the future, doesn't look surprised at all.

Mikhael, ever the peacemaker, says, "It's fine, Thaddeus. Hayliel, we're so glad to see you. What brings you here?"

"I know where Auriel is keeping Zeke and my parents, and I know that he's planning something big."

After a moment of silence, Shubael replies, "Please sit and tell us everything you know."

Raph, Theo, and the others step forward, but I don't budge. "I want assurances you won't try to stop me or my friends from joining the rescue mission. And before you say anything, please know I'd prefer we do it together, but I'm fully prepared to take on this task without your help."

21

HAYLIEL

After hours of discussion, we finally have a fully fledged plan.

Team A distracts while Team B sneaks in to rescue my parents and Zeke. It took a lot of convincing, since the entire council wanted us to wait. They said that if we had more time to plan, the odds would be more in our favor—but I'm tired of waiting. And after all the waiting we've already done based on their empty assurances, I refused to budge.

It wasn't easy, but it helped that Remiel took our side. Awfully handy when someone who sees glimpses of the future agrees with your plan. The longer we hold off, the more likely it is that something terrible will happen to the angels I love, and that just isn't worth it.

We have a plan. And a backup. Besides, I made enough damn weapons to arm everyone joining the rescue mission, so it's really only Auriel I'm worried about.

Still. All we could find was an old set of blueprints from an underground bunker in the area. Let's hope it hasn't changed too much because it's a pretty damn big part of our plan.

The council is dismissed, and we all head back to our shared room. We need pizza, and lots of it. Whoever had the foresight to order some in advance has every ounce of my gratitude because it's waiting for us when we arrive.

"I knew you had balls after you told Karena off at her own dining table, but I didn't realize they were *that* big," Briathos says around a mouthful of pizza.

I raise my slice toward him in salute, a grin spreading across my face as I chew. Damn right.

"Is it really true, then?" Rad asks. "About the whole Seraphim thing?"

"It is."

"Incredible." Rad looks at me with a spark of awe in his eyes, then he turns to his brother. "Please let me be there when you share the news with Mom. I want to see the look on her face when she realizes all the snide, shitty little comments she made about Hayliel growing up Fallen don't matter because she's literally an angelic class above."

I damn near choke on my pizza at his words, totally not expecting the dig at his mother. And even though I want to tell him yes, I know this isn't something for me to decide. Besides, despite what I might be, my views on angels haven't changed. None of us are better or worse. More powerful, maybe. Harder to kill, sure. But better? No. It's what's in our hearts that decides that.

When my eyes lock with Raphael's, I can tell he already knows what I'm thinking, but he also knows me well enough to understand how badly I want to see her eat her words. "Deal. I'll even try to snap a keepsake photo."

The group chuckles before silence falls again as we continue eating, but I can't stop the thought poking around in the back of my mind. "Briathos, you're a Fallen. How come she doesn't look down on you?"

He and Rad share a look before he shrugs and says, "Status."

"Because you're in the guild?"

"Well, that, and my Pure father held a rather prominent seat on the council before he retired. I think growing up in a household like that made me fit in a bit more with the Pures, so as long as Karena doesn't see my wings, she can pretend I'm just like her."

I roll my eyes. "The more I learn about her, the more I dislike her. No offense," I add quickly. Not that I think they'll mind. I know Raphael won't, at least, but Raduriel is still a mystery.

"Never any offense, sunshine," Raph says with a kiss to my temple.

Rad offers me a soft smile. "Despite how it may have seemed in the past, I'm not fond of her behavior either. Or Dad's, for that matter, but that's a whole other can of worms."

It's nice to see this other side of Raphael's brother, even if there's still a long way to go before these two siblings move past all their shit. "He seemed sweet, if I ignore the puppet strings tied to his every limb, that is."

"A puppet he might be, but it's still a choice he's making for his own gain," Raph grumbles from beside me. I squeeze his thigh, offering reassurances. Baby steps. We're making progress with Rad, and that's what matters.

"Speaking of puppets," Briathos says grimly, "I still can't believe Lieutenant Atlas is a traitor. We worked together a few times, and aside from being a bit of a snob, he seemed perfectly normal."

"Wait a minute," Raphael says, turning to Mira. "Your dad's a lieutenant. Had you ever met Atlas?"

"Probably. I've met a lot of guild members over the years," she says, looking a little pale. Her slate vibrates, and she jumps up, grabbing her plate of pizza. "I've got to take this."

Poor girl. She must be having a hard time keeping all these secrets from her dad. Maybe we should let her bring him into the fold after we get Zeke and my parents back.

Castiel clears his throat, breaking the weird vibes. "Well, we all have a big day ahead of us tomorrow, and I've got a few more books to go through before we leave. Rest up—we'll need it."

Theo watches him get up, and I know without him having to say a word that he wants to go with him. His thirst for knowledge is sexy as hell. Who am I to stand in his way?

Go, I say through our mental connection, offering him a smile.

You're too good for me, he replies with a wink before standing and calling out to Castiel. Then, through our shared connection with Raph, Theo adds, *Wear our girl out so she can sleep through the night, yeah?*

Raphael's smile turns wicked, and although I'm excited by the idea, I can't help but be a little distracted. Raduriel watches Raph with an intensity that might scare me if I didn't know they were brothers.

"We should be going too," Briathos says, standing.

Raduriel doesn't follow right away, continuing to stare at Raphael with wonder. When he finally breaks free of his trance, he rubs the back of his neck. "I'm really proud of you, Raphael. This bond you share with your friends is like a fairytale. I'm so glad you have angels like Hayliel and Theo in your corner." There's a beat of silence before he adds, "I'm sorry I haven't been the big brother you needed, but I'm grateful you're willing to give me another chance to make it right."

He leaves before Raphael can say or do anything. It's for the best, I think. Raphael can let the words sink in before he decides how to move forward. I, for one, am just happy to see his family finally do right by him—even if it's years overdue.

Now that everyone else is gone, it's only Raphael and me left on the couch.

He tucks a strand of hair behind my ear. "Are you tired?"

I shake my head. I really should be exhausted, but my brain

won't shut off.

"Go grab a sweater. I want to take you somewhere."

Searching his face reveals nothing about where we're going, so I rush to grab a sweater from our shared room. We still don't have our own clothes, but there's enough here for us to get by. I still wonder where the hell they all came from, though.

I'm back in less than a minute, which only makes him laugh. What can I say? My men have a history of taking me to the best places.

We walk hand in hand through the sanctuary. Down hallways and up stairwells, until we reach a beautiful stone balcony that overlooks all of Silver City.

Lights from each district shimmer under the fading light of the sun. This stunning view is my home, and despite the troubles I've had growing up in it, I couldn't imagine living anywhere else.

"Raphael, this is incredible."

"I wanted you to see it—this gorgeous place we call home. I've never seen this much of it at once, and it's crazy to think there are areas we can't even see from here."

"It's kind of intimidating," I laugh.

"Maybe. But it's also proof that, however big our foes might seem, we have an entire city backing us. We have Mikhael, Remiel, and Shubael. The council and the uncorrupted members of the guild. We aren't alone. How can we be in a place so vast?"

I lean against the balcony, taking it all in with Raphael at my back. "I want to preserve this view so I can always remember just how small I am compared to all this."

"After we get Zeke back tomorrow, we'll take a million group photos here." Raphael wraps his arms around my middle and squeezes. I'm not willing to consider we might fail tomorrow, and it's nice to see that neither is he.

"Thank you. For bringing me here. For accepting and loving me."

"Always, sunshine. No matter what."

Silence falls around us as we linger, taking it all in while the sky grows darker and the city lights below grow brighter and more defined.

"I wonder how often the Archangels come here and just look out at this view at the end of a long day," I whisper, not expecting an answer.

"I've been here twice before, and no one has ever shown up," Raphael says into my hair. He kisses the shell of my ear, the sensitive skin behind it, and down my neck. "It's only you and me out here, little sun. Just us above the entire city."

Tingles race down my spine as he piles my hair in his hands and wraps it around his fist. He tugs gently, causing my head to fall back against his chest.

I close my eyes and he tsks. "Open your eyes, baby. I'm going to fuck you right here—on top of the world. Watch the city sleep while I make you fall apart. Let them hear your bliss."

His free hand strays lower, dipping beneath the band of my pants where he cups my pussy. A moan escapes me as he glides his fingers over the dampening fabric. He's not in any rush, but I am.

I want him inside me. Need it more than oxygen.

"Raph, please," I pant.

"What do you want, little sun? Use your words."

"Fuck me. Now."

His deep chuckle travels straight to my clit, heightening my desire. "So demanding. But if you want me inside you, you need to let me in."

I fumble with my clothes until I finally manage to get my pants and underwear down around my calves. When I hear the jangle of his belt buckle, I can't hold back the needy, "Yessss!"

He doesn't waste a single second before sliding inside my already wet pussy and staying there as we both take in the shimmering city.

"I have never been happier than when I'm with you," Raphael says as he pulls almost all the way out before pressing all the way in again, oh so slowly. "You challenge me to be a better angel, and you make me believe that anything is possible."

He picks up speed, but it's still only torture. I need more.

"I love you, sunshine, and I plan to spend the rest of my life making sure you know just how much." He says the last words on a groan as he finally pumps into me exactly how I want.

Hard. Fast. Rocking my entire being.

Stars dance above us in the growing darkness, and I feel them converging inside me, ready to explode.

Then he stops.

"Nooo," I whine as my orgasm slips away.

"Just wait, baby," Raphael says as he withdraws and turns me to face him. He lifts me until I can rest my ass on the railing. As he slides back in, he says, "I want to watch you lose control."

In this position, I might not get the view of the city below, but what I get is so much better. Raphael—along with Theo and Zeke—are my world. They're the lights that guide me through the darkness. And when we get Zeke back tomorrow, I'm going to spend hours making sure they all know it.

Raphael's hands move up my spine while he kisses me. The tips of his fingers reach the sensitive area where my wings are hidden, tucked inside me, and I suck in a sharp breath.

"Raph. Please," I beg, but that only causes him to chuckle.

Asshole. I just want to get off, and I think I know how to make it happen.

I let my wings free, surprising Raphael. He stares at them in awe, but I don't let his reverent gaze distract me. Instead, I put my hands on the railing and transfer my weight there, lifting my hips off their perch. My wings beat hard, and the pressure forces me to sink farther down on Raphael's cock.

"Oh, fuck," he rasps.

I hook my ankles together at his back so he can't pull away as I fuck him with every beat of my wings.

"Fuck, little sun," he says again, his voice cracking. "You're so fucking perfect." His fingers find my clit, and all it takes is a few glides of his fingertips to make me tumble over the edge of bliss.

I lose control of my wings as I spiral through oblivion, but

Raphael doesn't stop fucking me. He pumps into me harder, faster, until I'm plummeting into another orgasm, but this time I take him along with me. His hot cum fills my pussy, and I swear the stars are shining even brighter now than they were before.

We might be standing over the entire world, but in his arms—or Theo's or Zeke's—I have everything I'll ever need.

22

THEO

I wake without an alarm, and it feels as though I've slept for all of five minutes.

Hayliel is already up and dressed, with imbued daggers strapped to her thigh and a sunblade sheathed at her hip. The rune-stitched clothes she wears have me wanting to drop to my knees and pray at her feet.

But I can't. Not now. Later I will, though. When we're back and know everyone is safe.

She's pouring coffee into a cup when I approach.

"Morning," I say, pressing a kiss to her temple while I reach for a mug.

"I see you slept about as well as I did," Hayliel replies, her tone filled with sarcasm.

She's not wrong. I hadn't had a nightmare in a few weeks, but they came back with a vengeance last night. My dad. Serah. Their faces all morphed and changed until I saw Zeke's face as he took his last breath. The next face I saw was Hayliel's. In my dream, she looked at me with so much blame and disappointment that it felt real.

Without thinking, I pull her into me, needing the reassurance that it was only a nightmare and nothing more. *This* is real.

Raphael joins us wearing a similar outfit to me—yesterday's shirt over a pair of shorts—and grabs a mug of his own deliciously hot coffee before we sit on the couch for what might be our last few moments of peace. Today is the day we bring our friends home, and I suspect it won't be easy.

Castiel exits his room at the exact moment I hear a knock at the door. He opens it to reveal Kirach, Zeke's father, standing on the other side with Azrael. They're each carrying several bundles of clothes.

"Oh, we're all set, actually," Hayliel says, pointing at what she's already wearing.

Azrael shakes his head. "I'm afraid not. It would seem the Archangels gave strict orders to the sanctuary guards not to let anyone pass without wearing the chosen gear."

Raphael says what I know Hayliel and I are thinking. "You've got to be fucking kidding me."

"Why?" Hayliel and I ask at the same time.

"I can't say for sure, but I suspect it's an optics thing. If they sanction a mission with you wearing whatever you want and things go sideways, it could look bad on them." Azrael sets his bundle down on a small side table.

"I guess I'll go change then," Hayliel says, clearly annoyed as she takes the outfit Kirach hands her.

"We'll worry about hitting them hard, you guys just focus on bringing them back safely," Azrael says to us, then he leaves to prepare his team. The plan is for them to act as our distraction while also causing as much damage as possible.

Auriel takes our angels? We ruin his secret base. It's a simple exchange.

Raphael and I grab an armor set and change. By the time we head back out to the main room, Mira is there and Hayliel damn near squeals.

"I knew you'd escape without getting caught!"

"It's only one of my many talents." Mira winks at Hayliel.

"Where did you escape from and what the hell are you holding?" Raphael asks, peering down at the velvet pouch Mira passes to Hayliel.

Unable to hold back, our girl tosses an excited glance in our direction as she unties the string, keeping it closed. "These are the potions Mira made for me to suppress and dampen my power signature. I figured everyone in our group should drink them to give us some added stealth."

I eye the glass vials she extracts from the bag and notice that Raphael looks like he'd rather pass entirely. "Great idea," I tell her, taking one. Turning to Mira, I add, "And very cool that you can make these. I'd love to talk once we get through this."

"Naturally."

Raphael watches the shimmering blue vial with skepticism. "So, uh, what exactly do these taste like?"

"Like not getting caught by demons and killed before we manage to rescue anyone," Hayliel says in a teasing tone, but it's no joke. Once Mira passes the vials around to everyone on our team, including Castiel and Kirach, Hayliel shouts a quick, "Bottoms up!"

The blue liquid is smooth as it goes down my throat, but the taste it leaves behind isn't pleasant. Like artificial blue raspberry gone wrong.

"That is foul," Kirach says with a grimace.

"Thank fuck someone else said it," Raph adds through a cough.

Even Mira shudders, looking at the now empty vial in her hand. "Look, ensuring these have the intended effect is easy, but the taste is never something I've been able to figure out."

"We'll make that our top priority after all of this is over," I tell her, half joking. My mind races with different options she could use to make them taste better, but without knowing the full list of ingredients, I can't be sure if they'd counteract whatever else is inside.

"I'll hold you to that. Now, these will only last a few hours—eight tops, but probably closer to six."

Hayliel checks the clock on her slate, and when her gaze meets mine, I know it's time to make our move. "Let's head out."

When Kirach opens the door, we find another angel waiting for us on the other side.

"Are we ready to go?" the unfamiliar angel asks. He's dressed in the same armor we're all wearing, but over it he's wearing a similar wing jacket to the one we bought Hayliel. Either he's a secret Seraphim too, or the poor guy has trouble regulating his temperature. Something tells me it's the latter.

"You're on the council," Hayliel says, stepping forward and eying the newcomer with confusion.

"Darok. I am but a gift from the Archangels, sent to help you achieve your goals."

Right. As if we needed some random council member to save our friends.

Hayliel sighs, and I feel her frustration flow down our mental pathway. "Well come on then, Darok. Try to keep up."

Examine the blueprints, they said. *It'll help you*, they said.

Except the blueprints we have are clearly outdated since the entrance we're supposed to be standing in front of is nowhere to be found.

"Dammit!" Hayliel whisper-shouts, letting her fear and frustration seep into the air.

This can't be it.

Reaching into the bag on my back, I pull out the blueprints and look at them again. Kirach comes up beside me, surveying the paper over my shoulder while Raph does his best to comfort a very frustrated Hayliel.

Darok doesn't move to help. He just stands there with a smile on his face like we're not paddling up shit creek with our hands. What the fuck is his deal?

"It should be here," I mumble to myself, tracing the lines marked into the paper. There should be a door right here, but instead there's only a tall sand dune that isn't marked on the map like all the other ones. A thought hits me, and I almost keep it to myself, but now isn't the time to shy away. "Could they have built this dune to hide the entrance?" I ask Kirach, whose eyes light up as he follows my train of thought.

He studies the pile of sand, then reaches toward a spot that looks perfectly normal to me. "Only one way to find out."

When his hand makes contact with the sand, it doesn't tumble to the ground or shift the thousands of grains. It presses in by half an inch, and the dune shudders as a door slides open, revealing the entrance we've been looking for.

No one moves for several seconds as we listen for any sign of movement from within. Finally, when we sense no immediate danger, Hayliel says, "We all know the plan, right? We get Zeke and my parents out while the others distract and destroy as much as they can. We're short on time, so we can't stray. Does everyone understand?"

I nod along with the others, a smile threatening to tilt my lips as I watch my firefly take charge. Raphael sends me a look that screams, *fuck, she's hot, isn't she?* and I'd have to agree.

But this isn't the time for ogling. I tuck those thoughts away until after. Once we have her parents and Zeke safely secured within the sanctuary, then we can shower our girl with all the love and praise she deserves. But right now, she needs my head in the game. And with demons most likely crawling all over this place, I'll need as much of my focus as possible to keep from converting to the shy, scared little boy who only wants to protect those he loves.

I will not lose focus today.

As silently and swiftly as we can, we make our way through the maze-like hallways en route to what we think—or hope—is where they're keeping Zeke. We found two areas on the blueprints that would be perfect for holding hostages. The first one is at the end of the hall. Let's just hope we're not wrong.

A commotion up ahead has my body tensing. Is it coming from the room we're heading for or one of the doors that branch off the hallway?

A booming, raspy laugh echoes from one of the side doors. Demons. But how many? My eyes lock with our group as I ponder our options. We can try to sneak past them, but that means we may need to fight them on our way out. Is it better to get it out of the way now than try to do it with our friends in tow?

A rock skitters down the hall and smacks into the door. The same door the demons are behind. We all turn to look at Darok, who starts fucking whistling. He stops when he notices us staring at him. "What?"

All fucking hell breaks loose.

Two demons rush into the hall. They barely spare us a glance before attacking. As fast as they are, Kirach is faster. He drops to the ground, sliding between the legs of one beast and thrusting his sunblade up through the demon's fucking taint, turning him to ash.

The other one doesn't go down as easily. He's a brute of a demon, but seven on one is no match. Castiel and Kirach keep him busy with their blows, and when his focus is on them, Mira drives an imbued dagger into his back and twists.

Hot damn. Maybe this won't be so bad after all.

We confirm there are no more demons hiding about, then rush to the room at the end of the hall. No sound escapes from behind it, but that doesn't mean anything. It could just be an empty room.

The door is heavy, but it opens without a sound, and we pile inside.

The scent hits me first, making me gag. Bitter and coppery. Pairs nicely with the blood and dark feathers littered on the floor.

Feathers from a Fallen angel. But that doesn't mean they're Zeke's. It could be anyone who displeased Auriel or the demons. We already know there are Fallen willingly choosing to align themselves with him, so it's not a far-fetched thought.

A tray of tools sits near the back wall. Kirach kneels to look at the dark object leaning against the frame. It takes me a moment to realize what it is, but when it becomes clearer, I almost puke.

A severed wing. The cartilage is sliced clean, but there are feathers missing in patches all over it. Most likely the ones littered on the floor. Whoever the owner of this wing is, they were tortured first.

"Oh shit," Darok says. "Is that from your guy?"

I'm going to fucking punch this piece of shit if he doesn't shut the hell up.

"It might not be his," Raphael tells Hayliel before tossing a glare Darok's way.

There's an unmistakable chill emanating from Kirach, but to my surprise he doesn't say anything. All he does is strap the amputated wing to his back and stride from the room without a second glance.

Hayliel, Raph, and Mira follow him out, but Castiel and I hang back.

Castiel blocks the door while I lean against the wall. "Listen, man. I get that you're on the council and the Archangel's sent you, but you've gotta give a little more thought to your words before you speak them. The last thing we need is for things to go south because of your inability to read the room."

"The Archangels didn't send me here to make sure your feelings weren't hurt. They sent me here as an assurance for your well-being."

Anger boils beneath my skin as I stare at this pompous asshole. We have enough shit on our plates today without him piling it on. Hayliel doesn't need it, neither does Kirach.

Castiel looks anything but his usual calm and composed self. "Our team had a good enough handle on our *well-being* when those demons attacked in the hall. So good, in fact, that you just stood by and watched. So if you're going to stay, do your job and keep fucking silent while you do."

Fucking A, professor. I stride past Castiel and back out into the hallway, finding the rest of our group a few feet away. Raphael looks at me, and I give him a nod. Hopefully, what we said to that fucker sticks, because next time I won't use words.

"Can we see the blueprints again?" Hayliel asks as I approach. "We've lost a bit of time, so I just want to make sure we don't lose any more."

I pull the folded paper from my pocket and hand it to her, watching as she finds our spot, then trails her finger along the path we need to take to arrive at the final room we think they may be holding prisoners. It's not that the room is far, but it's on a sublevel we have to get to first.

Castiel arrives as Hayliel folds up the paper and hands it to me. Then Darok runs to us from the room, seemingly out of breath for such a short distance. "I've just heard from Team A. The explosives in our suits will go off automatically in thirty minutes. They've advised us to place them in every corner and then get the hell out."

"Excuse me?" Hayliel asks, her tone as cold as the look Kirach delivers Darok.

"Explosives weren't part of the plan," Kirach adds.

"Well, plans change. These are our new orders. Any deviation will be considered treason."

That motherfuck—

Mira's fist launches straight into Darok's face, and he crumples to the floor, unconscious. "Holy shit, that felt good."

"Everyone, check your suits. I don't see why he'd lie about this, but we need to know what we're dealing with," Kirach says, taking charge.

In hidden pockets of our suits, we find three sets of explosives per angel, all flashing green.

Shit. "Everyone take out your slates and start a timer for twenty-five minutes. It seems we're on more of a time crunch than we initially planned for."

Hayliel pinches her brow, clearly frustrated. "I'm sorry, but as great as it would be to blow up their little fucking den, I'm not leaving without doing what I came here for—treason or not. And I don't give a shit what that fucks up for the Archangels."

Kirach nods. "I'm in agreement with you."

"Then we split up." Castiel steps forward, then taps Mira's and Raphael's shoulders. "The three of us will take the explosives and set as many as we can in the time we have left, while you"—he points to Hayliel, Kirach, and myself—"go save our friends."

I'm a little hurt that he left me off his team, but deep down, I understand why. With demons around, I'm a liability. And a liability with a bunch of explosives isn't a great mix. He needs angels around him he can trust to keep their shit together, and unfortunately, my track record for not falling apart isn't too great.

"As much as I hate to split up, he's right," Raph adds, taking

Hayliel's hand and placing a kiss there.

"Fine, but who's responsible for the asshole?" Hayliel asks, glancing toward Darok.

"We'll handle it and find you at the extraction point. Now go get you your man." Mira shoos us away. She doesn't need to tell us twice.

We speedwalk down a hallway and around a corner until we find the stairs that lead deeper down into the bunker. Despite our best efforts, they creak as we descend, but with our new deadline, we can't tiptoe around. There's no fucking time to slow down.

Bastards.

At the bottom of the stairs is a long corridor. The room we need to get to is near the end, just before another hallway that will lead to our escape. But guarding that door is another fucking demon. What the hell did Auriel offer them? From everything I've ever read about demons, they don't serve anyone but themselves and the demon king, so why are they acting as guard dogs for an Archangel?

The demon spots us quickly, but Hayliel and Kirach are already racing toward the creature with their weapons raised. I step forward, preparing to join the fray, but something distracts me. There, in the corner of my eye, down another passageway, I swear I see him.

The demon that killed Serah.

I blink, and he's gone.

My field of vision narrows, and everything shifts. I saw him, didn't I? That wasn't a figment of my imagination. I have to go after him. He must pay for what he took from me—for what he took from Serah.

"Theo?" someone calls, but I don't look to see who it is or what they want.

The moment I've spent my life training for can be mine if I just go. The fucker can't have gotten very far. I *just* saw him.

Theo.

I feel her. My firefly. She pours her love for me down the mental pathway we share, jolting me out of the haze of revenge. Now I have a tough choice to make. Do I go after the demon I've wanted to kill since I was just a teen, or stick with the plan?

One serves as vengeance for a dead friend, while the other serves the lives of the living.

23

HAYLIEL

*T*heo.

I don't know why he stopped. Is it a panic attack? Another flashback? I can't check on him until we defeat these fucking assholes.

What we thought was one demon turned out to be two. The first was easy to dispatch. All it took was Kirach's quick reflexes and one strike to turn him to dust. But this fucker? He won't go down.

I barely avoid the swipe of his claw and manage to graze him with my imbued blade. He screeches as he backs up a step, his eyes darting between the two of us. Then he just leaves.

My gaze swivels to Kirach, who looks just as confused as I am.

Why the hell would he run away? The asshole could have easily taken us both on.

"Come on," he says. "We don't know if they ran off for reinforcements, and I don't particularly want to be here to find out."

And we're running out of time on the damn fucking explosives.

I turn to check on Theo, but he's already at my side. *Is everything okay?*

I'm certain I saw Serah's killer just now and almost went after him, but that's not what we're here for.

From the emotion pouring through our connection, I know it took a lot for him to make that choice. *We'll make him pay, Theo. I promise you. Thank you for coming back to me.*

He presses a quick kiss to my forehead, and then we enter the room behind Kirach. The only light comes from a hole in the ceiling. It illuminates the doors of two cells, but doesn't reach any farther.

"Hayliel!" Mom calls out, and I rush to the farthest cell.

Thank the gods she's alright. "We're here to get you out," I say in a rush, trying to open the door, but of course it's locked. It's a damn cell, for fuck's sake.

"That demon you dusted didn't happen to drop a set of keys, did he?"

Kirach shakes his head.

"You should have enough heat to melt through the bars," Theo says, eying the keyhole.

Right. The powers my parents don't know I have. Well, this should be interesting.

"Are you both alright?" I ask, gripping the bars near the keyhole.

"We're fine, but ... Zeke ... Honey, he's not doing too good." They look in the direction of the other cell. I follow their gaze, but all I can make out is a lumpy figure beneath a threadbare sheet.

"We'll get him to a healer right away," I reassure them, not willing to let any negative thoughts enter. I can't. If I did, I'd crumble, and we don't fucking have time for that.

"We've got less than ten minutes before those explosives go off, and while I don't want to rush you, we've gotta get moving," Kirach says, spreading a sticky substance over the section of the cells where the door meets the bars. When he's done, he turns his anguished expression toward the prone figure.

Toward his son.

Without another thought, I move toward Zeke's cell and grip the bars. "Right. Mom, Dad, what you're about to see might be shocking, but I promise I'll explain it all once we're out of here." I find the pool of power inside me and direct it toward the bars. The metal heats beneath my skin, but I don't let up, not until I smell smoke.

"Stand back!" Kirach shouts, and I jump away just in time for a small explosion.

"You used a combustible agent to help speed up the process," Theo says in amazement as the door cracks open.

"You two check on Zeke while I get this door open," I say, but Kirach is already striding into Zeke's cell before I even get the words out. I shift my attention back to the door of my parents' cell, ignoring the heat of their stares. "Keep away until after, please," I tell them, then bring forth more sunfire. As soon as it's safe, I stride in and hug them both. "I'm so fucking glad you're alright."

Kirach makes a sound that has my head whipping toward him.

"My boy," he rasps out as agony spills from him.

"What is it?" I ask, rushing into the other cell.

"Firefly," Theo says, stopping me from getting too close.

"Stop it, Theo. Let me—"

The words get stuck in my throat as I finally see him. *Zeke.* He's pale, and his usually soft, dark hair is matted and patchy, like they've cut his scalp and took bits of hair in the process. His wings are out, but they look nothing like they used to. The one closest to me has had so many feathers removed it's bald in some places, and as my eyes trace the line of his wings, I notice what must have Kirach in such a state. Zeke's other wing is just ... gone. Cut clean off the bone.

Nothing remains but a stump.

"Zeke," I whisper, my eyes pricking with pain and anger so fucking hot, I swear I could burn the entire city to the ground. "But how? Why?" I ask, turning to my parents for answers.

"We have a lot to talk about, but not here. We need to get him to safety before they come back and do worse."

A single tear tracks down my cheek, scalding me.

"I'm going to tear them to the ground for this," Kirach promises, and I nod in agreement.

Auriel. The demons. They won't get away with this.

I place my hand on Zeke's remaining wing while Theo gives my parents water and food from his pack.

Zeke. I'm so fucking sorry, I say through our connection, but even though he's right here and I'm touching him, something blocks our pathway.

I feel a tingle from deep inside my well of power, and even though I don't know what it means, somehow I know it's nothing to fear. It builds until suddenly the power converges at my fingertips and flows into him. Before my very eyes, the open wounds where feathers were plucked from his wing close up, and new ones sprout in their place, shimmering softly—as if coated in glitter.

"By all that is holy," Kirach says, watching in awe.

I've healed him? But how? All I felt in that moment was anger for what they'd done to him and *pain*. Was it his pain ... or mine?

"Will it work on his wing?" Kirach asks, his voice pleading.

"I'm not sure, but I'll try."

He unstraps the wing from his back and holds the severed edges together. Bile rises in my throat at the sight, but I hold it back. Zeke needs me. Until a few minutes ago, I didn't even know I could *heal*. And if I can heal his feathers without conscious thought, surely I can heal this, too.

My hope bleeds into desperation.

"They removed it with an angel blade," Mom says softly from somewhere behind us. "Nothing can cure a wound like that."

I want to argue with her, to tell her *I* survived that very blade, except she doesn't know that, so I stay silent.

Digging deep into my power, I put my entire focus on raising those tingles, feeling the heat of my internal core, then push it toward the two ends of his wing. Nothing happens right away, but I don't give up, pushing and pressing despite the heat searing my insides, until suddenly, the cartilage shimmers, then glows a bright golden light that damn near blinds me.

Zeke screams, but still I don't stop.

When he goes silent again, I hold my breath. But it's there. Attached. Kirach isn't holding it anymore. Can it really be that easy?

"But how?" Dad asks, confused.

Ignoring him, I turn to Kirach. "How did you know to grab the wing?"

He shrugs. "Just a hunch—"

An explosion echoes off in the distance, signaling our time is up. *Fuck!* Another boom rings clear, shaking the foundation.

"Uh, guys?" Mira says from the hole in the ceiling, startling all of us. "Change of plans. We'll have to leave from here. The explosions blocked our other route."

Another blast, this time closer. Louder. We're running out of time.

With Zeke unconscious and the hole too small to fly out of, it'll be tricky to get out. But we've gotten through worse, right?

Well, maybe not worse, but still ...

Stay positive. I have to keep positive.

Kirach acts quickly, directing us to carry Zeke over to the hole while he jumps up with practiced movements and pulls himself out. Mira jumps down, and we all help to lift Zeke up enough so Raphael, Castiel, and Kirach can pull him through.

It takes more time than we have, but we finally get him out. Darok must have been wrong about his timing, because these explosives aren't going off at the same time. Just another reason to hate the fucker.

Mom goes next, even though she argues. And when Raphael and Theo demand I go next, I realize ... maybe my stubborn streak comes from my mother. But just as I ignored her arguments, Theo and Raphael do the same with mine.

Once I'm out, they pull Theo up next, leaving only Mira and my father down at the bottom. Another explosion goes off, halting our progress, but I take the time to talk to Kirach, sensing what he wants. "Take whoever you need and get Zeke to the sanctuary. Mom, go with him."

For the first time in my entire life, she *rolls her eyes.* "I'm not leaving Cam."

"Mom, don't—"

"You wouldn't leave us, sunshine," Raphael says, interrupting me. Fuck. He's right, even though I hate it.

"Castiel and I will manage while the rest of you pull the others to safety. We'll see you there. Be safe." Then, without another word, Kirach and Castiel lift Zeke and fly away.

A sound from below has fear rising in my gut. It's the door, banging against the wall. But who …

Then I see it. A demon.

"You wanted an explosion?" The big brutish fucker from earlier calls out, flipping something in his hand. "Here you go!"

Time seems to slow as he hauls his arm back and tosses an object into the room before disappearing as quickly as he came.

"No!" I shout at the same time as my mother, ready to jump down the hole and stop it from happening, but Raphael and Theo haul us both away just in time to avoid getting caught in the blast. Debris and chunks of sandstone rain down on the area where we just stood. Where my father and Mira were.

"Oh, gods," Mom wails, covering her mouth with her hand.

I move to her side, holding her tight in my arms and try to stay strong. We're angels, right? Bombs might hurt, but we won't die. So why is my mom so scared?

"They'll be okay, Mom. Dad will survive this," I reassure her.

"No, no, no," she cries. "They made special bombs loaded with angel blades. If they—" but she breaks out into another sob before she can continue.

Holy shit. If that's true, we're fucked, and my Dad … Mira …

"Stay with them," I hear Raphael say to Theo, but I don't look where he's going. I can't, not with Mom falling apart in my arms.

I don't know how long he's gone for. It could be seconds. Minutes. Hours. My entire focus is on the woman whose heart is currently shattering into a million tiny pieces at losing the love of her life.

"They're alive!" Raphael calls to us. He has to say it twice before the words sink in.

I stumble to my feet, hauling Mom along with me until we're staring down into the open pit that was once a room. Where the door was is nothing but rubble. A silver lining, I suppose. With that blocked, the demon can't come back with more force.

A strange, icy-blue mixture covers Dad and Mira from head to toe. Actually, it covers more than just them. It's on the nearest chunks of sandstone, too. What the hell is it?

Mira helps Dad to his feet. They're talking, but I can't make out the words. Then, Dad does the strangest thing. He hugs her. A complete stranger. Before I can do anything, the pair unleash their wings and fly out of the crumbling room.

"Cam!" Mom cries, rushing toward where my dad lands and jumping into his arms. As much as I want to run toward him and make sure he's alright, I know she needs a private moment with him, so I head toward Mira instead.

Raphael takes a quick scan of Dad while Theo does the same with Mira.

"How the hell are you two alive right now?" I ask. The pair of them are shivering uncontrollably despite the humid temperature. Adrenaline, maybe? They must both be in shock.

"Y-your friend doused us in something that m-made us cold enough to protect us," Dad says, walking toward us with Mom practically glued to his side.

"N-not fully," Mira adds, her teeth chattering. She's holding her arm to her chest. Broken, I suspect. Dad has a pretty nasty gash on his head, too.

I don't think that bomb had any angel blades in it, at least. For now, we're safe, but when they let that bomb explode, it will kill far too many angels. Pulling out my slate, I send a message to Castiel to let him know we're heading to the sanctuary. I ask him to notify Team A so they can fall back, and to warn them about a possible shrapnel bomb.

I glance around, not trusting our momentary peace. We need to get out of here.

"Are you well enough to fly?" I ask the group. Everyone nods, but then I realize we're down an angel. "Fuck. What happened to Darok?"

"He woke up and bailed. That asshole is probably back in the sanctuary, lounging in his council chair and pretending like he actually fucking did something." Mira kicks her foot toward a bag sitting a few yards away. "I don't think I can carry that. Not with this arm."

"I can take it for you," Raph says, rushing to pick it up. "As for Darok, I say fuck him. I'm glad he's not here."

"Agreed. What's inside?" Theo asks, nodding to the pack on Raphael's back curiously.

A triumphant smile grows on Mira's face. "We may have found a stash of weapons. I took as much as I could fit."

"Fuck, yes!" Raphael whoops. "Let's hope the rest get destroyed."

"Thank you," I mouth to her, hoping she knows just how grateful I am for everything she's done. I'm not sure I would have survived losing Dad, and I know for certain that Mom wouldn't have.

She bumps into me with her good arm, and then we take off, racing back toward the man I pray is awake.

24

HAYLIEL

I t's been a week since the rescue, and yet it feels like an entire year has passed.

My parents are safe, thank fuck, but Zeke ... he hasn't woken up yet. The healers tell me this is normal—encouraged, even, with their medicine. I guess losing one's wing does far more to the body than I realized, and with me reattaching it, things are even further out of our control. The healers say what I've done is unheard of, so their estimates of when he'll wake up are just that: guesses.

Still, I don't regret what I did. I just hate waiting. All I want is five minutes. Five minutes! To tell him he's safe. That I love him and we'll be here whenever he wakes up. Is that too much to ask?

Apparently it is.

If that wasn't bad enough, we finally found out why Castiel was acting so strangely. Turns out, I've been expelled from Silver City University—effective immediately. He kept it to himself all this time because he didn't want to add more to my plate. To be honest, I wasn't all that surprised. I'd already failed Wingology class and knew there were secret, important meetings being discussed about me.

The news might have shocked me once, but not now. And with everything else on the horizon, I can't find it in me to care.

"Hayles, wait up!" Dina calls from behind me. She was waiting for us at the sanctuary when we got back from our mission. I guess her dad has let up on her now that I've been MIA, so she doesn't have to fly home every day. Instead of waiting around and attending class like nothing was going on, she grabbed a few things and came here as fast as she could.

Gagiel and the others stopped her in the hall to check up on me, so at least I know not everyone hates me on campus. Though I'm sure Seraphina and Cadriel are thrilled to have me gone.

"Hey," I say back, though it's lackluster. A lot of the things I do lately are.

"Where are you off to?" she asks, falling in step with me.

"To check on my parents. I'm still not sure they'll ever be the same after ..."

"They'll get there. We all will. Mind if I join?"

What she doesn't realize is that I don't know if I'll get there, especially not while Auriel and the demons exist. "Not at all. They'd love to see you."

My parents finally know the truth about what I am. As soon as we knew Zeke was in the hands of the healers, they'd hounded me for details about the strange power I used on the cells. They'd already figured out it had to do with my change in wing color, but to say the truth shocked them is an understatement.

Just like it's always been, my differences don't faze them. They love me as much as they always have, and I know—in the very marrow of my bones—that will never change.

We finally stop in front of the room Remiel gave my parents. It's farther away than I'd like, but that can't be helped, or so I'm told. The door opens before I even have to knock. Dad stands on the other side while Mom is setting some food down on the coffee table.

"Come in, come in," Dad says. "Good to see you, Dina. Mari, we'll need another plate."

Mom puts another plate down and rushes over to us. "My two favorite girls!"

My nose burns, warning me of oncoming tears, but I fight them back. This all feels way too familiar. This place may not be our home, but everything about this visit is like before. Mom has been busying herself in the kitchen while Dad explores and waits to try whatever she puts in front of him. Now the four of us are hanging out like everything since my attending Silver City University never happened.

Damn. Maybe my parents are tougher than I ever gave them credit for.

We barely shut the door when a knock sounds.

"Expecting someone else?" I ask as a tingle of worry creeps down my spine.

"No."

Finding my well of power, I reach for the handle and open the door, ready to blast anyone who means us harm.

Remiel is on the other side, standing a few steps back from the door like he knew I'd be wary. "I'm sorry to interrupt, but your presence is requested in the council room."

I get the sneaking suspicion that *requested* isn't the right word. That would imply I have a choice.

"Of course. Just let me say goodbye—"

"No need. They're welcome, too. Come, or we'll be late."

Great. This is just how I wanted to spend my afternoon. I glance once more at the food Mom prepared for us and sigh. So much for comfort food.

We follow Remiel to the council chamber and find a heated debate about why the Fallen would ever agree to work with Auriel and his demons. Most of the council is made up of Pure angels, aside from a few Fallen—like Azrael—who I can't help but notice are getting the side-eye from everyone. Overall, this is the wrong crowd to understand what Fallen deal with on a regular basis.

Remiel makes his way to his seat next to the other Archangels, and the room falls silent.

"Ah, Hayliel. I'm so glad to see your parents settling in after their ordeal," Mikhael says, smiling warmly. "Thank you for coming. We were hoping you'd lend us your insight into a matter we can't quite seem to figure out."

"Of course. What do you need?" I'm still not pleased with the way things went down during our rescue mission, but it seems even they were played. The demand to drop the bombs and then leave never came from the Archangels or the distraction team. It was a rogue angel who infiltrated their way into our communications, hoping to take us out or make us angry enough at the Archangels that we'd go ballistic.

"Why do you think the Fallen would work with the enemy?"

I glance at my parents, noticing Mom has her hand raised. Cute.

"May we speak freely?"

Mikhael bows his head. "Please."

"Fallen have been mistreated for a very long time." The council room grows loud with aggravated grunts, but Mikkael only has to raise a hand to silence them, allowing Mom to continue. "We're given the worst jobs and paid poorly to do them. There are areas we cannot enter because of our wings and housing areas we cannot live in, even if we could afford it. Even now, we're sequestered to the Fallen district, a place more filthy than any other area in Silver City. While I don't agree with the Fallen who sided with Auriel, I can understand what they're trying to achieve."

The room is silent when she finishes. Put like that, I don't see how anyone could argue, let alone the Pures, who have never had to deal with those inequalities.

"My wife is right," Dad adds, grabbing her hand in solidarity. "I doubt the Fallen would have agreed to work with Auriel, or even the demons, if they knew what he was really planning. They wanted freedom and equality, but all they're doing is helping rid the world of their own population faster than before."

"What do you mean, 'if they knew what they were really planning'?" a woman with short curly hair and a pointy nose asks.

"From what we overheard in captivity, it sounds like their goal is to remove all traces of Fallen from the city. It's why they've built a bomb filled with broken angel blades and hope to drop them on the Fallen district."

If this information didn't come from my parents, I might not believe it, but these council members don't have the luxury of knowing my parents enough to trust their word.

My stomach knots just thinking about the offer Auriel made me. Of helping him with the promise of protecting my parents when what he wanted all along was their kind wiped out. "What we have to do now is work together. Not just against Auriel, but in the future, too. We need to win this war and continue to improve the lives of all our citizens, not just the Pure."

One of the council members groans and slams his fist down on the table. "No one is treated poorly. Has it maybe gotten a little out of hand? Sure, I can admit that, but to say that Fallen and Pure aren't equals is a load of shit. A look through history will prove it."

It's Darok. The piece of shit that came with us on our rescue mission. I'm immediately reminded of how much I hate him. How dare he sit there and carry on with this nonsense after what my parents and I just shared? As if he's known a day of hardship in his fucking life.

"Your privilege is showing, Darok. I agree with what Hayliel and her parents are saying," Azrael says, standing from his seat at the table. "We see it at the guild where only Fallen may work. But we have just as many Pure citizens, if not more, and I know several who would love the opportunity to fight for our city themselves. Fallen lives are not worth less than Pure, and I think it's time we changed the narrative so this becomes more widely understood by all."

I smile at him, glad to have him on this side of things.

Mikkael claps his hands once, drawing all eyes toward him. "It would appear we have some work to do. Camael, Maribella, would you two be willing to help us speak with other Fallen? We'd like to compile a list of all grievances and ideas on how we can improve things. If we can change their minds, maybe they'll give up on their plans with Auriel and those beasts. You have our word that, once we deal with him, we'll work on making things right in the city again. For every member of the community."

For a second, all I can do is stare at Mikhael. Did he truly just offer that? Alone, he likely wouldn't get anywhere. They need Fallen angels to reach other Fallen, and who better than my parents? The eternal optimists who have dealt with their fair share of bullshit. Personally, I love the idea, but I'm not sure what they'll think.

Mom and Dad are having a quiet conversation, but the moment their eyes find mine, I know their answer. They're going to do it.

"We will help, as long as your offer remains genuine," Dad says, gripping Mom's hand.

"Then it's settled—" Mikhael begins to say amidst another round of grumbling from a few council members, but before he can go on, someone knocks on the door. The messenger enters, but instead of heading to the Archangels like I expect, he comes to me.

"Sorry to intrude, but you asked to be told if there was any change with Zeke."

I suck in a breath, scared at what he might say next.

"He's awake."

25

EZEKIEL

Consciousness comes for me like a wraith.

It doesn't last long, not when my body feels weighted down and sore.

Back and forth, I wrestle to wake fully, not really wanting to. If I'm awake, I'll feel their torture, but if I remain in this state, they might harm Hayliel's parents, and I can't allow that.

Even on the cusp of what feels like death, I'd still do anything for her.

On my next bout of awareness, I listen. There's a low humming noise that wasn't there before. A rhythmic beeping that would probably annoy me if it were any louder. Have they moved me to a different cell? Beneath my fingers, I feel soft cotton and plush bedding.

Is this another of their tactics? Offer me niceties and hope I'll turn on my friends? If it is, I suppose I could enjoy it.

But no, it doesn't feel like their play.

I wonder for a moment if Hayliel saved me. Saved her parents like I tried, and failed, to do. But that would mean she ran straight into danger. Who am I kidding? She'd absolutely do that. Hell, that was her plan all along, wasn't it? To trade herself in order to protect her parents and everyone else. Of course she'd put herself in harm's way to save us.

Slowly, I crack my eyes open and immediately slam them shut. Bright lights blind me, their ghostly forms dancing behind my lids.

I hear the door click open, and a minute later, the room plunges into darkness.

"There. That should help your eyes adjust," someone says.

Shit. They know I'm awake. I guess my plan to feign sleep is dead.

Opening my eyes, I find a man standing at the end of my bed. He's wearing an unbuttoned white lab coat over a simple collared shirt and is looking over a stack of papers. I shift, testing my body, and instantly regret it. An ache races across my shoulder, making me hiss.

"I'm glad to see you're awake, Ezekiel. Your friends will be very happy."

"My friends?" I ask, voice hoarse. Is this another trick? Have they caught them, too?

"I'm not surprised you don't remember. There was a rescue mission, and they brought you here, to the Sanctuary. Camael and Maribella are safe, and now you are, too. You've been resting for quite some time. I'll admit, the reattaching of your lost limb isn't something I've heard of before, so I'm glad you've finally woken up."

Safe. They're safe. Wait. "Lost limb?"

The healer nods. "Your left wing. I'm told it was cut off with an angel blade."

My mind reels, and like a dam breaking, reality floods in. I remember. Auriel's torture. Plucking my feathers over and over again while demanding I tell him how to get to Hayliel. Then, when that didn't work, he pulled an angel blade and spent an hour sawing my wing off. He didn't need that long. He just wanted me to suffer.

"Here, have some water," he says, handing me a glass. "We'll continue with the serum that keeps your wings trapped beneath your flesh for another day or so, to promote the healing as much as possible. As soon as that's worn off, we'll begin the process of therapy to guide you through what your life will look like going forward."

That's what he doesn't understand. I'm not discouraged, not really. Am I happy that I've lost a wing? Fuck, no. But I wouldn't have been able to live with myself if it went any other way. I would gladly lose both wings and have to live life with the humans if it meant Hayliel was safe. She's worth far more to me than wings.

"Camael and Maribella are unharmed, truly?" I ask, still not convinced this isn't some mind-fuck orchestrated by Auriel. It's why I don't ask about Hayliel. Not yet. Not until I know doing so won't put her in danger.

"They're good as new, though I have them on a weekly therapy session to work through their trauma. Sorry to ruin the surprise, but you'll be doing the same once you're better."

Part of me wants to tell him I don't need therapy, but I hold back. Maybe I do.

"I won't lie to you, Ezekiel. The journey will be long, but we're truly dealing with a miracle here, so don't get discouraged," the healer goes on, confusing me.

"Miracle?"

"Unless you have another word to describe the rejoining of a limb previously severed by an angel blade, I'd say miracle is precisely accurate."

A game. That's what this is. Auriel is trying to confuse me—his next tactic in his crusade to get to Hayliel. But I won't fall for it, regardless of what he takes from me.

The sound of hushed voices grows louder outside the door. I struggle to listen past the low hum of the machines in here, needing to know if it's friend or foe, but all I can hear is the rushing of blood through my veins and the pounding of my heart.

This is it.

I'm about to find out if this is real or just a game to wear me down.

Then, like the sweetest symphony. I hear it.

I hear *her*.

"He'll appreciate seeing you guys, too," she whispers, and I hear someone snort. Probably Raphael.

"He'll appreciate us more if you go in alone. It's you he needs right now, not us."

The healer sets my chart down. "Well, that's all from me. Do you feel up to seeing your friends?"

"Yes," I croak, desperation clawing at me through the fear that this is all some clever trick.

"Happy to hear it. I'll let them in now. Push that button there if you need me," he says, motioning to a call button next to me. Then he's gone, and the door shuts behind him.

When it opens again, I hold my breath.

Hayliel walks through, slowly, seeming almost shy, and the moment our eyes lock, I feel whole again. Thank the gods she's alright.

"Zeke," she whispers, eyes roaming over where I sit propped up on the bed.

"Hummingbird."

She runs toward me, a sob tearing from her throat.

In this moment, I don't notice the pain or discomfort. All I see is her. All I feel is her.

She carefully sits on the bed, cupping my face like she can't believe I'm here.

"Fuck, I missed you," I tell her, looking over every inch of her beautiful face. My words only make her cry harder. "I'm here, baby. I'm here."

She curls against my side, and we lie like this for several minutes. Her, with quiet tears making wet marks on the blanket, and me totally content to just hold her.

"I'm so sorry," she says, finally breaking the silence.

What in the world? "You have absolutely nothing to be sorry for."

My words piss her off, but I don't think she's mad at me. She's mad at herself, and I don't understand why.

She buries her face against me. "It's my fault this happened to you. You were only there because of me! Fuck, if I had just told you what I was planning, maybe things would have gone differently."

Her words shatter my heart. "Hey, hey, hey. Look at me."

She shakes her head.

"Look at me, please. I need you to see my face when I tell you this."

Eventually she does as I ask. Her eyes are red and puffy from crying, cheeks wet. Gods, she's stunning, even in this state.

"You are not to blame for anything. Auriel is. He's the one who did this to me, not you." Another tear slides down her cheek. "Besides, if things didn't go down like they did, we may not have your parents back right now. But if what the doctor said is true, we do. They're alive. So am I."

"But Zeke ..."

I know she's talking about my wing, and maybe the loss hasn't sunk in yet or I'm delusional, but there are far worse things that could have happened. Things I wouldn't have survived—like her being harmed in any way. "No *buts*, hummingbird. If I had to go back in time, I would do it all over again."

"I love you."

"And I love you. More than I could possibly say."

When our lips meet, it's not romantic. Salt lines her tear-stained lips, and our teeth clash as we move in desperation. *She's safe, she's safe, she's safe.* The words repeat in my head like a prayer.

I'm finally home.

A knock on the door interrupts us, but she doesn't try to leave the bed. I wouldn't have let her go, anyway.

Raphael and Theo enter the room, and I almost can't decipher the looks on their faces. Relief maybe? With a hint of pain.

"It's good to see you, man," Theo says a little awkwardly.

"Yeah," Raphael adds. "Never thought I'd be excited to see your face, but here we are."

I laugh because, shit, are we bonding or something? "Enjoy it while you can. I'm sure the feeling won't last long."

There's an awkward silence as they stand by my bed, watching me. Theo is the first to break it. "Seriously, though. We're glad to have you back, and not just because our girl was in tatters while you were gone."

He elbows Raphael, who winces but adds, "Fine. It wasn't the same without you. You're part of our little family, and it sucked not knowing if you were alive and shit."

I grin, unable to believe the words coming out of his mouth.

If it were anyone else, I'd give him hell for being all mushy, but for some reason, I can't with Raphael. Admitting that, after all the crap that's happened between us, must have cost him a lot, and I don't want to diminish it with jokes.

"I'm glad to be back home, and that everyone is alright. Auriel, he said some shit, trying to get me to talk, but I never knew if it was true." My throat tightens as I remember the horrific things he whispered in my ear while I was delirious.

Hayliel sniffles, fresh tears falling from her eyes. "We tried to reach you every day. My parents, too."

I nod, believing with everything I am that she would have. "They gave me something to keep me weak. Whatever it was, they didn't give it to your parents. Fallen aren't taught how to use their abilities, right? So why waste precious product? Luckily for us, they didn't know you'd been working with them already. You saved us, hummingbird. You all did. Thank you."

"Your dad was a huge help, actually. He's been distraught ever since you were taken," Hayliel says softly.

I can't find the words to reply. I don't even want to think about what kind of pain he's been in and the memories that must have surfaced from my capture. Far too similar to my mother's death, I'm sure.

"How are you feeling?" Hayliel asks, her voice unsteady.

"Things are a little foggy. The healer said a few things that don't make sense. He kept talking about miracles and limbs and—"

"She put you back together again, man. Good as new," Theo

says, causing Raphael to roll his eyes playfully.

"Or at least as good as you were before."

I don't respond to his joke. My gaze turns to the woman in my arms as I stare at her, unsure if I can believe what they're all saying. She doesn't need to hear my question out loud—not when she can read me like a fucking book.

"I don't know how I did it or if I even really trust it, to be honest, but you have both your wings again. Auriel didn't take that from you."

Her words don't feel real, and yet the ache of my shoulders tells me it's the truth. "Thank you." I lean forward, resting my forehead against hers. "And for the record, the only thing I couldn't live without is you."

Raphael and Theo grab chairs and move closer, each one finding some way to remain in physical contact with Hayliel. All of us are clustered around my bed with her at the center. It feels right. Like the plates of the world have shifted and we're finally where we're supposed to be.

Fuck. Being tortured really did a number on me.

The door opens, slamming against the wall behind it. I'm still drowsy and weak, but I damn near jump into action.

No. They will not take this from me.

But it isn't Auriel or his horde of demon followers standing in the doorway.

It's my father.

"I tried to give you some time, but I couldn't wait any longer," is all he says, taking me in from a distance.

He looks terrible, and I tell him as much. "Dad. You look like shit." Worse than I remember him looking when Mom died, but that was a long time ago. Maybe my memories have faded. Archangels know I tried to bury them enough.

He barks a laugh. "Good to see your mental state is as good as it was before, at least." He takes a step into the room as another figure appears behind him.

Cam and Mari rush through, not bothering to keep their distance like Dad is. I'm not surprised. This is probably a step up from the last few times they saw me. There's no blood or other shit oozing from my open wounds, and I'm actually coherent.

"Thank the gods you're alright," Mari says while Cam talks with my dad, praising him for raising such a fine man and telling him how we wouldn't have escaped if it wasn't for me.

"What about you two? No injuries?" I look them over but don't spot anything out of the ordinary. Mari wears an apron, which doesn't surprise me in the slightest. Leave it to her to bake wherever she goes.

"Not a one," Cam says, and I'm glad to see that spark of joy hasn't faded.

Hayliel, Theo, and Raphael haven't moved from where they crowd around me, and it's only then that I remember all the fucking shit Hayliel hasn't told her parents. Her Seraphim news, our weird relationship ...

Her parents must sense it too, because their eyes immediately dart to where the guys are touching Hayliel. When she finally notices, she stiffens in my arms.

"Mom, Dad, there's something I should tell you," she says, before things can get any more awkward.

"Well, why don't you tell us over here, honey?" Cam adds, eyeing the guys. "We know how much Zeke, your *boyfriend*, means to you, but that bed is quite small for one person, let alone two."

Hayliel sighs but does as they ask, and although Mari tries to be quiet, I don't miss the words she whispers. "He just survived an ordeal. Perhaps it's not a good time to show affection to other men, right in front of him, no less."

Aaand it's more awkward. *Great.*

Hayliel laughs, her face turning a cute shade of pink. "That's what I wanted to talk to you about. Zeke is my boyfriend, that's true. But so are Raphael and Theo. We're all together."

The room grows silent as we wait to see how her parents will react.

"Did you know about this?" Cam asks my dad from the side of his mouth.

He shakes his head. "But now that I do, I think I'd rather go back to not knowing."

26

HAYLIEL

Two days later, I'm standing outside of Zeke's room while the healers finish another round of physiotherapy before releasing him. He'll still need to continue working his wing, but at least he can spend his nights with us.

Since he's woken up, I haven't left his side other than to get a few hours of sleep. I tried to deny the lead healer's suggestion to go get some rest, but his no-nonsense tone gave it away that I didn't really have a choice.

Being too far from him right now scares me. And not just because the fusion of his wing is still so unsure, or that I'm worried Auriel will somehow take him back from me. There are angels here I'm worried about.

The council has been desperate to speak with him since he woke up. We might have dealt a hard blow to our enemies, but it hasn't stopped Auriel. From what we've been hearing, all it's done is move up his schedule. But Zeke only just woke up. After what felt like an eternity of him being gone, I finally have him back. He's no longer kept in a cage like a stray dog, being tortured for information. The last thing he needs is to relive it all in front of a room full of unknown angels and Archangel strangers.

The door opens, and the healer walks out, smiling. "He'll be ready in a few minutes. Please make sure he checks in every few days and continues to do his exercises, but don't let him overdo it."

"I'll follow your orders, don't worry," Zeke says—and holy fucking shit. Is that a blush coloring his cheeks? Cute.

"It's been an honor working with you. The highlight of my career, if I'm to be honest." The healer's smile is so bright, it's damn near blinding, and his kind words only make Zeke even more uncomfortable.

Once I've had my fill of his blushing cheeks, I say, "Thanks again!" and then tug Zeke down the hall. We take our time, not rushing our strides. With Zeke at my side—his hand in mine—I feel whole again. I wish Raphael and Theo were here, too, but they've been trying to give me and Zeke some time alone. It hasn't gone unnoticed by either of us.

"Where are the rest of your shadows?" Zeke asks, teasing.

"They're waiting for us back at our section of rooms, but I

wanted to show you something first."

Zeke pulls my body into his until my back is flush with his front. "Does it happen to involve you and limited clothing?" He kisses my neck, making me melt into his touch.

"Not exactly what I had in mind, at least, not yet," I say, arching into him before teleporting a few feet away.

He stares at me, then rubs his eyes like he can't quite believe what he just saw.

"So, I can teleport now," I tell him, feeling a little self-conscious as I shoot back to his side. "It's pretty new. Mira helped me before, you know, everything fell apart."

His eyes grow dark, but not in the way I usually like to see. And when he speaks, his words are in complete contrast to the look on his face. "You amaze me."

He kisses the tip of my nose, causing me to giggle. We walk a little further in a comfortable silence, and when we pass by a set of stairs, Zeke stops.

"Be right back," he says, then climbs the steps two at a time. When he reaches the top, he takes a deep breath and then lets his wings unfurl from his back.

"What are you doing?" I ask, lurching forward like I can stop him. He spreads his wings wide, and even though my view is limited from this angle, I swear I can see the slight glow of gold that now emanates from where I reattached his wing.

"I only want to test it, to see if my wings can hold my weight."

"Zeke ..."

"I'd rather try it here with only you and this short distance to fall if it doesn't work. I promise I'll stop if it hurts, but I need to do this."

Despite the distance between us, I can tell just how much he means what he says, so I nod and swallow past my fear. If I'm honest with myself, it's not just fear of him getting hurt. I'm worried what I did won't hold, and I'll wind up disappointing him. Disappointing everyone.

I tried talking to Castiel about it, who spoke with Phiel on my behalf, but the old book he has doesn't give any indication on whether wing refastening is possible. It only mentions how easy healing another angel can be. As easy as breathing, the text said, and I suppose it was.

Holding my breath, I watch as he takes a small jump from the top of the stairs. His wings catch him and he grimaces, but he keeps them out, giving little flaps until his feet land in front of me.

It's only then that I suck in air. "You did it," I say, breathless. Relieved.

He nods, stretching out his wings again before letting them disappear. "It was harder to flap, like my muscles are weaker on that wing, which I think makes sense. But that's an easy fix. Far better off than I'd be if you hadn't reattached it," he says, gripping my chin. "Thank you. I can still fly because of you."

I wonder if he can tell how much comfort his words bring me. His wing *works*. All this doubt I've had tumbling around inside my head, this worry that I got his hopes up for nothing, it's eased off.

We stop in front of a door, and I don't miss the curious look from Zeke. This room is locked by a device that's similar to what we use at the dorms. Only this one has an additional step. Not only do I have to scan my wing to get in, but I also have to type in a nine-digit code. Annoying? Yes. But with so much uncertainty around who we can trust, we need the added security.

"Where exactly are you taking me, hummingbird?"

A shy grin spreads across my face. "Do you remember the first time I imbued?"

Zeke's eyes flash with heat. "That moment is seared into my memory, along with what came after."

I lean against the door, recalling the kiss, the way he'd devoured me on the workbench—and the awkwardness that followed. Not a day I'll forget, either. "Well, I put everything you taught me and every ounce of my fear and frustration to good use. Now close your eyes until I say so."

He immediately does what I ask, even covering his eyes with his hands for good measure. Opening the door, I pull Zeke inside. It clicks shut behind us, blocking out the rest of the world and leaving just the two of us and the hum of energy. "You can open them now."

His sharp intake of breath makes me giddy, and I watch as he looks around the room in awe. There are hundreds of weapons in here, in all different shapes and sizes, and all imbued with my sunfire. Swords, daggers, arrow tips, and each one casts the room in a soft golden glow.

"It's beautiful," he says, his gaze finally meeting mine. Within the depths of his green eyes, I see the golden light reflected back at me, making this moment almost surreal. "But how? There are so many." He reaches out, tracing his fingers along the hilt of several blades.

"I spent a lot of time here while you were gone. The Archangels and their council weren't too keen on letting us help at first. I felt so fucking useless, so I came here where at least I could put my energy into something worthwhile."

In one stride, Zeke stands in front of me. "You could never be useless." He moves a few strands of hair that have escaped my bun, running just the tips of his fingers along my jaw. "Even if you weren't a Seraphim. You kept me alive out there, and as mentally aware as I could be. *You.* Not what you can do, but who you are. Gods, there were so many times I was tired, hungry, dehydrated, crusted with blood, and barely able to make sense of the world. You were my guiding star. Every coherent moment I had, I thought of you. Your scent, the feel of your hand in mine, how much your parents mean to you. I thought of the way you taste and how you fuel my blood beyond compare. And I swear I felt you once, begging for me to come back."

My eyes sting with a wave of tears that I try to hold back. It's futile, especially when I realize the moment he's likely talking about. The night with Raphael and Theo, when they told me to put every thought I had into Zeke, hoping he'd feel my desperation for him to return. *It worked.*

"I love you," I whisper, voice gruff with too much emotion.

"And I love you." He dips his head, lips capturing mine in a fierce kiss that makes me want to jump his bones. But as much as I want to take this all the way, I want him to feel safe. Secure. Loved. He deserves all of that and more.

He grips my ass, and I know what's coming. He'll toss me into his arms, clear the desk behind me, and finish what we started in his dad's workshop. I still owe him for that, and it's time I pay up.

I stroke my hand down his chest and over the hard length of his cock through his jeans, distracting him. "I missed this," I croon, feeling him shudder beneath me.

"I need to feel you, hummingbird. I need your heat wrapped around me."

Dropping to my knees, I fumble with the button of his jeans. His hand covers mine, and when I look up, our eyes lock.

"I can handle fucking you, you know," he says, eyes full of hunger.

"I know." My voice is soft, almost shy. "But please, let me do this. Let me take care of you. You can fuck me later. For now, I just need to know you're here. You're alive. And I want to make you feel good, Zeke. Please."

He stares at me, hand still on top of mine. But then he nods, his green eyes growing hooded as he watches me on my knees for him. I free his cock and nearly cry at the sight of it.

He's here. He's alive.

There's already precum glistening beneath the glow of the imbued weapons. I dip my head, lapping it up, and sigh at the taste.

He's here. He's alive.

I grip the base with one hand, feeling his veins pulse with blood as he grows even thicker in my palm. Then I lean forward and suck his tip into my mouth. His groan sends little zaps of pleasure straight to my clit, but I ignore my need to get off. It's not about that. Not now.

Zeke spent far too long being tortured because of me. He deserves to feel something good for a change.

Twirling my tongue around his crown, I slowly take more of him until my eyes water and my breaths don't come. Then I back off and do it again.

His hands are in my hair, guiding my movements.

"Eyes on me."

I do as I'm told, and what I find in his gaze is enough to make me want to cry. Unbridled desire and love. He takes control, fucking into my mouth like a man starved. I don't care if my knees are sore or that saliva runs down my chin. I keep my gaze locked on him and push every ounce of love through our connection, just like I did before.

I know the second he feels it, because his eyes widen, muscles flexing. His dick jerks, balls tightening beneath my hand.

"I'm not going to last much—" His words die as I hollow my cheeks, swallowing him down.

Liquid warmth shoots down my throat as he roars his release. The sound he makes is primal.

He's here. He's alive.

And I won't let that fucker Auriel hurt him—or anyone else I love—ever again.

27

HAYLIEL

An hour later, Zeke and I leave the weapon chamber with smiles on our faces.

After he came down my throat and confessed his love for me a few more times, I let him watch as I imbued some weapons. Something about it had my skin flushing and spine tingling. To know that this strong and capable man not only loves that I'm strong too, but actually enjoys witnessing it?

Euphoric.

We're walking down the hall on our way to our shared lodgings when we run into Kirach.

"Ah, there you are. I went to the healers first, but they told me you had left. How are you feeling?"

"Fine," Zeke replies, and I can't help but notice just how strange their relationship is. What's with the one-word answers?

"I wanted him to see all the weapons we prepared," I say, adding more context. "He also tested his wing a little on the way, and it held his weight."

Zeke rubs the back of his neck, looking anywhere but at his dad. Things weren't this awkward after Kirach found us in a compromising position, so what the hell is going on?

"That's great news, son. You'll be back in the skies in no time."

Silence follows, one so awkward that I can't help but wrack my brain for anything I can say to break this weird tension.

I come up blank.

Kirach clears his throat, then says, "We tracked down who we think might be the traitor that tampered with the explosives and infiltrated our communications. I was wondering if you'd be up for helping with the interrogation?"

"You found someone? How?" I ask before Zeke can answer his father. Maybe I should have waited. It's not as if Kirach was asking *me* to help him interrogate someone, but holy shit. This is one more step toward weeding out the traitors.

Kirach nods but waits for an angel to walk past where we're standing in the hall before he answers. "We found the real uniforms Archangel Mikhael wanted everyone to wear, as well as some tech we think someone used to alter the explosives."

Zeke wasn't awake for the rescue, but that doesn't stop his

anger from rising. He hates a snake as much as we all do. "I'm in. Just give me the *when* and *where*."

"I'll come by to get you in the morning." Kirach takes a step back, then stops. "It's good to have you back, son." He leaves before Zeke can answer.

It's silent as we walk. My thoughts are spiraling out of control. I'm not sure if I should push him about his father or share my reservations about him assisting with interrogations this soon after recovery. In the end, I say nothing. Zeke is a doer. He's not someone who wants pity, which is exactly what he'll think my worry is.

Raphael, Theo, and Dina are lounging when we walk into the place we've been calling home these past few weeks. Dina is on her slate while the guys are reading.

"Well, well, look who's back on his feet," Dina says, sending Zeke a look I know he'll take as a challenge.

"My feet were never the issue."

"Food is on the way. We weren't sure what the healers were feeding you, so we ordered lots of extras," Raphael says, putting his book down and striding toward us to plant a kiss on my cheek.

Theo folds his notebook, then follows a similar path to my side. Instead of kissing me, though, he runs his knuckles along my jaw.

"Ugh. I forgot what it was like to be around you guys," Dina says, rolling her eyes, but her smile gives away her true feelings. I blow her a kiss, laughing.

"How'd your last session go?" Theo asks Zeke as we get comfortable on the couch.

"Fine. Wings can hold my weight, but the muscles need some work. Nothing I can't handle."

"Good, that's good." Raphael sighs, dropping his head in his hands. "My mother called earlier. I guess the school finally notified her of my absence."

Shit. I can't imagine that was a very productive conversation. "We've been gone for weeks. Isn't it a little odd that they're only calling now?"

"She's very important, you know. She doesn't have time for frivolous things like school calls," Raph says, his voice mimicking the butler I met when I had dinner with his family.

Dina grimaces. "The only reason my dad let me back on campus was because Principal Cael told him you were no longer a student."

"What the fuck?" Zeke seethes. Raphael and Theo do too, but they've had longer to deal with this bullshit. It's part of why Dina didn't come here right away. Her dad wouldn't let her on campus until I was taken care of.

It might have bothered me once too, but not now. How can I even care about school when the fate of the city is so up in the air?

"If only they knew what we were all up to, what we were trying to do for the entire goddamn city, they'd eat their fucking words." Raphael looks pissed, and I wonder if maybe I've been too dismissive of their feelings. They're not like Zeke. He'd never hide his emotions from me, but Raph would if he thought it would make me uncomfortable.

"Was Uriel still on campus when you left?" Theo asks Dina, making me grimace. Somehow, in the chaos of everything, I'd blissfully forgotten about that asshole.

"Yup." Her eyes dart my way, and for a second, I think she's going to hold back. Whatever she sees on my face must tell her to go on because she says, "That prick immediately went back to spewing more lies and rumors to the other students. For whatever reason, you're under his skin, Hayles."

"I'd rather he has no fucking skin at all," Zeke mutters, making me laugh. "I bet Malik would do something if he knew what was coming."

"That sexy motherfucker would look mighty fine on a battlefield," Dina says, sighing. "Actually, he asked about the two of you when I ran into him on campus." Her cheeks grow a darker shade of red, and I just know there's more to this story. As much as I want to pry, I don't. There are certain things that should only be discussed amongst the girls.

"Professor Isadora would help, too, not that I think getting their help would be easy," Raphael says.

Theo snaps his fingers. "Castiel could definitely help us convince them, or at the very least he'd tell us whether we're totally off base with our idea. I'll message him."

"Learn anything about the demon blood tree?" I ask, glancing at the discarded book on the table.

"Some." Theo sinks further into the couch, draping an arm

across the back. "On its own, the tree isn't harmful to anyone. In fact, if we assume the handwritten notes in the margins are true, the sap of the tree has certain health benefits for humans."

"Huh. How would anyone know that?"

Raphael shrugs. "Most angels who leave don't come back, but some do. It's rare, but not unheard of. Even so, it means the ash is only one compound of the mixture in those little pouches." He gestures toward where the sack Zeke stole from the guild rests next to their research.

"So, what you're saying is, we're shit out of luck." Zeke glances between Raphael and Theo, one eyebrow raised.

"Not exactly. I mean, sure, we'd need the leader of the guild to share the recipe with us, as he's the only one who knows it. The Archangels could request it on our behalf."

"But," Theo continues where Raphael left off, "We discovered its purpose. Whatever the ingredients are, when combined, cause temporary respiratory and neurological issues in demons. Unfortunately, they have a similar, though far less serious, effect on angels, which is why the use of them is cautioned."

Respiratory and neurological issues? That's a little vague. Even so, I can just imagine how much something like that could turn the tides in an emergency. "Probably not something we'll use then, though it may not be a bad idea to ration what we have out, just in case."

The food arrives—a tray full of ingredients to make our own tacos. I don't know that I've ever seen Zeke so excited about food. He manages to demolish two tacos—and already making a third—before I've even finished one.

"Fucking hell, this is good," he says, licking some juice off his fingers.

Damn, he's fine.

We're all silently digging into our meals when the door to Mira's room opens, and she comes out. "Sorry I'm late—"

Zeke stiffens beside me. "What the fuck is she doing here?"

Mira looks almost panicked as Raphael asks, "Ooooh, shit. What did you do to this one?"

"Zeke?" I say, confused. As far as I know, they haven't even seen each other since before the kidnapping, so why is he acting like she destroyed his favorite belonging?

"Fucking hell. They don't know, do they?" Zeke asks Mira, ignoring the rest of us.

"Don't know what?" I ask.

Zeke's laugh is bitter. "Do you want to tell them, or should I?"

Mira's silence is palpable, but eventually she says, "I'll do it."

Her response only confounds me more. What the hell is going on?

She turns to me, and I immediately put my newly built taco down. Mira looks almost scared, something I've never seen on her face before. I brace myself for my world to turn upside down yet again.

"First, I want to preface by saying I'm sorry I didn't tell you before now, and despite how it may look, I've always been on your side." She looks around the room, meeting each of our gazes. "My father ... he's the mole. Lieutenant Atlas."

My head swims as I try to make sense of her words.

"You're leaving out the best part, Mira. The one where you're working with him and reporting back on our movements like a fucking traitor." Zeke hisses the last words. I suspect he's using every ounce of his restraint to stay seated.

"That's bullshit! I found out at the same fucking time as all of you. I had no idea he—"

Zeke scoffs. "Like I'll believe the lies spewing from your mouth. Fool me once, and all that."

"Fucking hell. Can we just calm down for a second?" Theo says, rubbing his temple.

Raphael looks just as enraged as Zeke, but to my surprise he doesn't add to the outburst.

"Mira?" I ask, turning a cautioned gaze on my friend.

"I swear, I didn't know what he was up to. All I knew was that something about him had changed over the last few years. He kept pushing me away, and I couldn't figure out why. It's the reason I kept going to the guild. But the truth is I ... I guess I don't know my father at all."

I see the hurt in her eyes, the pain of feeling like the person you looked up to your entire life isn't what you thought they were. That's hard to fake.

"You're a good liar, Mira. Almost as good as dear old dad."

"Zeke. Please," I say, sparing him a glance. "I don't think this is as black and white as you're making it out to be."

His next words are quiet, composed, and somehow that

makes them more powerful. "Did you know it was your father who kidnapped me? He had the help of demons, as all Auriel's minions do, but he's the one who brought me to the Archangel."

"Of course I didn't!"

He stands so abruptly that I flinch. "You got close to Hayliel to help him, didn't you?"

"Zeke," I try again, but he ignores me.

"You nosed your way into our lives, all to help your father and this stupid crusade against the Fallen."

"Zeke!" All eyes turn to me. It might be the first time I've raised my voice like this, but it had to be done. "That's enough. Now sit down and fucking eat something."

"But—" Zeke tries, but I cut him off.

"Now, Ezekiel."

He looks pissed but sits anyway, though he doesn't even pretend to eat anything.

I take a deep breath, then release it slowly. "Mira, why didn't you tell me? After everything we've been through together, I thought we were closer than that."

"I'm sorry. I had my suspicions when I learned he witnessed you survive an angel blade. When I found out, I asked him about a rumor I'd heard at the guild. He always used to tell me the cool things he discovered on a mission, but this time he lied to me. Told me I needed to stop believing everything I heard, and then he just took off. I never would have guessed he'd sided with the likes of Auriel, and then when we found out, I didn't know how to tell you he's my fucking father. It doesn't even really feel like he is, not anymore. Not for a long time." She pauses for a beat, and the room grows silent. "I swear I never did anything to hurt you. He never knew where I was spending my time. In fact, I doubt he even knew I wasn't at home."

I watch her as she speaks, looking for any hint of deception, but I don't find any. "I understand. And I'm sorry. I can't imagine what that's been like for you. Finding out a parent isn't who you thought they were can't be easy."

"It's not exactly easy when you've known who they are all along, either," Raphael adds, trying to lighten the mood.

"Please don't keep stuff like this from us again. As far as I'm concerned, we're a family. I won't keep things from you, and I hope none of you will keep things from me either. We're stronger together."

Everyone but Zeke agrees, including Mira, who promises to share whatever she knows and offers to spill on all the details she's collected so far on her dad if it'll help.

"Why don't we do that now? It'll give these four a chance to, erm, settle things," Dina says. "We can do it in my room. You go ahead. I'll be there in a minute."

Mira disappears into Dina's room, and the moment her door closes, Zeke speaks. "You're just going to forgive her?"

"Yes."

"Just like that?"

I nod. "Just like that. If she wanted the same thing as her father, she wouldn't have protected my dad when we came to rescue you. He's a Fallen, after all. She could have just let him die, but she didn't. She helped me train and gave me a literal drink to hide me from demons—a drink that helped save you, I might add. And other than this one omission, she hasn't given me any other reason not to trust her, so I'm going with my gut on this one."

I take both of his clenched fists in mine and run my fingers along his knuckles. "I don't expect you to move past this as easily as I have, not with what her father did, but I need you to try, Zeke. We aren't the sins of our parents."

"I'm with Hayliel on this one," Dina says. "Besides, I can't imagine finding out something like that about someone I looked up to, and then having to deal with it all on my own."

"Exactly. She's been there for me, so I'm going to be there for her."

Dina leaves us then, heading into her room to chat with Mira about her father and leaving me alone with my three men for the first time in what actually feels like months. It's not exactly the reunion I was hoping for. None of us are in a very celebratory mood about what we just found out, but the fact is ... we're finally together.

Alive. Safe.

And that's what matters.

"Come on," I say, grabbing the platter of taco fixings. "Let's finish these off and then figure out how the four of us are going to fit into that room."

28

THEO

I count as I skip rope, not stopping until I reach two hundred.

Sweat drips down my back and stomach, and even though I'm tired, I give myself just enough time to catch my breath, grab some water, and towel off before I start the next workout.

Zeke is busy with his dad, Hayliel and Dina are trying to find some semblance of normalcy with Mira, and Raph is dealing with more bullshit from his family.

I'm alone in the gym, trying to work through the strange feelings that have plagued me since I let that demon get away. Strange, because I *know* I made the right choice to let him go, so why does it feel like I lost my only chance at justice?

Add Mira's news to the mess inside my head, and it's a fucking party. How did we miss who her father is? Thinking back to when we found out Lieutenant Atlas was the mole, I realize there were signs. They were subtle, a little tremor here, a furrow there, but if I'd just been paying attention, maybe I would have noticed. If we'd known, would everything have happened the way it did?

As mad as I am with her for keeping this to herself, I don't hate her. Not after everything she's done. She helped Hayliel—whether through training or by providing her with thoughtful potions. Plus, she saved Cam's life.

And just like that, I'm back to thinking about the demon who got away. Twice.

The sound of a bag hitting the floor has me nearly jumping out of my skin. Turning, I find Remiel placing his shit on a hook as if he's planning to join me.

Well, this is weird.

The knowledge-loving side of my brain is excited. The things this man could teach me would probably blow my mind. But the side that brought me here, the one feeling utterly lost and confused, he just wants to be alone. Besides, we're not feeling entirely trusting toward the Archangels at present.

"Do you mind if I join you?"

I realize I've been staring. *Great.* "Uh, sure. Yeah. Whatever you want." Smooth, man. Real smooth.

I return to my workout, completely forgetting which rep I'd been on before Remiel came in, but it's fine. Time for the real work, anyway. Ignoring the Archangel setting up beside me, I press a button on the wall and watch as the training dummy appears from behind a hidden panel. There's a remote control too, which makes the dummy strike and move, mimicking an opponent.

Say what you want about these suspicious assholes, but this room is seriously something else.

After making my selections with the dummy, I drown out all the noise in my head and focus on the fight. I strike like this is an actual fight, and my life is on the line. Still, the stupid dummy gets in a few good blows, one knocking the wind from my lungs and pissing me off.

If that were a real fight, I'd be fucked.

My breaths are ragged as I take another gulp of water and try to calm down the angry inferno inside me.

"Could I step in?"

Remiel gestures to the mat, and I eye him skeptically. I'm not really in the mood to fight an Archangel, but I can't ignore the benefits from doing so. Maybe he'll give something away that I can use on Auriel, if it comes to that. I nod in agreement, towel off, and take another gulp of water before joining him.

If someone were to walk in, I wonder what they'd think. I'm sweaty and clearly aggravated, while Remiel looks poised. The asshole could probably shoot covers for a magazine at this point. He's not even dressed to spar, wearing these thin beige linen pants and a similar button-down shirt. The sleeves are rolled up, and the top few buttons are undone. He looks like he should be relaxing on the beach.

We start off slow, each of us trying to learn our opponent and gain the upper hand. As we circle each other, I can't help but notice how lithe and graceful he is. This man might appear like the book-loving prophet, but he's got more tricks up his sleeve than I gave him credit for. Far better to be underestimated than overestimated.

I attack, he dodges, but not once does he press the advantage, even when I know he has one. Instead, he offers little anecdotes. At first it pissed me off, but the more I listen, the more I realize his words aren't full of malice or contempt. They're tips.

"That works best when your opponent is shorter than you. How can you tweak it to work on someone taller?"

"Demons will expect that move. Only use it to goad them or to fake them out for a more subtle attack."

I take in everything he says and adjust until I finally land a strike. If I were using more than just my hands, it might have caused him harm, but it'll leave a bruise at most. Maybe I should be worried that I just hit an Archangel, but I'm not. In fact, he seems happier about it than I do.

Remiel hands me my water bottle. "Well done."

I take it without replying. What am I supposed to say? Thank you? Instead, I give him this half smile, half grimace and swallow down the cool liquid.

"We're not so different, you and I," he continues. "We both lost someone important to us, and we both blame ourselves for it."

I want to ask him how he knows my past, but those aren't the words that escape my lips. "Who did you lose?"

"My sister. She was ... unwell. Looking back, all the signs were there. I should have caught it. Instead, she paid the ultimate price for my inattention."

"I'm sorry."

"There is nothing for you to be sorry for. Not for my sister, and certainly not for your friend."

Is it his visions that give him this knowledge? It has to be. I haven't shared Serah's story with very many angels, and the ones who know would never talk about it with someone like an Archangel. Still, I find myself saying, "How do you know what I went through?"

He pulls a black book from his bag. It's plain, bound in leather with a small ribbon to mark his spot. He doesn't open it, but from the edges of the paper, I see the dark smudges that hint at his drawings. "I see many things. Some are only glimpses and hard to pinpoint. Others, like your past, are clear."

"Oh." If he's truly seen that moment, then he knows how much I fucked up.

"Killing that demon won't bring back your friend, Theo. It won't even fully cure that space inside you that's festered and rotted all these years."

"I refuse to let him live, and I'll feel better knowing Serah's murderer has found justice. That's enough for me."

"Oh, I'm not here to talk you out of doing what you feel you have to. I just want you to understand that it won't be the saving grace you hope it will be. That will take more work in here"—Remiel touches his head—"and in here." He rests his hand on his chest, just above his heart.

He's not going to stop me.

I release a breath as this weight disappears from my shoulders. I really thought I was going to have to fight against Remiel and the might of the Archangels to kill the demon who harmed my friend. "I know it won't stop the hurt or cure my pain entirely. I've accepted that."

"Good. Now, if you're up for it, why don't we continue sparring, so you're as prepared as possible for the fight ahead?"

"I'd like that. Thank you."

Remiel sets his water down and strides to the mat, standing casually in the center. Before we start again, he says, "You might feel like you need this revenge, and in some ways it will help, but just know that you aren't going out there alone. All of us, including myself, stand with you in this endeavor."

29

EZEKIEL

I stare at myself in the mirror, wishing I was still asleep so I could wake up from this nightmare. The man who stares back at me looks similar enough. He has the same green eyes and sharp jawline as before, but the man in the mirror doesn't feel like me.

My hair is short now. I'm told I was a mess of patchy, half-shorn hair from shallow cuts on my scalp, so they had no choice but to chop it off. More than just the changes in my appearance, though, I feel different since captivity. Not just because of the wing or the scars that line my body from his blade. There are mental ones, too.

It's partly why I think the others accepting Mira's betrayal is affecting me so deeply. If we can forgive her, what's to say we can't forgive Auriel? Uriel? Hell, even her father? I *can't*. But I have to find a way through these deep-rooted feelings. It's why I've done my best to bury them when Mira's around and hide them from my friends. We have enough outside bullshit to contend with. They don't need to fear I'll blow up at Mira.

Again.

Besides, according to the others, she saved Cam and helped Hayliel out with her potions and tinctures.

We are not our parents.

I think of Dad and the time we wasted during the interrogation yesterday. Not only were we unable to find anything helpful, but everything we uncovered only added more questions. We have legit evidence tying Darok to the rigged bombs and armor, but the asshole doesn't seem like he has two brain cells to rub together, let alone pull off something so big. Dad agreed, so we brought our findings to the Archangels.

They promised to look into it, then took advantage of my presence and pestered me with as many questions as possible about my time with Auriel. I gave them everything I could remember. The sheer volume of demons I encountered, every whisper I overheard, every question Auriel asked me. As hard as it was to relive those moments, it was even worse seeing my dad flinch with each recounted piece of torture.

I ran out as soon as I could and spent the next hour by myself, stretching and testing my wing in quiet solitude, trying to erase his horrified expression from my memory. Sleep didn't come easily last night. I woke myself—and the others—twice with nightmares.

Now, I find myself heading back to the council room, this time with a select group of angels to discuss our next steps to deal with Auriel. Something must have happened for them to haul us here before any of us had coffee.

I'm walking down the hall with Hayliel, Raphael, Theo, and Dina when we run into Castiel and Mira. I hate that she's here, hate that I have to hide my distrust of her from everyone, and even hate that she's in on this planning session. I don't smile at her, but at least I don't say anything offensive.

Sorry. I guess I'm just not perfect.

As we wait for the doors to open, I spot Dad coming down the hallway with Briathos and Raduriel in tow. Despite the strides I'm told Raphael has made with his brother, he still stiffens when he notices who's approaching. But Raduriel doesn't come toward us like the others. He turns as if he's going to leave.

Raph hesitates but then whispers to Hayliel and takes off toward his brother. He's only gone for a few minutes before returning alone. He says nothing out loud, but through our joint mental pathways he says, *I told him he should be in there with us, but he insisted we go in first with this group and then decide who we need.*

From everything I've heard about Raph's brother, this certainly isn't the response I expected, and it looks like Raphael didn't either. Perhaps he and his brother can truly turn things around.

The doors open and we're invited inside the council room, a room that has been transformed since the last time I was here. The table where all the council members sat and judged me earlier is now laden with plates, cutlery, and other things one would expect to see at a fancy brunch. On the other side of the room is another table with bagels, bacon, sausage, pancakes, and even a whole-ass ham. Beside it sits the biggest carafe of coffee I've ever seen. I'm instantly salivating.

"Thank you for your prompt arrival," Mikhael says. "Grab a plate and load up. We have a long day ahead of us, and it doesn't end here." We make two lines, with most of us going for coffee first—myself included. Only once we're all sitting down with our food does Mikhael proceed. "As some of you know already, Auriel moved up his attack plans. We found out this morning from a trusted source that he intends to attack tomorrow. We've developed a plan, which includes evacuation measures and a discreet broadcast warning angels of the impending fight, but we need your help to perfect it. I implore you to listen closely, ask questions, and speak up should you have any concerns."

Tomorrow. Something must have spooked him to act so rashly. That, or he's trying to force our hand and have us unprepared. I don't like either reason very much.

Remiel begins the briefing with what we know of the attack. It's not just the Fallen district they plan to hit, but the production district as well. As I chew, I listen and think. If their intentions are to *cleanse the impure*, it makes sense for them to attack both. There are very few Pure angels that work in the production district, since it's considered lesser work. And if their entire goal is to wipe out the Fallen in Silver City, they wouldn't go for areas with a heavy Pure population.

Mira clears her throat and asks, "Have we considered that the mole in the guild might also try to strike there, given they're our largest group of protectors and all happen to be Fallen?"

Mikhael nods. "We have."

"And?"

The Archangels exchange a look, but it's Remiel who replies. "And we have no reason to believe that will happen."

"With all due respect, I disagree." Mira glances at Hayliel, who gives a slight nod. "The mole is my father, and while it's clear that I no longer know who he is, I still understand how he operates. He knows the ins and outs of the guild. Their defenses, their strategies. He won't just pretend they don't exist. For one, he'll have assisted Auriel with a plan for each of the guilds' threat responses, but I believe he'll do his best to sabotage them, too."

The room falls silent. I expect outrage from the Archangels at learning Mira's secret, the one she kept from all of us until recently, but they don't seem bothered in the slightest. They glance at one another, probably having a private mental conversation about how best to proceed, but finally, Mikhael nods. "Perfect. Just as we hoped."

All the color drains from Mira's face. "Excuse me?"

While I hate to agree with the traitor's daughter, in this instance I have to. What the fuck?

Remiel gives her the oddest look under the circumstances. A

smile. "We've known who you are from the moment the mole's identity was revealed. I suspected you weren't a willing participant in your father's treason, and this just proves us right."

My mind is about to explode with this news, and I sense the others feel the same way.

"You've known?" Mira asks, disbelieving.

"Yes. But everything I saw in my visions showed me which side you were on—all except for this one today. If you didn't speak up about your father here, I'm afraid you'd have gone down a path there's no coming back from."

Dina, who's sitting beside Mira, places a hand on her forearm and squeezes. Well, shit. If the damn Archangels are offering her a clean slate, what gives me the right to hold a grudge?

Except emotions and trust aren't that easy to win back. Her betrayal feels far too personal for me.

"Now that that's settled," Mikhael says with a grin, "how should we handle the situation at the guild?"

Kirach clears his throat. "I suggest we speak to the leading general about this. He knows about Atlas, but if we have any hope of winning the battle tomorrow, we need his—and the guild's—full cooperation."

Mikhael raises his mug in salute. "On that, we can agree. In fact, I already sent off a request to meet—off the record. He'll be joining us soon. How do you propose we split our forces?"

We go through scenario after scenario, with the Archangels listening to each idea and giving it their full consideration. It's nothing like how I expected things to go. These are the rulers of our city and the famed god killers. Yet they're listening to us.

Before we break for lunch, I finally speak up with an idea that's been bouncing around in my head since discussing it with the others. "Like Castiel, there are other professors on campus who might help. Angels we trust. I think it's a good idea for us to reach out and invite them to join us. As much as we don't want to spread fear, with all due respect, we're going up against a rogue Archangel, his demon army, and the angels he's persuaded to his cause. Given how small our trusted group is, I believe having multiple plans in motion—each known to only a few—gives us an advantage against any hidden traitors."

"These angels Zeke speaks of are strong in combat and abilities," Castiel adds, offering me a smile. "I believe they'll aid us a great deal."

The Archangels do that thing again where they're clearly having a private internal conversation, and when they're done, Shubael says, "Give us their names before you exit for lunch, and we'll vet them. Don't stray far. We need everyone back here in thirty minutes."

Three and a half hours later, we have a pretty decent plan. Castiel just left to meet with Malik and Isadora, and if they agree, they'll help us with a secret mission at the guild that only a select few will know the details of. Dad's fighting with the main army, as are Briathos and Mira.

Hayliel, Remiel, Theo, Raph, and a few other guards have

their own mission—one to draw out Auriel and take him down. Dina is staying at the Sanctuary, despite wanting to fight with the others. But she'll be here with Mari and Cam, working on a structure for our city's future.

Everyone seems to know their place but me.

The Archangels have more food brought in, but I'm no longer very hungry. Not when we're talking about an all-out war on the horizon. One I know the angels I love won't stay out of. It's terrifying. "Where are you putting me?" I finally ask. I'm tired of waiting around.

It must be the wrong question, because suddenly, there's a shift in the air, and I know I'm not going to like what comes next.

"Well," Shubael says, looking more uncomfortable than I've seen him today. "We'd like you to stay here and defend the sanctuary, should the worst happen."

"Absolutely the fuck not." They can't be fucking serious.

"We don't feel comfortable putting you on the battlefield given the injury you sustained," Mikhael continues, only pissing me off more.

"I'm fine," I growl, sitting taller in my chair like that might prove my claim. "I don't need a wing to kick demon ass, so with respect, the answer is *fuck* no."

"He's right," Dad says, and for a second, I'm not sure which of us he's referring to. "Ezekiel is a fine fighter with great instincts. It would do our chance at victory a disservice to keep him out of it."

Briathos lifts his glass of water, the ice cubes clinking. "I agree with the lieutenant. From what I've seen of Zeke's ability to fight, the wing he lost—and regained, I might add—won't hinder his ability to turn our enemies to dust."

The Archangels study us while I do my best to keep my anger in check. An outburst wouldn't serve me well here.

It's Remiel who breaks the silence. "Hayliel. What do you think?"

I almost don't want to look at her, too afraid of what I might find behind her eyes. She's been so worried about me and the wing she reattached that I prepare myself for the flinch I know her words will cause. But what she says isn't what I'm expecting.

"I think you're both right. Zeke shouldn't be sidelined at the Sanctuary, but I don't think you should be put in the center of it all, either." She says the last words directly to me. They cut, which I know isn't her intention, but it hurts all the same. "Just hear me out, please," she says, imploring.

All I offer is a nod, because I don't know what will come out if I open my mouth.

"We know your wing is reattached, and aside from some muscle loss, it appears to be working just as it was before, but do we really want to test that in war?"

"I won't need my wings," I say, my voice gravelly.

"Not with demons, you're right. But we're not only fighting demons, Zeke. There are angels out there, too. What happens if your muscles give out and you can't fly to safety? It's too risky." Hayliel's gaze softens, like she hates being honest but knows she needs to be.

I drop my chin to my chest in defeat. "I can't stay here, caged within the Sanctuary."

"I don't want you to be. Take a position on the outskirts. Something equally important, but outside the inner fray. Please."

"He could man the ballista," Dad adds, pulling my attention. "With me."

Hayliel's brow shifts, confused. "What the hell is a ballista?"

As the pieces come together in my mind, I reply absentmindedly, "A two-person crossbow hidden within the mountains of the guild. You've already imbued bolts, actually, so this could work."

"No." Mikhael kills the idea before it can fully form. "Kirach, you're needed with the main army, not just for your skill or rank as lieutenant, but for the guild's image. For inspiration. Briathos, do you know how to work this weapon?"

"No, sir. But I can learn."

"I know how," Mira tells Mikhael, who looks pleased, but I only feel sick.

"Yes, this could work. Mira and Zeke, you'll work the ballista. Be our advantage against demons in the sky and take them out before they can wreak too much havoc."

I want to argue, but before I can, Remiel says, "This is the only way we'll agree to have you fight, Zeke. Do you accept?"

Ugh. On top of visions, can this guy read fucking minds or something? It's like he knows I want to say no and request literally *anyone* else to assist. But with options like these, what can I say? So instead, I give a restrained, "Yes. Thank you."

It doesn't make any fucking sense how someone like her, a Pure with no goddamn official training, was originally fighting alongside my father while I'm being tucked away like a liability. I might have lost a wing, but it's been re-a-fucking-ttached. We're not even supposed to fly around demons, so I don't see how this was ever an issue in the first place. And now this? Having to work a machine *with* her? I don't even trust her not to stab me in the back. How am I supposed to trust her with a massive weapon?

Already, my mind whirls with thoughts of what she could really want. Maybe the plan all along was for her to work that weapon, only instead of firing at demons, maybe her father ordered her to shoot us down instead. If she so much as makes a single step out of line, I'll handle her. Even if it means having to work that goddamn weapon by myself. It's not impossible, really. It's just far more work, and it extends the time between rounds, but I'll figure it the fuck out if she proves to be the snake I suspect she is.

The meeting ends, and I can't escape fast enough. I just need a moment, one fucking moment to myself. I keep walking until I push open a door and find myself outside. The cool breeze brushes over my skin, providing immediate relief. I breathe in once, then pull in another gulp of air before slowly expelling it—then I do it again. Apparently, it's a special breathing technique that's supposed to help with stress, and even though I was skeptical at first, it actually seems to help.

A little.

The door behind me opens, and I stiffen.

"Can I join you?" Dad asks. I don't bother turning around. Instead, I wave to the empty space around me in open invitation.

After a beat he says, "I'm sorry about the decision in there. I know that can't have been easy."

"It's shitty," I say, then sigh. "But I guess I can understand. I'm just glad not to be sidelined entirely." That's not the whole truth. I'd be even more glad if they weren't saddling me with the traitor's daughter, but I guess I can't win them all.

"I'm proud of you, Zeke. What you've endured and the way you're handling this." He swallows. "Your mother would have been proud, too. She would have hated the way I behaved after … when she …"

"It's fine, Dad, really."

"No. It's not fine. I might have lost my wife, but you lost your mother, too. And then I became closed off. Distant. I tried so hard to be strong for you that I completely missed being there for you. In a way, you ended up losing me, too."

For a moment, all I can do is stare. Dad and I have never really talked about feelings, not since Mom was alive, so that he's doing so now is much bigger than I can wrap my mind around. "You've always been there for me, even if it looked a little different. I've always felt it."

"I'm glad. And I'm so happy you found someone like Hayliel

who supports you. Cherishes you. The friendships you've made with Raphael and Theo, with Dina, and even with Mira, which is why I suspect her secret hit you so hard. Those are connections I could have only dreamed you'd have."

His words burrow deep, spreading through me like wildfire. I didn't realize how much I needed to hear them. The fact that he can sense all of this already makes me smile. "I lucked out pretty hard with them."

He pulls me into a hug that eases a pain in my chest from long ago. "When we get through tomorrow, I promise things will be different. We're going to spend some much-needed time together, and we're going to remember your mom the way she deserves to be remembered." He pauses, then adds, "We'll even have weekly family dinners. Not just with the two of us, but with Hayliel and her parents, too."

I laugh. "Ah, so you've experienced Mari's cooking then, have you?"

"What can I say? That woman can cook."

30

HAYLIEL

"Where are you taking me?"

Raphael and Theo placed a soft scarf over my eyes five minutes ago, and we've been walking ever since. Zeke is here too, somewhere up ahead.

"So many questions," Theo teases, lightly trailing a finger down the back of my arm.

"You could try answering at least one," I pout, though there's no conviction behind it. I don't really mind that I'm blindfolded and being led to some undisclosed location by my boyfriends. After the day we've had and what's coming for us tomorrow, I can't imagine anything better.

I listen, hoping something will give away our location, but

other than the sounds of our feet, all I hear are crickets. With the breeze on my cheeks, it's not hard to guess that we're outside, which tells me they're taking me somewhere private. But where?

The ground shifts from cobbled stone to something smooth, and my guides help me navigate a few short steps. Up ahead, a door creaks open, and I know the moment I step inside the building. There's a faint scent of ink and leather, but it isn't overly familiar. This isn't a library. Not a barn either. So where could this be?

The door shuts behind me, making me jolt in surprise, and then Raphael says, "Are you ready for this to come off?"

I purse my lips and nod, then the scarf is pulled away to reveal a large open room. The glass ceiling is tall and domed around us with a perfect view of the night sky, but it doesn't meet at the top. Instead, it's like the walls have retracted to allow free access to the outside world. In the center of the room is a large machine that I can't decipher. Is that a huge-ass telescope? Beyond it is a makeshift bed made up of blankets and pillows. There's a table laden with fruits and cheese next to a bottle of some type of sparkling beverage that's resting in a bucket of ice.

"This is ..." I trail off, unable to find the words. Everywhere I look, I find something new. A bookshelf filled with leather-bound tombs. A desk with quills and ink pots resting beside aged parchment. It's like we've stumbled into another dimension.

"We wanted to do something special for you, and when Theo found this place, we knew it would be perfect." Raphael leans in to press a kiss on my forehead.

My eyes sting with tears, and I laugh. "I don't know what to say."

"You don't have to say anything, firefly," Theo says, holding out his hand. "Come explore!"

Without hesitation, I take his hand and do just that. I pass by Zeke and offer him a dazzling smile and kiss before perusing the shelf beside him. They're full of books on planets, stars, constellations, and meteors. It's incredible and impossible to pick only one to read.

"I'm really glad we're all here for this. Thank you for putting it together." I reach out to each of them, holding their gaze and hoping they sense how much I mean the words.

"While we're on the topic of gratitude, I don't think I ever properly thanked everyone for rescuing me." Zeke's deep voice is raw with emotion. "I know we haven't always seen eye to eye—and that's mostly my fault, which I deeply regret—but you put yourselves in danger for me anyway. I'm still working on overcoming my baggage, but when I'm with you guys, it doesn't feel like it's between us. Here with you, it just feels like home."

My gaze is glued to Zeke—mouth agape—because holy shit. Did he just apologize, thank Raphael and Theo, *and* admit how he feels all in one go? The guys must be equally in shock, because it's silent for several moments.

"Too much?" Zeke asks, looking abashed for maybe the first time ever.

Theo steps forward and places a hand on Zeke's shoulder.

"Unexpected is all, but in a good way. We feel like home to me, too."

"A family—one we get to choose instead of being saddled with," Raphael adds, placing his hand on Zeke's other shoulder.

"I love you. All of you," I tell them. I'm not sure whose mouth finds mine first, but suddenly, the room feels extra charged, heavy with tension. They pass me between each other until I've felt each of their lips on mine, but they don't progress things further because Theo speaks.

"Wait, wait, wait. The telescope first."

"The telescope?" I ask, breathless.

Zeke sighs, his chin resting on my head. "Right. Okay, let's do it, then she's all ours."

My stomach flutters at his words, and part of me wants to tell them to screw the telescope. I don't need to see shit. I just need them. But it's clear they put thought into whatever they want to show me, so I go along with it even though my pussy throbs in dissatisfaction.

Next to the telescope sits a stack of papers. Star charts, I realize. All I catch from the top is the word *nebulae* before I'm parked in front of the telescope and Raphael commands me to look.

It takes me a moment to get the right angle, but when I do, I find the most beautiful thing. It almost looks like the inside of a geode, full of glittering specs and colors. "What is this?"

"That's the heart and soul nebulae. Two distinct nebula where stars are born, and sometimes you can even witness them mingling together," Theo whispers in my ear, his breath hot on my neck. "You are *our* heart and soul, Hayliel."

A shiver races down my spine, but I don't stop looking through the telescope.

Raphael is on my other side, his fingers dancing along my thigh. "It's because of you that we're here, together, fighting to unite our city."

"You make us better men," Zeke says from behind me, his hard body pressing against my back. I hear him breathe in against my hair, and it takes everything not to let out a moan. I lift my head, but he carefully pushes me back. "Enjoy the view while you can."

I do as I'm told, but I can't focus on the sight through the telescope while they shift around me. Every touch makes me jump and squirm with the need for more. Someone shifts the telescope, and although the view is different, it's also not. The nebula are linked, inexplicably, just like us.

Hands find the button of my jeans, then my zipper.

"Oh," I manage to get out.

"That's right, little sun. We'll give you what you need, but you have to earn it."

"Earn i-it?" My mind refuses to focus on Raphael's words while Theo is undressing me.

Zeke pulls away, and I immediately feel the loss.

"That's right, baby." Raph tilts my head, his lips locking with mine in a kiss that has my head swimming. Theo rises, my pants still trapped around my legs. He turns me toward him while

Raph takes over undressing me. Their kisses, while similarly passionate, are so different. Raphael's is intense, with nips of his teeth, while Theo moves slower, his tongue gliding across mine in a way that has my core spasming.

I feel like a pinball, bouncing between them. And I love it.

There's a sound from somewhere in front of me, then I hear Zeke command, "There. Take another look, hummingbird."

I almost object, not wanting anymore of this damn telescope when I'm currently naked from the waist down, but they don't give me a choice. Theo and Raph pull back enough to nudge me forward.

Well, looks like I'm stuck using this damn thing again.

I barely manage to see something blue through the telescope when I feel it. Two sets of hands on me. Then fingers dip between my thighs and swirl through my wetness. I suck in a gasp, my legs trembling already.

"Keep looking if you want to come," Zeke says, not letting me off the hook. "All you have to do is name that planet, and they'll make you feel good, won't you, fellas?"

"So good, firefly," Theo whispers against my skin while he and Raphael tease my entrance.

"Oh, fuck." I whimper, unable to focus at all. Planets? What the fuck are those? I can't think straight, and they want me to name a fucking planet?

"You want to feel good, don't you, little sun?" Raph asks, pressing a single digit inside me and withdrawing it completely.

"Yes," I say on a breath.

"Then be a good girl and do what Zeke says." This time, it's Theo's finger inside me.

With a shuddering breath, I lean forward and look through the scope. There are two circles; one white and one blue. Two planets? Or maybe a planet and its moon.

Just as I think this might not be so bad, two fingers enter me at once. When I glance down, I find my two men working together, each fingering me at the same time in alternate strokes.

Oh, gods.

I look up to find Zeke sitting in a chair, cock in hand, and my panties wrapped around his shaft as he strokes. He looks dark and dangerous, his shirt unbuttoned, chest bare. He's getting off on this.

Theo and Raph shift, each inserting another finger until somehow I have four inside me. They take turns licking and sucking my clit until I feel like I'll collapse. I'm so fucking horny.

"Please," I moan, utterly desperate as my hips gyrate, helping them finger-fuck me.

Zeke grunts, and I see the satisfaction in his gaze. "You know the rules. Name the planet and you'll get to see stars."

Fuck. I barely know my own name right now. How the hell am I supposed to name a stupid fucking planet? As if sensing my frustration, Raphael and Theo have backed off a little, and as much as I hate it, it's enough for me to find one singular ounce of concentration.

When I look through the lens again, they hike it up a notch, nearly making my knees give out, but I put everything I have into focusing. If I want to come, I have to do what Zeke says. That's what they told me.

Eventually, I'll recall how hot this is, but now I'm desperate, horny, and needy as hell.

Blue. Which planets are blue?

Neptune is the obvious one, but I know there's another. Uranus maybe?

Theo's tongue increases in pressure against my clit, making me shout out, "Uranus! Fucking hell, please be Uranus."

The licking stops and the four fingers inside me grow still, my orgasm fading.

Shit!

"Neptune. It's Neptune!" I shout, my voice high and whiny.

"Thank fuck," I hear Raphael say against my neck as everything begins again. Fingers thrusting, tongues lapping. It's everything and too much at the same time. I shatter, seeing the stars they promised, but not through any telescope.

You're so fucking beautiful, Zeke says through our mental connection.

As my orgasm fades, I feel a finger teasing against my ass, and know Raphael is there. I want what they promised me before. I want them both at the same time.

"I need—" I start but don't get the words out as my mind turns to mush beneath their expert touches.

Theo tugs my tank top off over my head so that I'm completely naked, while they're all mostly clothed. Against my ear, Raph says, "Zeke looks a little lonely, doesn't he, baby?"

My gaze jumps to Zeke who's still sitting in that chair, fisting his cock with my underwear. Precum glistens on the tip, beckoning me toward him. I only manage one step before Theo whispers, "Crawl to him."

A shiver races down my spine as I sink to my knees. I should hate this. I should fight back. But instead, I move closer to Zeke on my hands and knees, desperate for a taste of him. Even when I'm in front of him, his strokes don't stop. They don't even falter.

My mouth waters at the sight of my underwear in his fist, choking his cock. I haven't forgotten what this man likes. "Can I help?" My voice comes out grittier than I expect, so I clear my throat and try again. "I really want your cock in my mouth, Zeke. Please."

His throat bobs as he swallows, sparing a glance at the guys. I follow his gaze and find them naked, stalking toward us.

"Only until they're ready to make you come again," he finally says, and I turn back to him with greedy eyes, not waiting another moment.

I don't toss the underwear aside, and instead keep it there beneath my fist and immediately lick at the tip, savoring the taste of his arousal. I swirl my tongue around it before taking as much as I can down the back of my throat. He grunts, and I hum my approval.

"Raphael and Theo want to share you. Do you think you can handle them both, hummingbird?"

My pussy clenches around nothing as I nod vigorously.

"Mmhmm," I say around a mouthful of cock.

"Good girl."

Raphael's hand skates across my back while Theo's lips wrap around my nipple. I gasp, feeling overly sensitive, and Zeke takes the opportunity to withdraw his dick from my mouth. I whimper, but he only chuckles.

Theo lies on the bed while Raphael and Zeke help me straddle him. The moment his thick cock slides inside me, stretching me, I need more. I need what they promised me in the training room all those months ago.

Something cold slides between the cheeks of my ass. Lube. Raphael spreads it around, then presses a finger inside me.

"Oh, fuck," I mumble as Raphael inserts a second finger. Theo's the thickest of my three men, and I feel so full already. Will there be room for Raph's cock?

Zeke squirts another drop of lube on my backside while Theo slowly pumps into me with deep, shallow thrusts that have my mind fracturing. How am I this close already? *Fuck.*

Slick sounds penetrate my mind, but I don't have to wonder where it's coming from for too long, because Raphael's cock is notched against my ass, and he says, "Are you ready, little sun?"

"Gods, yes."

Zeke puts pressure on my shoulders until I'm leaning over Theo, my hair cascading onto his face, but Zeke notices right away and collects it. He wraps it around his fist and pulls just as I feel Raphael's cock press through my tight ring of muscles. The stretch burns, but the tug on my scalp holds some of the pain at bay, forcing me to split my attention.

"You're doing so good, baby," Raphael says, settling for a second while I adjust to the new sensations.

Theo's hand is on my breast, twisting and pinching my nipple just enough to distract me further and allow Raphael to gain another inch. And when Zeke traces circles on my clit, I clench around both cocks inside me. Raph and Theo curse at the same time, and my laugh turns into a moan as Raph finally seats himself all the way inside me.

We stay like that, suspended in time for what feels like a lifetime.

"You good?" Theo asks.

I don't know how to tell him I'm good. Too good. I feel like I could detonate at any moment, and they haven't even moved yet. With Zeke's fingers on my clit, the fullness inside me, I might just be going mad.

"So full," I mewl. "But ..." I hesitate, feeling delirious. I need to come. I need them to move, but I also need *more*.

"What do you need, firefly?"

I turn my head and lock eyes with Zeke. It's like he knows without my having to say a word. "You want my cock, baby? I can fill up that last hole of yours, hummingbird. All you gotta do is ask."

My pussy clenches again, and I beg. "Please." I shift closer to him and open my mouth. He grips his cock and traces my lips with his tip, then places it on my tongue.

"Now be a good girl and suck."

I do as I'm told, all the while staring up into his forest-green eyes. He looks away from me, and something passes between him and the others. Permission maybe, or instructions, I don't know. But Raphael begins to move. Slowly at first, he pumps in and out of me, and the move has Theo's cock rubbing against my inner walls.

I detonate. It happens almost instantly. The buildup having already put me on edge and sensitive. Zeke fucks my mouth, uncaring of the scream that tears up my throat. In fact, I think he enjoys hearing the muffled sound, wet and garbled, around his shaft.

"Fuck," Theo hisses at the same time Raphael growls, "So tight."

They don't let up, and my orgasm goes on and on. It doesn't even feel like it's my body anymore. My mind has transcended to a higher plain, and for the briefest moment, I actually think I catch a glimpse of us from somewhere else. An onlooker. A witness.

I know Raph is close, his cock thickening and quivering inside me in the seconds before he comes. Theo is quick to follow, filling me with his warm cum as it pulses inside me. And still, my orgasm doesn't subside. They thrust for as long as they can before it becomes too sensitive.

Sweat beads on my skin as Zeke pulls his cock from my mouth, and I collapse onto Theo's chest. My body quakes with little aftershocks of pleasure as I lie here, drained and stuffed and content.

Except, no. There's still one more thing to do.

"Zeke."

All three of my men know what I need, and they also know that I'm far too exhausted to do much more than provide a hole and vessel for his cum.

Raphael pulls out first, then Theo. Cum drips out of me, trailing down my leg, but Zeke doesn't seem to mind as the guys position me and spread my legs for him.

He watches my pussy, seeping with Theo's cum, and then, in a move that shocks me to my core, he scoops it up and presses it inside me. It's one of the hottest things I've ever seen this man do. My broken boy is finally on the path of mending.

A tear rolls down my cheek, and Raphael kisses it away.

Zeke lines himself up with my entrance, then pushes in slowly. His eyes never leave my pussy as, inch by inch, he buries his cock inside me. The moment he's settled, something shifts. It's like he's possessed.

He's like a rabid dog, and I'm the prey. He drives into me with the force of a madman. It takes everything for Theo and Raph to keep my legs spread wide, each of them sucking on a peaked nipple. And when Zeke grips my hips, shifting me slightly, his cock rubs against that sacred place on my inner wall, and I lose all function as the orgasm hits me. My muscles seize, head rising with a shout that Raph swallows with a kiss. It's sloppy—I'm incapable of anything but feeling, melting, exploding.

"You're doing so good, baby," Theo whispers, his breath cool on my wet skin.

Zeke lasts longer than I expected him to. When he comes, he grabs my neck and pulls me in for a kiss—Raphael's taste still on my lips.

A little while later, the four of us are curled up on the makeshift bed. I've been stewing for the last ten minutes, trying to figure out how to broach a subject I'm not so sure I should mention, but the more I think about it, the more convinced I am. Who knows what tomorrow will bring? Anything could happen, so I might as well put everything on the table now.

With a deep breath, I jump in. "So, I was thinking." I sit up, wanting to see each of my men for this. "I know this thing between the four of us is pretty new—"

"Not new," Raph interrupts. "We were inevitable, all of us. Even Zeke knew it, though he didn't want to admit it."

Theo laughs, but it's Zeke who says, "Well, I hate to admit *this,* but he's right. Sort of, anyway."

"Right, well, do you remember when we read Isaac's journal scrap about Octavius and Ingrid? It mentioned a ceremony that irrevocably bonded them." Silence is all that greets me, though I feel three sets of eyes on me, so I continue. "I just thought that maybe, if we survive tomorrow—"

"*When* we survive tomorrow," Theo corrects.

I smile and squeeze his knee. "When we kill Auriel and survive tomorrow, perhaps we can investigate the ceremony and see if it's viable for us." Fuck. Doubt settles over me like a cloud. "If you'd want to, of course. No pressure."

"Yes. Absolutely, yes," Raphael says.

"Without a single doubt," Theo adds.

I turn to Zeke, holding my breath. If he says no, what will this mean for us?

"I would love nothing more than to be linked with you."

"You sure, man?" Theo asks him. "You'd be linked to us, too."

"Forever," Raphael adds.

"I'm sure. Even if it means being linked to you *Pures*." He says the last word like he's disgusted, but I see past it to the smile beneath. And then I curl back up with my men in absolute bliss.

31

HAYLIEL

I slip the rune-stitched shirt over my head and pull it down, reveling in the soft fabric. It still baffles me that this clothing, as beautiful as it is, has added protection to it. Whoever the rune weaver is, she's an artist.

Assessing the weapons laid out on the dresser, I put each one into its proper sheath, including the secret pockets I discovered when I put this on the last time we went into battle. If only we'd been able to wear them then.

This time, the Archangels didn't even try to get us to wear their special clothes. Probably Remiel having seen the fight we'd have put up for it if they tried. But after the explosives incident from last time, I don't think anyone can blame us for being reluctant.

We can trust these clothes. At least, as much as we can trust the rune weaver. Okay, so maybe that's not very much either, but I trust Raduriel's judgment. He wouldn't have given her information to us if it would put his brother in danger.

As soon as I'm dressed, I head out to the main room in our private quarters and find my parents waiting for me. Mom sobs when she sees me, and Dad looks just as worried for me while trying to console her.

"I'll be fine," I assure them, pulling on the optimism they instilled in me. "Basically invincible, remember?"

This has Dad rolling his eyes and Mom's crying turning into laughter. "Well, I guess there's that, huh?" she says, wiping the tears from her face.

"We'll be throwing ourselves into planning for the future. It's about damn time we mend the relationship between Pure and Fallen," Dad says, looking somber.

"I've already got a ton of ideas," Dina says, coming out of her room with a notebook tucked under her arm. "Destroy those fuckers and be safe, alright? I need my bestie at my side in this new future." She looks from Zeke to Theo to Raphael, and then back to me before adding, "Ugh. Sometimes I hate that you're the chosen one," she teases.

She's not wrong. They do look damn fine in their armor.

I hug them each as tightly as I can, but refuse to say goodbye. None of us are dying today.

Another tear tracks down Mom's cheek as she stands in the

doorway. "I'll have something tasty waiting for you when this is over, so come back in one piece, okay?"

"You heard the woman," Raphael says. "End this as quickly as possible so we can eat Mari's famous food."

When they're gone, I turn and survey what's left of our group. The guys look incredible in their rune-stitched clothing. It's criminal, really. I hope that whatever happens today, those clothes don't get ruined, because I can think of quite a few scenarios I'd like to use them in.

Roleplay, anyone?

Castiel isn't here. He came back from his secret rendezvous with the trusted professors but only stayed long enough to grab his things before heading out. They're keeping the plan pretty close to their chest, but it sounds like everyone we expected to say yes did, and even Phiel agreed to help. If Atlas tries to take over the guild as Mira suspects, he won't get far.

As if hearing my thoughts, Mira comes out of her room looking gorgeous in her rune-stitched clothing. Her outfit is different from mine, more fierce somehow. I wonder if that was done by request, or if the rune weaver could sense that about her.

Mira hands me the power suppressant elixir, this one modified to only diminish my power to mimic a normal level instead of hiding it entirely. Then she hands me the antidote.

We'd made this plan only yesterday, which meant Mira had spent most of the night working on both liquids. One so I could blend in, and the other to make me stand out and hopefully lure the bastard Auriel to my position.

Mira clasps her hands behind her back. "I've already given the main army a few bottles of that power spray, too."

"Clever trick, using their strengths against them," Theo tells her, sounding infinitely impressed. If I didn't trust him fully, I might worry that he was interested in her romantically, but I know he's only curious about the making of her potions. This one is new. A spray that mimics the power essence of an angel. Kirach and his team will douse the Fallen district down in the hopes it'll confuse the demons enough to not come after me when I use the antidote.

"It was actually Dina's idea. With her, Mari, and Cam, we'll probably have hundreds of viable options to fix this rift between Fallen and Pure."

From outside our rooms, I hear the alarm blare. The scouts Mikhael sent to keep track of enemy movements must have found something. It's our cue to get going so we can be in position before shit hits the fan.

Kirach and the main army already have their boots on the ground in the Fallen district, which I'm told had already been evacuated quietly. Same with the production district, though the machines are still pumping out smoke to appear as normal as possible.

We won't know whether we've fooled Auriel until his army swoops in.

Zeke stops by my side, carrying a bundle of imbued crossbow bolts. He pulls me into him and kisses me like he never wants to stop. Like he needs the very air from my lungs to exist. And when we break apart, I think maybe we do. I need them just as they need me. "Please be safe. Don't be reckless."

There's a glint of mischief in his eyes, but it passes when he says, "You come back to me in one piece. Take care of each other out there."

I offer a nod to Mira, and then they're gone. The power suppressant tastes just as awful as it did before, but I swallow it down, hoping it's the last time I'll ever need it.

With one final check to make sure we have everything, Raphael, Theo, and I head out to meet Remiel on the cliffs overlooking the guild and Fallen district. We make it in record time, not wasting a single second in case we miss our chance at spotting Auriel. It's him I need to find and destroy. It's him only I can take care of.

There's an uncomfortable silence as we stand on the cliff watching the empty landscape. Didn't the scouts report movement? Where is everyone?

Something shifts on the horizon. My eyes stay glued to the spot, and I try not to blink for fear of missing anything. There's a hint of darkness that grows until a horde of demons seems to fill the sky. How are there so many of them? On and on they come, flying like a cloud of locusts. There are more demons than angels, but I still spot a few feathered wings among them, and not all of them are black. Pures have joined Auriel's cause.

Standing on the ground below them is Auriel. His four wings are set free and spread wide behind him like a damn peacock.

He's not alone. I spot at least one angel and demon with him, but all the group has done is watch as the demons and angels in the air grow closer to the Fallen district.

This asshole doesn't intend to fight with the others. He wants to watch. He's going to fucking sit back while the rest of the city fights for their lives, then he can swoop in when it's all done and lay claim to a Pure city.

Over my dead fucking body—and I'm damn hard to kill these days.

"We could go to him, since he's mostly alone, but if we want to keep the element of surprise in an area we know well, we'll have to lure him like we planned," I say, whispering even though I know the bastard can't hear me.

"When the battle begins, we'll get in position," Remiel replies with authority.

"When will—" Raphael starts as a barrage of imbued arrow tips flies through the air toward the oncoming horde. Some manage to hit their target, turning demons to ash in seconds, but enough of them miss to be a problem.

The ones who survived dive toward the shooters. Why aren't their forces splitting between the Fallen and production areas as expected? Unless ... someone fed us false information. Again.

Fuck!

I turn to Remiel. "Our intelligence was compromised. Call off the forces at the production district. Now. Have them join the army here as quickly as possible. It's our only chance—"

"Already on it," he assures, but we may already be too late.

A sickening sense of dread seeps into my bones.
There's no turning back now.
We cannot fail.

32

HAYLIEL

We stay close to the cliff wall as we descend. As much as I might want to join the fight, we need to remain unseen for as long as possible. And even though it makes more sense to fly to our lure point, the demons would spot us and everyone knows the golden rule of fighting demons: remain on the ground. No matter what.

We walk for what feels like ages, and although I can't really see the battle, I hear it. Distant booms have me worried about those specially made bombs, and snarls that sound far too close—even though I know they aren't. The wind is carrying them to us.

Worry gnaws at the edges of my mind. Did the army merge in time? Do we even have a chance at our plan still working? The questions are pointless. All they do is fuel more fear and unease, so I do my best to shake it off.

Someone would tell me if things took a turn we couldn't survive. I need to trust that.

At the halfway point, we find the small section of land without cover. Aside from our descent from the cliff side, this is the part I'm most worried about. Images flash through my mind of the last time I was here. It might not be the exact coordinates, but this is close to where that scarred asshole stabbed me with an angel blade.

Even though I survived, it hurts to think about. I swear I can still feel the blades as they stabbed into me. If only we'd known about Lieutenant Atlas then, instead of thinking he was some savior. He probably never even tracked down the demons who survived.

"We move quickly," Remiel says to no one in particular before swinging his gaze to Raphael and Theo. "And remember what we decided. The goal is to get Hayliel to the lure point, with me at her side to help incapacitate Auriel. Ideally, we do this as a group, but if we need to split up, we split up. Is everyone still in agreement?"

"Yes," I tell him, nodding. The Archangels explained that my sunfire is the weapon that will end Auriel for good, but not just imbued into a weapon. I need to hit him with pure sunfire, something I haven't managed to do on command yet. Of course, Remiel couldn't give me the exact specifics without it "affecting the outcome." He said I'll know it when I feel it though, like that's helpful. Guess I've got to figure it out myself. No pressure.

The guys exchange a look, but it's Raphael who says, "She's the only one who can end this. We'll do whatever we can do to support that, even if we don't much like it."

"Her chances are higher with you three," Remiel says to them, and I know right away he's referring to Zeke as the third. "Let's go."

We move quickly and quietly, doing our best not to draw attention to ourselves. Except even our best isn't enough to get through undetected. In a flash, two demons and an angel drop from the sky and attack. I'd been so focused on the path ahead, worried we'd be running directly into a group of them that I never even thought to look in the sky. It was empty before we came out here.

The demons are no match for our imbued weapons, but the angel is another story. No one wants to fight one of their own, and that hesitation allows him to kill one of our guards before Remiel uses the angel's own blade to end his life.

The sight is something I don't think I'll ever be able to clear from my mind.

"You didn't have to do that!" Theo says the very words I'd just been thinking.

"I did," Remiel replies, brooking no argument. "If I let him live, he'd have killed him later." He points to Raphael, and the breath in my lungs turns cold. I hate everything about the scenario we're in, but no one threatens my men. No one.

"Well, in that case," Raphael says, forcing a laugh.

The longer we stand here, the more likely it is someone will spot us. "We need to move."

"More are coming," the Archangel adds almost cryptically.

"Then we fight," I say, pulling the short sword from its sheath.

"No." Remiel stares off in the distance. I follow his gaze but see nothing of interest. When he continues, I understand. "Hayliel, Theo, and I must forge ahead. The rest should stay here."

What he saw hasn't happened yet. As much as I want to deny it, this is the exact scenario we'd discussed earlier. I might hate separating, but the mission depends on it.

"Be safe," I say to Raph before pulling him in for a quick kiss. "I love you. Go save the city."

Theo grips Raphael's forearm in this cute bromance hand-shake that would have me melting under different circumstances. Now though, all I can do is leave one of the men I love behind and head toward what might just be the biggest fight of my life.

The sooner I defeat Auriel, the sooner everyone, not just those I love, are safe. We'll still have the demons to contend with, but is it too hopeful of me to think they'll back off if they no longer have a powerful ally?

Remiel, Theo, and I take off toward the forest. The same forest we found Roderick in all those months ago. From what I can tell, no one has seen or heard from him since.

I didn't know it at the time, but I teleported in that forest.

We're almost to the edge of the tree line when I see a dark figure off to the right. Theo notices too, his spine stiffening as we get a better look at the creature's face. It's only when I see the scar that it clicks.

This must be the demon who killed Serah. Why else would Theo go so still?

The thought has barely registered in my mind before something strange passes between Remiel and Theo. Then he gives me one pleading look and takes off toward the demon.

I want to go with him, but Remiel stops me, guiding me back in the direction of the lure point. "He has to do this, and we need to let him."

His words might not give it away, but I know from the look in his eyes that he's seen this play out. And even though I shouldn't trust the Archangels after everything they've put me and my friends through, something tells me I can trust Remiel with this.

"Besides," he continues, "we don't need further delays, nor do we want that creature to follow us or sound the alarm before we're ready. We'll soon be out of time."

At the cryptic note in his voice, I go against every single instinct urging me toward Theo and push onward.

Yet as we walk, I can't help but wonder if every decision we've made so far today—separating from Raph, and now Theo—has been the wrong one.

33

THEO

I n this battle, we all have a job to do.

Hayliel's is to take out Auriel. Ours is to make sure she gets to her position intact. Going after this demon is technically still doing what I'm supposed to do—it just has the added bonus of filling another need inside of me, too.

I only give myself five seconds to feel guilty before I remind myself that Hayliel supports my need for vengeance. She understands why I can't just walk away.

Because of all the training I've done recently—with Remiel and on my own—I'm ready. It feels like every trial in my life before now has led to this moment, but I don't let myself linger on how momentous it is that I'm here. Instead, I focus on the steps in front of me.

The beast doesn't get very far, and something tells me it's not because of how quick my strides are. Does this demon remember me? I've changed a lot since then, maturing from a young boy into an adult.

I've trained against fierce warriors and even fought against the very creatures who haunt my nightmares. Nothing quite compares to this, though.

But as much as I might have changed, this asshole clearly hasn't. He's here, ready to slaughter more angels. I'd be a fool to believe Serah was his last kill.

When I've taken two more steps, the demon turns around. As soon as our eyes lock, my vision grows blurry around the edges. Suddenly it's harder to breathe, like some heavy, foreign object sits on my chest.

No, no, no!

The last thing I need is another panic attack now when I'm this fucking close.

My foe doesn't move to attack. He only watches as I struggle to keep my composure, like he knows something is off, but whether he understands is a mystery.

I breathe in slowly, hold it, then exhale. Next, I name five items in my surroundings, trying to ground myself to the moment, but my eyes never leave the creature in front of me.

He's shirtless, just like he was that day so many years ago. The scar is still there on his face, but there are others, too. One on his jaw and three curved around his ribs that look like claw markings. What could have left that mark? A sunblade, perhaps? I doubt he got it from his own kind.

"Your power is familiar," the demon coos. "Have we met before?"

Even though I didn't expect him to, the fact that he doesn't fully remember only pisses me off.

"I'm not surprised you don't remember. I'm sure the angels you kill are all forgotten once you wipe the blood off your blade."

"You are here, no? Surely I did not kill you." He tilts his head to the side. "Ah. So I killed someone you loved. A friend? Family? Or a lover, perhaps?"

He's goading me. Probably trying to make me angry so I'll be ruled by emotion and do something stupid. It's a smart tactic, one I wouldn't have thought these meatheads would think of. Still, it's unfortunate for him because I won't fall for it. "Something like that. Today marks the day of reckoning for your crimes. Are you prepared to face them?"

"From you?" He grins. "Gladly." The demon pulls an angel blade from his belt but doesn't step toward me. He must want to see what I'll do first.

I pull out my own weapon, this one a curved, double-edged blade. It glows brightly, powered by Hayliel's sunfire. This isn't the typical style our fighters would use against the demons, and I hope it gives me the upper hand.

Of course, he notices the difference immediately, but if he's afraid, he doesn't give any sign. "If you want to kill me, you actually have to stab me with something. The daggers in your eyes don't count."

I only shrug. I suspect he's trying to taunt me, but all he's doing is giving away how much my inaction bothers him. He knows how to fight. To maim and kill. But this pussy-footing around isn't something he knows how to deal with, and I can use that to my advantage.

I look beyond him, pretending to check out the territory without ever really taking my sights off him. This only unnerves him more. He thinks I'm unbothered and doesn't know how to react. If he only knew how much I'm itching on the inside. The need to kill him is burrowed deep in my psyche. But the murdering son of a bitch in front of me isn't nearly pissed off enough.

So I wait.

I swear I can sense the moment he's about to snap. Something in the air shifts, like an electric current that barrels toward me moments before he does. It's probably the only reason I dodge his first strike so well, and that's the last thought I have before every ounce of my focus is on the fight.

He attacks with so much anger that the force is far greater than I expected. Even when I block the incoming hit of his angel blade with my sword, my feet skid back on the ground like I'm trying to hold off a freight train.

Twisting away, I break free, but I'm not quick enough to avoid the swipe of his claw against my abdomen. There's a moment of pain, but it's him that yelps.

What the ...?

We both pause and stare at the smoke rising from the claw that just cut me. Then I look down and see the wound. It's minimal, thank fuck, but it cut through my rune-stitched shirt. What the hell is this thing made of?

Whatever it is has the demon in front of me absolutely enraged. He comes at me with force, shaking me from my thoughts until we're right back where we were before. Him attacking with me on the defensive. But he's learning.

He feints a jab, and I move to block it, but don't get to because a searing pain shoots up my right arm. I stumble back and chance a look down. The fucker's claw got me good. From wrist to elbow, there's a deep gash. Blood flows freely down my palm, dripping onto the ground.

The demon grins, looking pleased with himself. He probably thinks he just gained the upper hand, and while it *is* a lot of blood, it won't stop me from ending him. I'll do it or die trying.

I transfer the sword to my uninjured arm, the move only making the asshole's smile grow wider. After that, all pretense is gone. He's done with our little back and forth, and he's more than ready to end me for good.

He lunges forward, and I dart out of reach, barely escaping another clash with his claws. I need him to think I'm weak, then he'll let his guard down.

Little does he know, I can fight just as easily with either hand. I made sure that particular disadvantage wouldn't be one I ever suffered.

My breaths come in and out in fast bursts, partly because it's a workout and a half to stay alive, but I play it up a little. He, on the other hand, doesn't look at all tired.

In that moment, something shifts. The next thing I know, he's on me with no reservations. His hits are hard, but I don't back down. Even when my wounded arm aches. Even when the wind is knocked out of me. I push through and use everything I've learned over the years—every ounce of knowledge gained from Remiel's instruction.

It's like I've stepped out of my conscious body and become a bystander, watching on in utter fascination as my blade plunges deep into the demon's chest. The look of utter horror before he turns into dust will be seared into my memory forever.

As I catch my breath, no fireworks go off in celebration. There's no victory horn blasting around me. But I swear my soul feels lighter. I take a moment to look up at the sky, closing my eyes as I think about Serah. "Be at peace now, my friend," I whisper up to her as if she's listening.

Hayliel's voice pops into my mind, along with a rush of affection. *You did it, Theo! Are you alright?*

How she knows I killed him is a question for later. My focus needs to be on taking down the piece of shit threatening to take over and dismantle our city.

I glance down at my arm to find the blood has slowed, and the wound has already closed a little. That's good. *A little banged up, but nothing serious. I'll come—*My telepathic thoughts are cut off when I catch sight of Raphael in the distance.

The angel he's with falls to the ground in a heap, leaving my best friend to fight off three demons all on his own.

34

RAPHAEL

The guard fighting beside me—Yael, I think?—is good, but he's no guild member.

I can tell he's had some of the best training out there, but that's all it's been. Practice. Today might actually be the first day he's ever been face to face with a demon, and it's not going well. So far, he's blocked most of the attacks, but he hasn't gotten a single hit in himself.

All he's done is put off his own death long enough for me to step in.

I throw an imbued dagger toward the demon, who's distracted by trying to kill Yael. It arcs through the sky, throwing beautiful shafts of light around, before sliding into the demon's skull where he turns to dust.

The ashes fall onto Yael's face, some even going into his mouth. He sputters—heaving as he tries to shake the remains of the dead creature off him. I help him up, instantly regretting it when he says, "Ugh, that's disgusting! Could you be a little more mindful next time about where the body will go?"

Is he fucking for real right now?

"How about you kill it yourself next time, then, yeah?" Ungrateful asshole. I turn to leave, desperate to get back with Hayliel, Theo, and Remiel, but five demons now stand between us and the forest. And they don't look very happy.

Yael gulps audibly beside me, making me frown. Great. Keeping my voice low, I say, "Listen up. You've been trained by some of the best fighters in our city, including the Archangels themselves if the rumors are true. Would you cower like a little bitch if Remiel was still with us, or would you fight with everything you've got?"

"I—I—I—" he stutters, testing my patience. The demons are closer now, clearly ready for a fight.

How the hell did I end up with this sniveling coward?

"Decide!" I shout just as the demons make their first move.

I lose sight of him as I fend off two demons at once, blocking and attacking in a steady rhythm that eventually earns me a pile of dust when one of them falls onto my blade. I'm left with one demon to fight when I notice Yael has three, and it looks like they're toying with him.

Probably because they sense he's weak.

My focus is pulled again as the demon in front of me, who seems a little pissed that I just killed his friend, comes at me in a fit of rage that makes him reckless. Eventually, our fight has me turned enough that I can see Yael in my periphery.

Somehow, in a feat that actually impresses me, he impales one of them on his long sword. "Holy shit," he screeches. "Did you see that, Raphael?"

I did see it, just like I see that his gaze isn't on the remaining two demons. No, he's watching me, looking for what? Approval? Instead, all he gets is death.

One of the demons thrusts an angel blade straight through his chest and lifts, holding him up like an offering. I swear, the demon near me laughs as Yael's limp form is kicked clean off the blade, falling to the ground in a heap and leaving me alone with three angry demons.

They all rush me as one, not giving me the opportunity to fight them individually. A claw hooks through the fleshy part of my thigh, making me fall to my knees in agony while the three demons draw closer around me. Should I use the small sack of ash? They said it's only for emergencies, and this is feeling more and more like one.

I try to stand, but whatever muscles they hit must have been important because holy fucking hell does it hurt. The odds of my surviving become dimmer with each passing second. I feel my heartbeat in the wound like a second organ as blood spurts out in a disgusting rhythm that only seems to delight my enemies.

Three demons, three angel blades. And only one me.

I fumble to access the pocket, no longer caring what the ash will do to me as long as it incapacitates them. I'll gladly take pain if it means Hayliel survives and takes Auriel down. Then this will all be worth it. Whatever happens to me is meaningful if she succeeds, but as hard as I try, I can't get the pocket open.

The demon in front of me holds an angel blade high in the air, ready to strike, and at that moment the only thought flowing through my mind is that I wish I had more time with Hayliel—with the family we created.

The pulse of something very similar to fear spreads through me from the mental pathway with Theo. It's so sudden and powerful that I look around, eyes wide. The demons must think it's fear for my death because they cackle.

It doesn't last long, though, not when Theo barrels into the closest demon, catching him completely off guard and turning him to dust in the same moment.

That distraction, despite it lasting only a few scant seconds, gives me enough of a chance to heal—or maybe it's my adrenaline. Either way, I finally make it onto my feet. I'm still not at full strength, but these odds are far more manageable.

Theo lost the element of surprise, but he must be riding a high of endorphins because he doesn't seem to slow at all, even when an angel blade lances across his cheek and blood trickles from the wound.

A demon growls, bringing me back to the fight in front of me just in time to stumble backward. I'm not quick enough to avoid the knick of the angel blade across my chest. I wince, but the pain isn't nearly as bad as it could have been.

The demon drops the blade, yipping like a hurt dog as he stares at his fingers. I look down at my clothing and smile. I'm completely clueless about what the fuck just happened, but one thing is clear. The rune weaver sure knows her fucking stuff.

Theo joins me and the last remaining demon—who still hasn't picked up the angel blade he dropped. He must think it was the blade that caused his injury—not the clothes—but that's fine. Let him fear the weapon.

It makes this far easier for us.

Instead of attacking us, he spreads his wings and takes to the skies. His wings beat twice, then a third time, but doesn't make it a fourth. There's a whoosh and a whistle before a sunfire imbued bolt falls to the ground along with the ashes of the demon.

I glance up to where I know Zeke and Mira are working the ballista and send gratitude down our mental connection, then I turn back to Theo.

"Why aren't you with Hayliel?" Now that the danger is gone, I have time to panic. He's covered in blood, more than just from the cut on his face. "And what the fuck happened to you?"

"She's fine, and so am I," he says, soothing my worries. "We got separated. Serah's killer showed up, so Remiel and Hayliel forged on while I got rid of the problem and took care of a long overdue life debt."

"No fucking way," I say, slapping my hand on his back. "Serah can finally rest now, thanks to you."

"Now let's go make sure we don't need to avenge any more angels, yeah?"

35

HAYLIEL

Each step brings me and Remiel closer to our destination, so I send a shot of love down the mental pathways to my men.

With Theo on his way to Raphael, I can breathe a little easier. Although the elation I felt from Theo still lingers, Raphael is in pain. Whatever is happening, I need Theo to get there in time.

Instead of focusing on that line of worry, I concentrate on Zeke. Through our connection, I know he's bored. Angry. He doesn't want to be sidelined, and he sure as shit doesn't want to be stuck with Mira, but it's good for him. Maybe it'll allow him to move past what happened.

Still. If we make it through today, I never want to be separated from them again.

A sound catches my attention, and I turn just in time to see an angel pass behind a tree so thick no creature could wrap its arms around it. Was that Darok? What the hell is he doing here?

But no, it can't be, because what emerges from the other side isn't an angel. It's a demon.

He walks toward me casually, like he doesn't have a care in the world. "My, my. What are you doing so far from the action, Hayliel?"

He says my name like we're friends, like he's not on the opposite side of this war. The wrong side. "Do I know you?" I know we don't have much time to waste, but there's something about this demon that has sirens going off in my brain.

He laughs. "Clever little thing, aren't you? Too bad, though. You might have gotten away from the bombs, but you won't make it out of the forest."

The bombs. Is he saying what I think he's saying? But if he is, that would mean demons had access to those uniforms and maybe even access to the sanctuary. A chill rolls down my spine at the thought.

"Very valiant of you to try, but you can't stop what's coming. The demon king will prevail." I know the minute he sees Remiel, because he pauses his tirade, most likely reassessing the situation. Then he smiles. "Look what we have here. A two-for-one deal. How lucky am I?"

Apparently done with his monologue, he attacks. As far as demons go, he isn't the most formidable one I've fought, but he isn't the easiest, either. On my own, it would have taken longer, but with Remiel here, we turn him to dust in under five minutes.

"Do you think Auriel sent him here?" I ask Remiel as we continue our way toward the lure point.

"It's possible. But with the way he spoke, it's more likely he came on orders from the demon king himself."

"Don't really like the idea of being on his radar," I mutter, already hating it enough to be on Auriel's.

"Best not to think of it, then. Come on. We're almost there."

Easier said than done, but I suppose he's right. I've got enough on my plate to worry about now. Worries about the demon king can wait until after we deal with Auriel.

The forest grows thicker and denser the closer we get to our destination, accompanied by the earthy scent of moss and colorful mushrooms that make my nose twitch. The undergrowth is thick with vegetation and broken branches, making it difficult to maneuver, but we finally break through.

Sunlight dances in from the break in the leaves above, and a few feet away from us sits a large stump. We approach with caution, just in case we haven't been as subtle as we think.

When we're close enough, I reach out and touch the old tree. There are far more rings than I can count, and I marvel at how perfectly flat the top is. Whoever cut it down must have taken great care and precision to make it this clean.

I wish I could ask them why. What did they hope this would become, and what would they think about it now if they knew what we were about to do here?

I pull the antidote from within a hidden pocket and nod to Remiel before drinking it down. For our plan to work, Remiel had to take some of Mira's potion earlier too, or else we'd both have been easily recognizable. He doesn't take the antidote, though. We want Auriel to believe I'm here without an Archangel.

For a second, I think I might feel the antidote working, flowing through my bloodstream and canceling out Mira's earlier potion, but maybe that's all in my head.

Every moment that passes is an eternity, and I begin to worry that our carefully laid plan won't work. Did we fuck up somewhere? Is there another traitor among us?

Something shifts on the breeze, then a twig snaps from somewhere nearby, and I know before he even steps foot out of the trees—it's Auriel.

He's alone, looking far calmer than I hoped he would at finding Remiel beside me. It's one thing to fight me, but his own kind? Someone he's spent countless years ruling beside? Auriel appears only happy at the revelation. Gleeful, almost.

"How cute of you to bring the bookworm," Auriel says as he continues taking slow steps toward us. "Senseless, perhaps, but cute. He can't protect you like he promised."

His words are confusing, and even though I want to probe for more details or lash out about not needing protection, I know Auriel is only trying to get under my skin. So instead, I put it back on him with the hopes he'll give something up. "Oh, really? How exactly do you see this playing out, then?"

"If you're smart, you'll kill him and join me at my side. If you're not"—his grin widens—"you'll have an up close view of your friends and family dying before I end your life."

"You can't kill me."

"There are far worse things than death, little seraph."

Once again, I don't take the bait—even though it dangles there, tempting me. He must sense his tactic won't work because he changes gears.

"It's funny how you'll refuse to work with me, but have no trouble siding with them," Auriel says, tilting his head toward Remiel. "Who do you think is to blame for the current state of our city? They didn't stop me from separating the Fallen because they simply do not care. If you truly hate me, then you'll have to hate them, too. At least with me you know what you're getting."

Gods, I hate this man. "You talk too much, you know that?"

"Maybe. But it served my purpose flawlessly." His grin turns absolutely feral. "I've worked with the council for ages. Did you really think I'd be dumb enough to show up without reinforcements?" Then, as if he's summoned them by words alone, I see what he means. Demons and angels, all rushing to this very spot. Some flying, others coming through the forest.

There are too many to count, and when they arrive, I'm afraid we'll lose every chance we have of ending Auriel for good.

36

EZEKIEL

I peer through the scope on the ballista, watching the fight unfold.

There's not much I can do to help the crowd of fighting allies below—not when they're all so close to each other. It would be far too easy for me to hit someone on our side. Besides, with the walls of the Fallen district, there are blind spots.

Auriel probably had them built that way.

Still, I can keep an eye on things like I did with Raphael and Theo, or like I'm doing now with my father, using telepathy to pass information along to him. I suppose that counts for something.

So far, I've managed to ignore Mira and the other angels sent to protect our position. Not only have I been sidelined with the traitor's daughter, but they sent us with fucking babysitters.

It's bullshit.

I spot a few angels trying to get the surprise jump on Dad and pass along a message to him, watching as he and his elite group secure them with ease. One angel slips free, nearly stabbing my father with an angel blade before he winds up paying the ultimate price himself. I can't imagine it would be easy to kill our own kind, and I know Dad would do everything in his power to avoid it, but it's not always an option.

There are only a few on our side carrying the deadly weapon. Only those we trust implicitly.

Mira taps on my shoulder, jolting me from my thoughts. I stiffen, not wanting her anywhere near me. Hell, I consider ignoring her completely, but that will only make her tap again. "What?"

"I want to look."

"Fuck off."

She doesn't back down. "Five minutes, that's all."

"Fine. But only because I want to check in with the others." Sighing, I step back. Even though I don't like it, I can't pass up the opportunity to make sure Hayliel is okay. She wasn't with Raphael and Theo, and that makes me nervous.

Searching down the bond, I find them all breathing. Theo and Raph seem to be in less pain than the last time I checked, and Hayliel only feels anxious. Anxiety I can handle. It means they're still alive.

With my checks complete, I turn, fully intending to tell Mira her time is up, even though I know it hasn't been five minutes. She's frowning, her movements frantic as she tracks something through the scope. "What is it?"

I don't wait for her to respond, instead shoving her out of the way so I can take a look.

"My father." She barely gets the words out before I see Lieutenant Atlas through the lens.

That piece of fucking shit traitor.

"You," I say to one of the babysitters. "Help Mira man this weapon. I'll be right back."

"But, sir," the guy squabbles at the same time Mira says, "Fuck no. I'm going with you whether you fucking like it or not."

She turns to the rest of the angels with us. "Zeke and I need to go handle a traitor. Take over this machine and help us reach victory. We'll be back when we're done."

Mira's ready to fly, but she takes one last look at her father through the scope. "If we head to the corner of the city, he'll run right into us."

I let my wings free, feeling a slight twinge in the muscle around my reattached wing.

"You good?" She looks over my shoulder at the ring of gold that signifies where Hayliel attached it.

I roll my eyes. "I'm perfect."

We probably shouldn't be flying, not with so many demons around, but there's no other way to get from point A to point

B. We just have to hope they're all too busy fighting for their lives to notice.

Staying low, we fly over the small river that runs parallel to the production district. The closer we get to our destination, the more destruction there is. The ground is filled with pieces of rock and brick, and there's a massive hole where the wall once stood. Through that hole, I see my father. He's fighting like a pro, slicing and avoiding, stabbing and receding. I've always looked up to him for so many reasons—and this is one of them.

A gust of wind hits my wings, causing a fierce pain to lance through my left one. I want to shout, but the pain holds my voice hostage. All I can do is crash to the ground.

I flip over, tucking my wings as best I can, but the pain is too much. When I finally stop skidding, I'm near the wall with Mira at my side, trying to figure out what's happening. Even through the pain, I hate that she's here.

Dad shows up next, but as I sit, I feel almost lopsided.

There's a dark shape a short distance away, and I know instantly what it is.

My wing.

"Let me see," Dad says, peering at my back. I don't fight him. All I do is breathe as the pain slowly diminishes to a dull ache. His brows draw down, and he says, "Whatever Hayliel did, a part of it is still there. The wound is closed, but son, I—"

"I know," I say, my voice far stronger than I feel. "The wing is gone for good." I don't know how my voice sounds so calm, but here, in the middle of this battlefield with Atlas so close, I need to keep my emotions under wrap. "It's fine. Atlas is close. Let's just—"

Five demons filter out through the hole in the wall. The smallest guy notices my discarded wing on the ground and laughs. "We've found ourselves a flightless bird!"

Then it's utter chaos.

I stand too quickly, and the regret is immediate as my head swims. Dad is there, protecting me like not only a fierce warrior but a father protecting his young.

There are too many of them for my dad and Mira to handle alone.

Even though I'm not at full strength, I have to do something.

Yanking out my multi-weapon that Hayliel imbued for me, I launch into an attack. Every twist of my left arm tugs at my shoulder and makes me hiss, but I power through it as best I can, and for a second, I think we're winning.

That's when I catch sight of Mira from my periphery.

Three demons surround her. She's standing in the middle, circling to not give one of them her back for too long.

Two of them have their angel blades drawn, but the other either doesn't have one or has it tucked away somewhere. The two with the weapons are toying with her, and when one of them lunges forward, he barely makes it a step before he dissolves into dust.

When the ash and dust clear, Atlas stands behind him, his face filled with an emotion I've never seen him hold. Fear.

"Zeke! Behind you!" Dad yells, kicking my instincts into full gear. I block a swipe of claws, but the sudden movement forces an embarrassing yelp past my lips.

I will not give up.

The fight takes every ounce of my concentration, and by the time Dad and I are done fighting, so is Mira. Except she's anything but victorious.

She's kneeling over a body. It takes me a second to recognize who it is.

Atlas.

Immediately, I wonder if she killed her own father. Yet as bad of a man that he was, I can't imagine her doing it. Even if she hated him. Even if she was never working with him.

Dad and I approach her slowly. He scans the ground and skies for demons while I focus on Mira—the liar and the traitor, yet I can't quite see her that way right now.

"Mira?"

When she looks at me, I expect to find tears running down her cheeks, but her face is dry.

"He took the blade meant for me. I killed the one who did it, but the other one got away." Her voice comes out monotone, as if she's on autopilot.

"I'm sorry," I say. I don't mean that he's dead, only that she had to witness it. It's almost worse that he died protecting her. It blurs the lines of his wickedness and probably makes his death harder to swallow, or at least it would for me.

All she says is, "He chose his side."

I can't tell if she's referring to him siding with the demons or choosing to protect her in the end, but I don't ask. Something tells me she wouldn't know the answer.

Despite what's just happened, we still have more work to do before this battle is won. "Let's get back to the ballista," I say without thinking.

But I can't go back without both wings. I can't fly *anywhere* with only one wing.

Dad's whispered voice has me looking up. "By the grace of God."

I follow his line of sight, my heart sinking as I find a swarm of creatures flying through the sky, all zeroed in on one particular area.

It's surreal how familiar this feels. Just like that day on campus when Hayliel was in danger.

"Change of plans."

37

HAYLIEL

Watching the horde of enemies land is like watching the waves crash against the shore, except the water is toxic waste filled with mutant sharks.

They land in a circle, trapping us in a way that reminds me far too much of the well on campus. I got out of that pinch because of a fluke. My transformation. That won't happen today.

How the fuck are Remiel and I supposed to get out of this alive and do what we came here to do?

We stand near the stump. The demons and few angels—both Fallen and Pure—accompanying them are antsy, desperate to make a move.

One of the Pure angels rushes toward me, and in a flash,

Auriel is there, stabbing him with an angel blade. He pulls it out as easily as one would a splinter. Except, unlike a splinter, the angel doesn't survive extraction.

Auriel just killed his own follower.

The circle closes in, stepping over the dying angel as if he were nothing more than a branch discarded on the forest floor. Auriel's nonchalance doesn't go unnoticed by the other angels, and for a moment, they seem to realize just how dispensable they are to him. But with two taps of his scepter, it's as if a fog descends. The flicker of realization vanishes, and their anger turns back toward me.

Remiel mutters low under his breath, tracing the pages of his book in a pattern that appears random, but I sense to be intentional. Whatever he's doing, he doesn't fill me in.

Whether Auriel notices what Remiel is up to, I can't tell. That stupid, gleeful look remains on his face, and I want nothing more than to wipe it off.

"Last chance, little seraph. Side with me and my new world by choice, or face the consequences."

"Bring it." I draw my imbued short sword and brace for the fight of my life.

No one attacks us, but they do move. The circle grows smaller and smaller as the demons and angels take step after step forward, and just as half of them surge forward, I hear something.

It's rhythmic, this pounding of footfalls or wings. I can't tell which.

But are they friends or foes?

I have my answer when Auriel turns toward the sound, but he quickly realizes it's not just coming from one direction. It's coming from everywhere.

My mental connections light up and I smile, knowing who it is.

Backup.

They crash into the outer circle like a battering ram, but I can't focus on *who* or *where* or even *what* because the demons and angels who surged toward me and Remiel are swiping and stabbing, trying to take us out. I fight with everything I have, doing my best to keep Auriel in my sights. He's like a slippery fucking snake though, because he blips in and out of existence, moving around the battlefield with every blink.

I back up into someone and turn, ready to defend myself, only to find Castiel and Isadora instead. They're battle-worn, covered in blood and ash, but otherwise unharmed. Something must have happened at the guild, as we expected, but what are they doing here? There's no time to ask. "I need to get to Auriel," I tell Castiel before a Fallen angel barrels toward me with an angel blade in hand. Fuck!

Fighting demons is one thing, but fighting angels? It makes me queasy. Even though I know they've betrayed us, it doesn't make hurting them any easier.

Going up against the angel when I've been attacked by demons is almost a walk in the park. It helps that he's behaving strangely. One second he's ready to strike, and the next he looks almost confused. Second thoughts, maybe? I take advantage of his next hesitation and knock him out, then Isadora quickly restrains him.

Maybe it isn't smart to subdue instead of kill, but it's a choice. One we can live with.

"We'll take it from here," Castiel says, his eyes filled with pride. "Go end this."

I spare him and Isadora one last look before scanning the crowd. Demons and angels fight all around me. I don't see Auriel right away, but I find Remiel instead. He's on the outskirts of the fight, lips moving like they were before, and I can't help but wonder what the fuck he's doing. But no. It's not the time for that. I have to trust that whatever he's doing is helping and just focus on finding Auriel.

It takes two more passes before I find him, cutting through one of the Sanctuary guards. I teleport closer until I'm standing face-to-face with one pissed off looking Archangel. I've never seen anyone look so unhinged before, and I swear, if he could make it happen, he'd shoot lasers out of his eyes and kill me right here.

Too bad I won't give him the chance to try.

I twist the weapon in my hand and watch Auriel for any sign of his next move. The air around him seems to shimmer, and then he disappears and reappears to my left. I watch him once more, sensing something in the air before he blips away—something I think I can use. On his next attempt, I teleport near the spot I think he's going to go, and to my surprise—and his—it works.

His shock wears off quickly, replaced by a smirk that chills my bones. If I thought that was enough to win this fight against him, then I'm a fool. He's had years of practice honing his abilities, while I've barely had any time in the grand scheme of things.

We blip in and out, reappearing all over the battlefield. I try to keep up, I really do, but this power just hasn't been trained enough. My limbs shake, my mind feels frazzled, and I start to fall behind. He appears before I do, and I barely have time for my feet to land on solid ground before I'm finding him again. Every time he blips back into existence, his staff hits the ground, making this clang of noise that's really getting under my skin.

On the next blip, he's waiting for me. "How's your boy healing up, little seraph?" he taunts, wrapping a hand around my wrist. I feel his evil presence on the outskirts of my mind, my anger at his words somehow doubling in size. What is he ... But this is it, isn't it? This is how he's convinced those angels to do such horrible things. Instead of purging the wicked thoughts and desires from his followers, he's igniting them. That must be why Remiel is chanting. He's trying to dispel the wicked thoughts that Auriel's planting.

Like a battering ram, he tries to invade my mind. The feeling is strange and has me gripping my head, desperately wanting him to leave. For a moment, I forget about the battlefield and the war raging on around me. I forget that I should be scared to have him touching me. He's an Archangel, after all. The saviors of our city.

Then I remember the sight of my parents in a cage and Zeke's limp form, his wing cut off, and everything comes tumbling back. Auriel is a monster. An evil, vile creature who needs to die.

Anger sparks my internal sunfire to life, burning away his essence until my mind is clear.

Take that, motherfucker!

But my victory is short-lived because he's no longer near me.

A muffled cry echoes from somewhere behind me. I recognize the voice, though I've never heard him make that noise before. Spinning around, I pray my eyes are playing tricks on me. No, no, no! This can't be real.

Castiel is on his knees. Isadora screams from somewhere off to the side. And Auriel ... he stands at Castiel's back, twisting the angel blade that protrudes from his chest.

Everything around me fades. Color. Faces. Sound. Until the only thing I hear is my whispered "no" and the burning inferno that's bubbling in the very depths of my soul.

Not Castiel. He was kind. He was good. A protector. A friend, even. Auriel can't take him. But I know with that blade, there's no stopping this. Just like that man I witnessed die all those months ago, there's nothing I can do.

I refuse to accept that.

As if on instinct, I teleport to Auriel. He tries to blip away but I throw my arm out, a whip of pure sunfire extending as if a part of me and wrapping around his torso. As much as he tries, he can't teleport, and he can't break free.

I clench my fist and watch as the band of sunfire curls tighter around him, making him shout in pain. The thought mingles with the raging beat of my heart, and I feel him trying to access my mind, to force his evil intentions on me once more.

For a second, I let him in. The dark, oily stain of his wicked mind makes me want to run, but I stand firm, somehow knowing what needs to be done. Just like Remiel said I would.

I loosen my grip, just enough for him to smile through the blood currently dripping from the corner of his mouth.

He thinks he's won.

Quicker than I ever thought possible, I open up the core of power in my chest and let it flood through me, aiming it directly toward his vile mental path.

Auriel thought he could take control of my mind and make me submit to his diabolical ways, but all it did was give me the power to destroy him.

I feel his presence in my mind fall away, feel the surge of my power filter down the mental connection and into his mind. The warmth in my chest pulses as he screams, and then, just like that, he's solidifying. Turning to stone.

Without thinking, I shove his solid form over. When it hits the ground, a blast echoes out around me as it breaks into pieces, and a wash of golden light spreads across the forest. The closest demons die on impact, turning to dust in an instant, just like they did at the well.

We did it.

Auriel is dead.

But that thought is soured by the dying angel at my feet.

38

HAYLIEL

A s the light fades, every angel around me stands still.

The demons who didn't burn up in the blast halt their attacks. The Fallen angels who sided with them lower their weapons.

It's like the entire world pauses.

Auriel is dead.

Dead.

I glance once more at the broken statue of Auriel's body, still not quite believing it.

"It is done," Remiel says. It's the first time he's spoken to me directly since he began chanting. He kneels over Auriel's broken form, his lips moving with silent words I can't piece together, then he picks up the flame-tipped staff. He looks strange holding onto it, his book still held in the opposite hand.

Mentally, I send out a message to my friends.

Auriel is dead.

The demons must realize this too, because half of them hop in the sky and take off without a second glance. The others turn to us, ready to fight once more, but with half of their survivors having disbanded, the army around me makes short work of them. Some they kill, some they capture for questioning.

They do the same with the Pure and Fallen angels who were on the wrong side of this war.

"I'll need to question them," Remiel tells me, as if sensing my thoughts. "I should be able to tell who acted purely under Auriel's influence versus those who chose to take up arms against their fellow angels of their own free will."

The battle might be over, but the work is only just beginning.

I turn and catch a glimpse of Castiel's unmoving form. My legs move on their own until I'm crouching down beside him. Isadora is there, holding his hand. If my powers could heal Zeke's wing, maybe I could do something there.

Digging deep, I coax my power forward, willing it to enter Castiel's wound and save him. Please. Please save him. Tears fall freely as I stare at him, watching as the hole in his chest glows with pure sunlight. The light is far too soft, too dull.

"You did it," he rasps, a smile tilting his bloodstained lips.

A sob tears up my throat at the pride I see in his eyes. "But I wasn't quick enough."

"Hush now," he says, placing his free hand on mine. "You did good, Miss Hayliel. This old man is fortunate to have had the chance to get to know you."

"There has to be a way," I whisper, desperation clawing at me.

"What's going on?" Zeke's voice comes from behind me, causing the tears to fall even harder.

"Auriel got him with a blade," Isadora tells Zeke, Raph, Theo and Mira as they crowd around Castiel's form.

"I tried using my powers, hoping I could help him like I did with your wing." It has to work. Then I see what Zeke just dropped on the ground beside me. His severed wing. I meet his eyes and find nothing but love there. "But how?"

"With all things, there are limits," Remiel says as he approaches with Phiel.

"Thank you ... for the privilege," Castiel tells me, his voice weak, but I'm not ready to say goodbye.

"Please don't go," I whisper through the pain in my chest.

We must have used up all our miracles for the day, because a few minutes later, his eyes shut and they don't open again.

A fresh wave of guilt and sorrow damn near drowns me. He died because Auriel sensed he meant something to me. If Castiel had never been kind to me, if he'd stayed away, maybe he'd be alive right now.

Someone pulls me up, Raphael, I think, and I burrow my head into his chest. "Are you injured?"

"Nothing that won't heal." He presses a kiss to my head.

"I hope you didn't get attached to his perfectly sculpted

chest," Theo says, his tone full of false light. "That cut is gonna scar."

Pulling back, I glance down at Raphael and really look at him for the first time. His pants are covered in blood, and there, on his chest, is a thin line crusted with blood. When I look up at him, he's grinning at Theo.

"You're one to talk. Look at your cheek."

"I can try..." I say, then drop it when I sense how empty my power reserves are.

"It's alright, firefly," Theo says.

Zeke rubs a thumb against my cheek, wiping away my tears. "It gives them character."

Laughter tumbles up from my throat that quickly turns into a sob as I glance back down at Castiel's body.

"Don't cry," Phiel says. "He died defending the city he loves, which is exactly how he would have wanted to go."

I close my eyes and take a deep breath. There will be time to break down later. Right now, there's still work to do.

"Have you heard from your father?" I ask Zeke when I open my eyes.

He nods. "He's with Briathos. They've cleared out all remaining demons in the district, but now they're trying to find Malik. Briathos saw him with a woman not too long ago, but the building they went into collapsed."

So many questions flood my mind at once.

Why did half the demons leave?

What was Auriel offering them to make them fight?

What was Malik doing in the Fallen district, and who was the girl?

I don't think I'll get any answers right now, so all I say is, "We should help them and the wounded."

"If it's alright with you," Isadora says to Remiel, who still hasn't left my side. "I'd like to bring Castiel to the sanctuary and prepare him."

My eyes prick, hot with the promise of tears, but I hold them back. Later.

"Of course. I've already notified the guards to keep the gates open." He turns to me then, eyes soft. "It may not feel like it right now, but you saved the city. We can handle the wounded, if you want to accompany Castiel's body."

I spare another glance at Castiel's unmoving form. As much as I want to, I'm afraid. This grief feels too big, too suffocating. I'm worried if I let it in, I might never find my way out. "I can do more good out here, but Isadora, please let me know where he is, so I can see him after."

She offers me a sad smile, and then she and Phiel grab Castiel's body and leave with Remiel.

Raphael, Theo, Zeke, Mira, and I walk in silence toward the ruins of the Fallen district. The damage here is extensive. Irreparable. Which is good, I think. Going forward, we will no longer sequester Fallen angels away from society. This area can go back to what it once was. A place for guild lieutenants and their families to live—except now it'll be for all angels regardless of wing color or background.

Hopefully, the house Zeke grew up in remains intact. With so many memories of his mother there, I'd hate for him to lose anything more in this war.

"Bombs?" Raphael asks as we grow closer to the decimated brick that once was a wall. Chunks of it lie scattered on the ground.

Zeke nods. "But I don't see any blade shards, so they must have just been normal ones."

"That's good. I hope they were destroyed in the bunker," Theo says as we step into the throng of moving bodies. Time passes in a blur as we busy ourselves in the search for wounded angels.

Malik checks in from the sanctuary after rushing another angel there for healing, and I'm relieved that another professor isn't dead because of me. I know my friends would tell me it's not my fault, and maybe someday I'll believe them, but not today.

So instead, I focus on making myself useful by healing as many angels as my power supply will allow. Sweat coats my skin, but still I don't stop until there's no one left. We head back to the sanctuary, with Raphael and Theo helping Zeke. He doesn't look nearly as frustrated as I feel.

Later, I'll have time to mourn. For Castiel. For the other dead angels. For Zeke's wing.

I tried to save everyone, and I failed.

It's going to be a long road to recovery for all of us, but at least now the city can heal.

Maybe someday I will, too.

39

HAYLIEL

I wake a few days later with Raphael and Theo still sleeping beside me. The spot where Zeke slept is empty, the sheets cold, but that doesn't surprise me.

He's done this every morning since the battle—getting up early to take in the sunrise. I suspect it has something to do with his lost wing, because he still refuses to talk about it with anyone. Other than reassuring me that it isn't my fault, he changes the subject every time it's brought up. Even when the Archangels offered to procure him a prosthetic wing, all he did was take the information provided and thank them.

Somehow I'm more concerned than he is, but I guess all we can do is give him time to process in his own way and support him as best we can with whatever he decides.

It's been a strange few days. My emotions run haywire more often than I'd care to admit, and I suspect today will be no different. The Archangels set up a broadcast this morning to discuss recent events and what it means for the future. Not only that, but they've requested our presence.

I glance at the time on my slate. Shit. We overslept.

"Time to get up," I whisper to Raph and Theo, jumping out of bed before they can trap me between them.

"The war is over. Can't we sleep in?" Raph mumbles.

"If you want to look frumpy on every slate in the city, be my guest."

This has him sitting up in a panic. Yep. Knew that would do the trick.

We get dressed quickly, putting on our freshly cleaned rune-stitched clothing at the request of the Archangels, then we make our way to the designated recording spot, which happens to be the balcony where Raphael and I fucked. How fitting.

The Archangels are just wrapping up their speech about Auriel and the atrocious things he's done when we arrive, and I spot Zeke talking with his father, who's standing next to Azrael and Briathos, each wearing their guild uniforms.

"Hi," I say, approaching the group.

"Cutting it close," Zeke whispers as he presses a kiss against the hair above my ear.

The guild members are called to approach the podium. Everyone except for Zeke heads to stand with the Archangels and receive a certificate of honor. While we watch, Raduriel comes up to stand next to his brother. Their relationship is rocky, at best, but it's come a long way. Raphael still isn't sure what to make of the shift, but he's trying, and that's enough for now.

Malik, Isadora, and Phiel are brought on next to receive a similar certificate. Castiel receives an honorable mention for his bravery and unwavering support of our city. I'm shocked to my core when Mikhael states they will create a new statue to honor him and his sacrifice. My heart sinks when I learn it'll be on the grounds of Silver City University, a place I'm no longer welcome.

I don't know what my future holds. Without SCU, what will I do? Maybe they'll let me help Mom and Dad or even stay at the sanctuary. I know there are positions to fill here. Even if Darok wasn't a suspected traitor, he hasn't showed up for duty. Whatever he did for the council, I'm sure I could handle it far better than that idiot could.

The Archangels call us up next. My stomach somersaults as we walk up to stand in front of the railing. Cameras trail us and I feel a trickle of sweat run down my back. *Ugh.* I hate this. Having angels watch me is something I've grown to dislike over the years, and that hasn't changed just because we've saved the city.

They can't possibly get us all in the same shot. Not with Raphael, Theo, Zeke, Mira, and me standing beside the Archangels.

"It is with honor and appreciation that we offer these fine angels a medal of valor. Without them, Auriel and his traitorous followers would be well on their way to eradicating the good Fallen citizens of our great city," Mikhael says, then proceeds to hand deliver a medallion and pin to each of us. He moves slowly so the cameras catch every second of the interactions. When he gets to me, he announces, loud and proud to the entire fucking city, that I'm a Seraphim, the first in several generations, and a liberator for the whole city.

My face feels flame-hot, and I really hope this broadcast isn't recorded. I never want to watch it.

We step out of frame as the Archangel's call my parents and Dina up to talk about the new equality department. Mom and Dad will run it, while Dina acts as the official project manager. I'm so happy for them and for what this will mean for all of Silver City's Fallen community members.

Part of me is still skeptical, but a greater part is just happy to see us moving in the right direction with angels I trust at the helm. My parents will kick ass, and I know Dina will, too.

"We can't reveal everything to you yet, but Cam and Mari wanted to share two important initiatives we'll be focusing on in the coming months," Remiel says, extending his arm to my parents.

Mom beams at the camera, looking like she might burst with joy. "The first might be the easiest of our challenges, which is to open up the guild to new members. Angels of all types will now be able to apply, not just Fallen."

"I already know several members of our community who will find this information quite exciting," Mikhael adds.

Dad clears his throat, looking totally, adorably uncomfortable but plowing through anyway. "The second will take a bit more work, but is no less worthwhile. Areas and districts will no longer be separated by angel types, and all jobs will be reassessed to ensure proper earnings are received. We look forward to providing you with more updates soon."

They exit the balcony and the Archangels wrap up the broadcast by announcing a new holiday to commemorate those who fell during the battle. As soon as the broadcast is over, slates buzz all around me.

Raphael receives a video call from his mother. He answers it, and she immediately starts with the shitty little remarks. Raduriel chimes in, sticking up for his brother in a way that has pride shooting through me. Fucking *finally*.

Dina's dad calls, but she steps away before I can hear how it goes. Hopefully, he's proud of her. He should be. She'd gotten a little banged up after somehow getting trapped in a crumbled building in the Fallen district with Professor Malik. I still haven't gotten the full scoop on what transpired there, but I trust she'll open up to me in time.

Theo's grandparents call him, shouting about the fact that he let Lorna ramble on about Seraphim without telling her she was standing in front of one the whole time. I laugh before silently excusing myself to search for my parents. I want to tell them how epic their interview was and how excited I am to watch them change the fucking world. They're surrounded by journalists, all vying for more information, so I hang back and watch on from the shadows.

Until my slate vibrates.

Principal Cael's name flashes across the screen, making my stomach drop. I immediately move to tuck it back into my bag, but then he calls a second time.

Shit. Maybe it's important.

With my heart racing, I swipe to answer. "Hello?"

"Thank you for answering, Miss Hayliel," he begins. "I'm sorry I didn't contact you sooner, but Castiel swore me to secrecy until this matter was done."

Castiel swore him to secrecy? On what? All I can get out is a mild, "Oh?"

"Please come to my office tomorrow. It's better if we talk face-to-face."

I drag my feet on campus, flip-flopping between wanting to avoid the principal's office and wanting to get out of the open. My friends—who also returned to campus this morning—offered to walk me in, but I said no. They've been with me through everything. The good and the bad. This is something I need to do myself, and, surprisingly, I feel strong enough to handle it on my own.

The path to the main hall makes me think of my first day when Castiel met me at the gate. He was so nice to me, even from the beginning. But what was it he swore Principal Cael to secrecy on?

When I enter the outer office, the angel behind the counter isn't the same one working when I was last here. This woman lights up, gushing about meeting a Seraphim in person and how she'd seen me on her slate the day before. I don't know how to react, so I say nothing, face growing redder with every moment that passes.

She must sense my unease because she immediately covers her mouth, eyes growing wide. "I'm so sorry. That isn't at all why you're here." She doesn't give me the chance to respond before saying, "Principal Cael will see you now."

I enter the office like I have several times before. It looks much the same. Tidy, with the principal giving off an air of curiosity. I wonder if he's going to ask me to take out my wings again so he can study them. To my surprise, he doesn't.

"Please, sit."

Awkwardly, I slump into the seat across from his desk and fold my hands in my lap.

Principal Cael shuffles through some papers, and then finally sets them down on his desk. "First, thank you for coming today. I don't imagine it was easy to step onto a campus that has been the location of such discomfort for you."

"I appreciate you letting me return, even if only to have a discussion. You mentioned Castiel, and I—" I have to pause and swallow past the growing lump in my throat.

"Castiel was a great man," Cael says, giving me a break from trying to get my shit together. "Not only was he a fine professor here at the university, but he sensed things about angels that others didn't. Like you, for example. Castiel was a staunch supporter of yours from the very beginning."

He speaks softly enough that I have to look away, hoping he won't notice the tears building behind my lashes. "I did not deserve him, but I'm grateful for every kindness he offered."

Cael chuckles. "I think he would fiercely disagree with the first part of that statement. He advocated for you at every turn, and I regret that I had to do things I would have preferred not to."

Finally, I look up and meet his gaze. "I'm sorry, I'm not quite following."

"Your expulsion, for one. As you know, this school is the best in the city, but with that title comes certain ... pressures. Castiel came to me not too long ago and laid everything on the table, or, at least, everything that I believe he could have at the time. He understood that I needed it to look like I'd expelled you, though we both hated doing so."

"What do you mean?"

"Precisely as I said. Expelling you was never officially submitted, so you're still a student here, if you'd like to continue."

"I ... I don't know what to say."

"You don't have to say anything just yet, because I have more news. As of last night, Professor Uriel is in the hands of the guild; he's being questioned about his association with the rogue Archangel, Auriel. In fact, he's already named students and other accomplices. We've suspended them as of this morning, but I believe you should have the final say on whether it escalates into expulsion. You were the one they harmed, after all."

My mouth falls open, and all I can do is stare. Is he for real right now? "Uriel is truly gone?"

"Yes. And I spoke with his replacement. Given what transpired, we don't believe the failing grade you received has any merit, so we'd like to offer you a redo. If you're interested, of course."

Part of me doesn't believe any of this to be true. It's all too clean, too kind. I'm not used to it, but deep down, I'm desperate for this to be real. "Thank you. I'd like that. As for the students, I don't want anyone's future harmed because of what happened. I don't need to know names, but I believe an expulsion is unnecessary. Perhaps a compromise? They could remain students at SCU, but only through distance learning. If that's not too much trouble, of course."

"Not at all. I see Castiel was right about you in all things. You are gracious, indeed. Now, we only have a few more things to discuss. The first being Seraphina Beckett. Because of her lightning attack on a fellow student and the destruction of the Fallen house library, she is no longer a student here."

That was Seraphina? All this time I thought it was Auriel—the cloaked figure acting in a fit of rage after being unable to find me. But it was her.

"You seem surprised," Cael says, watching my reactions unfold.

"I am. Isn't Seraphina's family quite important?"

"They are, yes. But we're entering a new era in which spoiled children need to be held accountable."

I try and fail to hide a smile. "Well, alright then."

"Lastly, I'll need you to remove the banned rune from the cave near Somersault Falls. Cadriel Hammerman was found there only recently after having been trapped and paralyzed for days. While I understand your need for protections, given the circumstances of the last few months, I don't think you'll be needing that anymore."

It takes every ounce of self-control I have not to burst out laughing. Damn, I would have loved to have seen Cadriel all trussed up in vines. Would it be inappropriate to ask if Cael snapped a photo? "We'll get that cleared up right away."

"Perfect. In that case, we're all settled. I hope you'll consider my offer and continue on as a student." Cael stands, extending a hand for me to shake. "Silver City University will be among the first schools to assist the Archangels in developing real change for our citizens. That's a promise."

I take it and offer him a smile. "I'd love that. If there's anything I can do to help with Castiel's statue, please let me know. He was the best of us."

Exiting Cael's office, I smile at the receptionist and take my leave, but before I make it out the back doors, a familiar stack of papers catches my attention. News articles. Harold the Herald just doesn't quit. I reach for the shortest pile but think better of it. There's nothing in there for me but trouble.

And with everything we've sacrificed lately, I don't need any more of that.

I walk past the fountain and through the tree-lined path to Fallen house without anyone stopping me. It's almost strange to move around campus without the fear that someone is waiting for me behind the next bend. Strange, but in a good way.

As I approach the front door, my steps slow. Taped to it is another article, this one with today's date on it. Without thinking, I reach for it, pluck it from the door, and read the headline. *Gilded in Gold: The Gift We Didn't Know We Needed by Harold the Herald*. Something about it feels oddly familiar, and even though I know I should put it down, I keep reading.

> *So far this year I've written several articles about an angel named Hayliel Gracelin. If you'll recall, she's a first-year student whose attendance at Silver City University created quite the stir. With gray wings turned gold, the rumor mill hasn't stopped churning with ideas to explain the wild phenomenon that was her transformation. After the events of late, I'm here to clear a few things up.* □
>
> *Hayliel Gracelin is a godsend. You read that right. A godsend. And I, for one, would like to issue a formal apology to the angel who saved our city. She*

and her friends faced certain death, and instead of looking at the world through a different lens, I took the easy way out. I let the rumors and accusations fill my page without even once doing what a good journalist does: investigate, fact-check, and use trusted sources. As ashamed as I am, take this as my debut article. As of now, I will do better, and I have Hayliel to thank for that.□

The first angel I sought was someone I interviewed in the past. Gagiel Nisbet. He reiterated what he said in his last interview, stating that things have only gotten better with her around. So much better that his friends Sidriel, Tabbris, and Yofie began attending classes in person again after meeting her. "She stood up for us, supported us, and it's why she's earned my lifelong gratitude. For the first time, I'm excited about the future and hope to be the kind of angel who deserves her friendship."□

Gagiel isn't the only one to step forward and offer support to Hayliel. Professors from our elite school have reached out in support of her, stating, "If more angels had her compassion and understanding, our city would be a much better place."□

I hope someday to speak with Hayliel myself, but until then, I'll do my best to make this column something I can be proud of.

Along the bottom is an arrow. When I flip the page over, I cover my mouth in shock. There are several handwritten notes from friends and other students. I only recognize half the signatures, most of which are my friends or boyfriends. Who are the others?

I read words like *extraordinary. Unique. Remarkable. Selfless. Generous.* Tears slip from my eyes and onto the page.

The door opens, and I look up to find a group of angels waiting for me just inside. Zeke, Theo, Raph, Dina, and even Mira are here. I spot Gagiel holding hands with Sidriel—that's new!—and Tabbris and Yofie nearby, too. Marina is near the back, along with other Pure and Fallen students I recognize but can't remember their names. They hold a banner that reads, "Welcome Back, Hayliel!"

As I look around the room, my heart expands until I'm bursting with joy.

I glance up and send a shot of gratitude to Castiel for helping make this moment a possibility. He may not be here physically, but I feel his calm presence all the same.

Raphael pulls me inside, then raises my hand in the air to the sound of everyone cheering.

My smile has never been so wide.

40

HAYLIEL

Several months later

I stare into the mirror and don't recognize the woman looking back at me.

Logically, I know it's my reflection. I'm the only one here, so it can't be anyone else, but it doesn't look like me. My long hair is pulled back into an elegant bun while a few soft tendrils frame my face. Mira helped me with it while Dina did my makeup. I asked them both for subtle, natural beauty and they more than delivered.

Esther, the owner of the photo parlor, graciously allowed me to borrow a dress from her shop for the occasion. The straps hang delicately off my shoulders while the rest of the fabric hugs my body like a glove. Someone told me once that purple was my color, and in this dress I believe them.

Today is the day we've waited so long for. Our bonding ceremony. My first year of university might have only ended last week, but none of us wanted to wait another second longer. We spent hours researching between classes, late nights rereading Isaac's old letters and talking to historians to find the missing pieces.

There's a soft knock on the door, and I rise from my place in front of the mirror. My parents are waiting for me on the other side. Mom is already crying, and Dad looks halfway there himself. They are so damn adorable.

"Are you ready, Haylie-bear?" Mom asks, dabbing under her eyes to keep her makeup intact.

"More than ready."

I follow them out of the large pop-up tent, then loop my arm with theirs. We couldn't decide on the best place to have our ceremony—until the guys surprised me with an option. The island we escaped to all those months ago so I could practice my flying maneuvers away from Uriel. I said no at first. It's not an easy place for Zeke to get to with only one wing, but he refused to let his affliction stand in the way of what was otherwise a perfect spot. More and more, he's growing to accept the loss of his wing and allow others to help him. Maybe he'll take the Archangel's up on that prosthetic wing after all.

Warm sand acts as a cushion for my bare feet as we grow closer to the others. We set up on the beach instead of the mountain peaks. Turns out none of our family would allow this to be a private ceremony. Not that we fought too hard against it.

Turning a corner, I see them.

Zeke, Raph, and Theo stand near the makeshift altar, each wearing the same linen pants and pale purple button-down shirt. As I grow closer, I notice how they each have a different number of buttons done. Theo has the most, Raph's is open enough to reveal his chest, and Zeke's is unbuttoned entirely. I'm not surprised in the least.

Sunlight hits the scar on Theo's cheek, and I know if I look down at Raphael's chest, I'll find his scar there, too. They serve as a reminder of what we lost and also of what we gained. But even I know that sometimes the most devastating scars are the ones we can't see. Like Zeke, who rarely takes his wings out in public.

As if sensing where my thoughts have trailed off to, my men push their love for me through our mental pathways until I can't help but smile.

Today isn't about the past. It's about us and marks the beginning of our future.

Phiel stands behind them, acting as the officiator of this special bonding and sitting on blankets in the sand between me and my men are the rest of our family. Mira and Dina are there, sitting across the aisle from Raduriel. Perhaps the most shocking of our guests is their father, Andras. He's really stepped up over the last few months and is even taking some time away from his wife. A separation, I'm told, but I wouldn't be surprised if it became more permanent. In fact, if he hadn't found more of Isaac's journals, we may not be here doing this at all.

Theo's grandparents are here, too. They helped us decipher the rune, and we used Kirach's workshop to build the last object we needed for the ceremony. My parents, who are both crying again, drop me off with my men and step back to join Kirach on the blanket.

You look breathtaking, Theo says through our shared mental connection.

So gorgeous, Raphael adds.

Stunning, though you're wearing far too many clothes if you ask me, Zeke teases, his green eyes flashing with heat.

Speak for yourselves, I tell them, smiling between the three of them.

Raphael looks up at the familiar mountain peaks and then asks, *Don't you have favors to cash in on?*

He's right. How could I have forgotten about that? A mischievous grin has my cheeks aching as I push words through our shared mental path, *Now that the city isn't in danger, I'm sure I'll come up with something.*

"Are you ready to begin?" Phiel asks.

We all nod. When we first asked him to officiate the ceremony, I wasn't sure he was going to agree, but he did. Without hesitation. Having him here makes me feel a little closer to Castiel. He's the one who brought us together. I wish he was here for real.

"Thank you all for joining us on this momentous occasion. A bonding ceremony like this one is rare, but powerful. Hayliel, Raphael, Ezekiel, and Theo, have you each brought a feather with you?"

Tingles race through me as I nod and we all reach for the feathers we'd plucked earlier that morning while we were naked and tangled together.

"Hayliel, please step forward and tie your feather to the center of the pendulum."

Beside Pheil hangs the item Kirach made for us. Two three-dimensional diamond-shaped pieces of metal make up the outer area, and in the center are two spinning circles made of silver. I tie the top of my feather to the utmost peak of the diamond, loop my feather through the circles of silver, and attach the stem at the bottom.

Phiel calls on Raphael next, and he ties the stem of his feather to the diamond point on the left side. Theo does the same with the right side, and finally, Zeke attaches his to the bottom.

"Stand around the pendulum and recite the words we discussed," Phiel says.

The four of us encompass the runed object and repeat the words together. "I deliver this feather to bind us."

I watch in fascination as the runes etched in the metal diamond glow with a subtle light, fusing our feathers to it. None of us really knows what to expect, but I'm surprised by the prickly sensation currently traveling along my shoulder blades and the sudden pop as all our wings unfurl.

A sudden mist seems to manifest from the very air itself. It coats our wings, tugging us closer as if all four of us are held together by the same string. Blinding light sears my eyes, and when it fades, I'm awestruck.

Across from me, I stare at Theo's wings. Where they were once all white, now they're speckled with golden feathers. Raphael's wings are the same, white with gold interspersed throughout. But it's Zeke's that have my heart nearly thumping out of my chest, because his are peppered with black and gold, but that's not what has a gasp tumbling from my throat.

Where there was once only one wing, now there's two.

He has two wings again.

I blink, needing to make sure this isn't a trick of the light, but they don't fade. My eyes prick with tears, and he flexes both wings, flapping them gently and rustling the loose strands of hair around my face.

I cover my mouth with my hands, my heart beating out of control as the reality of it crashes into me. As hard as I tried, my powers were never strong enough to fix what he lost. Until now. Our shared bond. This love the four of us have for one another. It's strong enough to take on anything.

When our gazes lock, I see the astonishment and joy hidden within his green depths. Raph, Theo, and I rush toward him, whooping with excitement as we fall into a group hug that I somehow feel on more than just my skin or my heart.

Now the four of us are intricately linked by our souls.

HAYLIEL

One year later

"Is this the last one?" I ask Mom while placing what must be the fifteenth tray of food on the table. When I agreed to let her throw us a small grad party, I didn't expect *this*.

"It is," she replies, worrying her lip as she looks around her dining room. "Do you think it'll be enough?"

"Mom. Just how many angels do you think are coming? At this rate, I hope you have extra containers, because we'll all be taking some home with us."

She smirks, then opens a cabinet door revealing the prepped containers. Of course she'd already thought of it.

The doorbell rings, and even though I race to answer it, Dad beat me to it. Mira walks through the door first, still wearing her guild uniform. "Sorry, sorry. My shift ran late. Any chance I could borrow a room to change?" She holds up her bag, looking sheepish.

"Of course, of course. Up the stairs, second door on your right."

Zeke walks in next, and I damn near melt. He's wearing a black button-down shirt with the sleeves rolled up. *Yum.* He offers quiet pleasantries to Dad before beelining it to my side and wrapping me in his arms. "Gods, you look good enough to eat," he whispers in my ear. "Are you wearing it?"

I laugh, then whisper, "Yes."

The guys had given me this weird contraption and made me promise I'd wear it today. The box said it was a wearable G-spot stimulator. At first, the sensation of a foreign object in my pussy was strange, and it took longer to get used to the feel of something pressed to my clit, but it's getting easier.

I hear the doorbell again, then Raphael's moaned, "Oh, my gods. What smells so delicious?"

For some reason, Zeke doesn't let me go say hello. He exchanges a look with Raphael and Theo, who just passed through the threshold, then pulls me into the house and out onto the patio. The moment we're alone, I ask, "What's going—"

But my words cut off as the toy inside me begins to move. It's subtle—at first. A slight pulsing against my inner walls. Then a low hum starts on my clit, the vibrations utterly silent.

"Here, sit," Zeke says, pressing me down onto the chair. The moment I do, the sensations increase. I suck in a breath, then try to hide it as I hear someone approach. Theo grins, stepping up to plant a slow, teasing kiss to my lips. Raphael comes next, placing a plate of food down.

"Hungry, sunshine?" Raph asks.

"Yes," I say, then hiss as I hear a soft click and the pulsing toy grows more erratic.

He pops a juicy slice of watermelon into my mouth as Mira, Dad, and Mom join us on the patio. I twitch in my dress, fidgeting to relieve some of the pressure, except it doesn't work.

"Are you warm? You look a little flushed," Mom says, cupping my cheek. "Cam, can you bring out some water, please?"

"Oh, I'm fine," I say, trying to keep my composure. Thankfully, Raph must sense my awkwardness, because he clicks the button again and the toy settles.

"Have you heard from Dina? Will she be able to make it?" Mom continues, blissfully unaware of what my sneaky, kinky men are up to.

I shake my head. "She isn't back yet, but she promises to stop by when she is."

Dad hands me a glass of cold water. "And you still don't know who she's dating? Seems awfully suspicious if you ask me."

He's not wrong, but who am I to judge? I'm currently in a happy relationship with three guys and kept it a secret for as long as I could. Dina is more than entitled to do the same.

We sit around the patio table, talking and eating. Mom asks

Theo about his plans now that he's finished school, and even though I know the answer, I smile every time he talks about it.

"I'll be back at SCU, actually. But this time I'll be on the other side of the desk."

"A teacher?" Dad asks, pride in his voice.

"Eventually. But first I'm helping Cael with the new state-of-the-art library facilities. With the old school housing structure abolished, we're building one giant library. We'll have physical books and digital ones. A few of our nerdier friends from campus have already started translating old original copies into digital files. Eventually, we'd like to have an archives room with rare originals, but we're still fighting for that." He looks at me, then up at the sky, and I know what's coming next. "Once that's set up, I'll be taking over Castiel's class and teaching history."

"How wonderful," Mom tells him. "I think he'd approve."

"I owe it to you both, and Dina, for everything you've done to remove the Fallen divide."

"We're proud of what we've done so far, but there's still a long way to go," Dad says. "Mari has been itching to open a cafe, though, so that's why we were hoping Dina was back. See if she'd be interested in taking over for her."

"That's amazing!" I say, and I mean it. Mom would kill with a bakery. Plus, she'd get to see so many angels that it would probably give her some insight into the daily lives of others in the community. She could still help overall.

The topic shifts to demons, souring the mood. Zeke stiffens like he knows they aren't supposed to discuss this with us non-guild members, but Mira has no such qualms.

"Sightings are low. One, maybe two a month since defeating Auriel. After that epic loss, I doubt they'll do anything foolish for a while."

"We can only hope," Mom adds, then changes the topic to ask Raph and me about our upcoming work with the Archangels. I'll be assisting with city regulations while Raphael works with their change management and innovation team. It's not where either of us expected to end up, but it brings us both purpose and that's what matters.

The next few hours pass without incident. To my surprise, the guys didn't start up my toy again. Even though it's not buzzing, I've been on edge all afternoon. We play crokinole and a terrifying game of spoons that reveals just how competitive Mira and Zeke are. My parents called a tie before things escalated. He's come a long way since Mira's secrets came to light, and I'm just happy they get along again.

When it's time to head out, I stop in the hallway and stare at the newly framed photos on the wall. After the bonding ceremony, we went back to Esther's parlor and had more photos taken, this time with the four of us. I think we might have spent an entire eight hours there, but the shots we got were worth it. Some are serious while others are goofy. Even Zeke, my handsome grump, let loose.

Eventually.

"Thank you for this," I tell my parents as I hug them good-bye.

"Any excuse for your mom to cook," Dad says.

She laughs, playfully swatting his arm. "See you in a few days for family dinner!"

Mira offers us a little wave, then heads back to the guild. I swear that woman lives there. It can't be healthy, but she's been struggling after everything that went down, and this is how she copes.

The moment we're in the air, I feel Zeke's presence in my mind. *Fair warning, hummingbird*, is all he says before the toy in my pussy comes to life. My wings nearly give out, but Theo and Zeke are there to catch me. All I can do is wrap my arms around their necks and hold on while an orgasm barrels through me. It comes on faster than ever, but I guess that's what happens when you're on edge all day.

From the corner of my eye, I catch Raphael pocketing the remote with a grin. *Smug isn't a good look on you*, I tell him when I catch my breath. The toy hasn't stopped, but if I hold my legs just right, it takes the pressure off enough for me to think straight.

"We're just prepping you for when we get home," Theo whispers in my ear as Raphael approaches.

He grabs my legs and holds them together just long enough to have my body shaking with need, then he spreads them.

"What's happening when we get home?"

Zeke *tsks* against my neck. "That's a surprise."

Raphael puts pressure on the toy until I'm on the verge of coming apart once again, but then he pulls it out. Immediately I feel empty. My whimper gets carried away by the wind.

Do you trust me, sunshine?

You know I do.

Good girl, is all he says before I feel the toy, already slick with my arousal, between my ass cheeks. He pushes it in, slowly. There must be a button on it because it no longer pulses like it was before, and all that's left are soft vibrations.

The guys bunch my dress up, exposing my pussy to anyone who dares to look, but up here in the clouds, it's only us. As Raphael trails his fingers along my inner thighs, jolts of electricity dance in their wake. "What are—" Then I feel the first drop of water hit my clit.

Weather manipulation. Is he really going to …

He ups the pressure of the water until it pounds against my already sensitive nub, and I shatter. Zeke and Theo keep my legs spread while Raphael works me over again. One orgasm rolls into another until I swear I lose time, because suddenly, we're descending from the sky and landing on the balcony of our apartment.

Raph has the door open while the guys carry me inside and set me down on the plush carpet in our living room. My mind is reeling with a post-orgasm haze, but I'm not ready for this to be over yet. I reach for Raphael's pants and make quick work of freeing his cock. It's stiff beneath my palm, weeping at my touch. "Get undressed," I say, hoping it came out as the demand

I intended.

Swirling my tongue around Raphael's tip, I tease him until Theo and Zeke join us. They stand around me in a circle, cocks out and ready for me. It's a heady sight.

I grip their shafts, stroking up and down in the same rhythm that my mouth moves on Raphael's cock. When my head bobs faster, my hands match the pace. None of them try to stop me or take control. Not when I take turns giving each of them the same treatment. All they do is take what I offer them. I didn't expect it to turn me on so much, but clearly it does, because I'm dripping down my thighs.

When I pull back next, Zeke practically tears the dress off me until finally, blissfully, we're all naked. From my perch at their feet, I look up at them—my bonded men. They stare back at me with lust-filled gazes that make my toes curl, but when a smile plays on their lips, I just know I'm going to enjoy whatever comes next.

Theo shifts to the end of the sectional, lying on his back with his thick, pierced dick in his hand. He watches me with a hunger I can't resist. I crawl to him, kissing every inch of his body I can get my mouth on before I straddle him. Our eyes collide, and without needing to say the words, he knows what I need.

"Stuff that cock inside you, firefly. I want to watch you take all of me."

I'm still wearing the plug. Somehow I forgot it was even there, but now, as I sink onto Theo's waiting length, I can't ignore it. My pussy is wet enough that what might have usually taken a few minutes to accept all of him took no time at all.

I rock my hips slowly, loving the feel of him rubbing against my overly sensitive inner walls. Someone comes up to stand behind me. *Raphael.* My nipples pebble as I think about what happened the last time we were in this position.

"We wanted to try something new this time," he whispers against my neck.

"Anything." The word comes out on a single breath as I keep moving on Theo.

"We couldn't decide who gets your sweet pussy, so we're both going to use it."

I shiver as I feel Raphael's finger, already slick with lube, press into me beside Theo's cock. "Oh gods," I pant, halting my movements as I realize what he means. They're both going to fuck my pussy.

At the same time.

"Say you want it," he says, biting down on my shoulder hard enough that I gasp.

"I want it. Please. But ..." I hesitate.

"But what, firefly?"

"Will you both fit?" I ask the question just as Raphael inserts a second finger.

"We've prepared you all day for this, baby."

The teasing. The toy. They planned this all along. My core clenches at the thought. "What about Zeke?"

"Such a greedy little thing, aren't you?" Zeke murmurs from where he kneels on the carpet. "Don't worry, hummingbird.

You'll take my cock, too."

Raph withdraws his fingers, making me whimper, but then his cock is there, pressing against me. He goes slow, letting me adjust to every inch he fits inside me. When the burn becomes too intense, Zeke is there, stroking my clit as a distraction. Once he's settled in all the way, I take a few deep breaths. Gods. I've never felt anything like this before. With two cocks in my pussy and the toy still in my ass, I can barely manage to breathe, let alone anything else.

Theo stays still while Raphael pulls out almost all the way, then thrusts back inside. I nearly crumble then, but the couch shifts as someone climbs on top of me. My eyes pop open—*when the hell did I close them?*—and I peer over my shoulder to find Zeke squatting over me. He presses a button on the toy, turning the vibration up to full blast for only a second, but it has the three of us cursing. Can Raphael and Theo feel it, too?

Gently, he takes the toy out, then squirts more lube onto me and then himself.

"You're doing so good, baby," Theo coos. "Taking us so well."

When Zeke rests the tip of his cock against my ass, I hold my breath. Can I really take all three of them at once? My skin is slick with sweat as I wait for him to press into me. Theo tugs me down so I'm resting on his chest, which must give Zeke a better position because he's suddenly there, pushing past the tight ring of muscles.

Zeke curses, and the groans from my men only turn me on

more. At some point, he stops. "You good? You've gotta keep breathing, hummingbird."

"Good," I mumble, drunk on the feel of them. Am I drooling? *Shit.* Yup. I definitely just drooled on Theo. Wiping my mouth, I say, "Give me more. All of it. I can take it."

Zeke chuckles. "You hear that, boys? Our girl wants it all." Then he's thrusting forward, and the pressure is almost too much. It feels as though I'm being torn apart from the inside, but somehow, not in a bad way. My pussy clenches, and all of my men turn rabid. Raphael thrusts, which makes Theo's cock rub against that special spot inside me.

I detonate. Behind my eyes are colors I've never seen before. A myriad of bright blues and greens and oranges that shatter into a kaleidoscope. The more my body convulses around them, the higher my orgasm rides, until I think I might actually pass out from the overwhelming pleasure.

"Shit. Fuck," Raphael hisses, and then I feel the hot ropes of his cum burst inside me. He stops moving, and Zeke picks up the pace, making me twitch with oncoming bliss. Can I even handle another one?

Slowly, Raphael pulls out and comes to stand beside us. His cock is covered in both our releases, chest dripping with sweat, but it's his eyes that have me captivated. They're the darkest shade of blue I've ever seen. Almost black and blazing with so much love, I'm afraid it'll consume me if I don't look away.

"Look at the mess you made," Theo whispers in my ear as Zeke shifts his position behind me. "I think you should clean it up."

I lap at Raph's cock, tasting the two of us on my tongue. I barely get my lips around his half-hard dick before Theo and Zeke move. They fuck me with inverted strokes that grow increasingly more volatile. I lose control of my body, no longer able to do more than keep my mouth open for Raphael's cock to rest in as I scream.

And scream.

And scream.

When I come to, I'm in bed. The guys are snuggled around me, talking about our plans for tomorrow like they didn't just completely destroy me in the best possible way.

"If we all imbue a weapon, I say our prize should be doing that again," Raphael says.

I groan.

"Ah, I think she likes the sound of that. Are you finally awake, firefly?"

I shake my head, then mumble, "Not tomorrow. Need to recover."

Zeke clucks his tongue. "It's cute that you think you have a choice, hummingbird. But you're right. We should probably hold off on giving our girl any orgasms at all for at least a few days—maybe even a week."

My eyes flash open to find my men staring at me with shit-eating grins on their faces.

VICTORIA PAULEY

"Oh. Is that not what you meant?"

I narrow my eyes, which only makes the three of them laugh.

"Don't worry. That's not a pleasure any of us would deny ourselves," Raphael says.

Closing my eyes, I smirk and burrow further into my men. "I love you, assholes."

"And we love you," I hear them say in unison as I finally drift off to sleep.

Acknowledgements

Finishing this series feels bittersweet. While I'm happy the characters got their HEA, I'm sad to see them go. I have a ton of things planned for the future, some of which I even hinted at in this book (did you catch them?). Hopefully it won't be the last time we see Hayliel and her men. I want to thank my editor, proofreader, formatter, and cover and graphic designers for putting up with me and helping make this one hell of a book. A massive shout out to Chloe Rouxel for alpha reading this one and hyping me up. I'm not sure what I would have done without your friendship! And finally, thank you to all the readers who took a chance on me. I'm sorry you had to wait so long for this one, but I appreciate your patience! Without you, this wouldn't be possible.

I hope you enjoyed the final installment in this series and will stick around to see what I've got coming next. Join my newsletter to stay in the know.

About the Author

Victoria is a Canadian girl with a love for travel, music, books, games, and mayonnaise. She spends her mornings writing before work, and hopes to one day write full time. Friends say she gives the best hugs and you can usually find her laughing at her own lame jokes.

Website: victoriapauley.com

TikTok: @victoriapauleyauthor

Instagram: @victoriapauley.author

Facebook Group: /victoriasvillainousqueens

Facebook: /victoria.pauley.506

Linktree: /victoriapauley

Also By Victoria Pauley

Standalones

Caged (*MF Gang Romance*)

A Night of Indulgence and Sloth *(MFM, Office, Dark Romance)*

Series and Duets

<u>Creating Destiny Duet</u>
(Double MF Fantasy Romance, Greek Mythology)
Guided by the Stars
Fighting for the Stars

www.ingramcontent.com/pod-product-compliance
Lightning Source LLC
Chambersburg PA
CBHW070756120726
47910CB00001B/187

* 9 7 8 1 0 6 8 9 2 0 7 1 4 *